THE TATTOOED MUSE

Also by Kent Harrington

Dark Ride (1996)
Día de los Muertos (1997)
The American Boys (2000)

THE TATTOOED MUSE

Kent Harrington

2001

FIRST EDITION
Published November 2001

Dustjacket and interior artwork
by Scott Musgrove.

ISBN 0-939767-40-6

Dennis McMillan Publications
Tucson, Arizona
http://www.dennismcmillan.com

DEDICATION

Now, whenever the opponents are real maulers, the ring small and smokey, and me, as usual, without a corner man, I don't worry. You see, I have a great trainer back in Sausalito—gulp—who is a *painter, sculptor, philosopher.* I smile and pull up my trunks, confident. OK, I says to myself. How would my old Art-as-ten-rounds guru, Ross Curtis, knock this guy out . . . and then I think sure, of course! Why, it's going to be a piece of cake. Why, he won't stand a chance, poor bastard. *Gracias,* Ross!

Writing, at its best, is a lonely life.

—Ernest Hemingway

ONE
San Francisco

Martin Anderson leaned against the open door of the blood bank gripping his battered skateboard, waiting for his strength to return. Blond and handsomely disheveled, he was feeling almost anonymous since he'd decided to stop telling people that he was a writer. He'd gotten tired of answering all the attendant questions. His friends from Cal had gone either into investment banking or B2B and were full of pointed jibes at parties. Inevitably, the final one was thrown down as a challenge to his veracity by the gainfully employed: *Have you* sold *anything?* The answer, of course, was a resounding yes–at the blood bank.

He'd found the one thing he produced that America *did* want to buy: his blood–he had a very uncommon type. He sold as much as he was allowed to. He glanced at the plate of sugar cookies near the door and wondered if he should take some, but he just couldn't stomach them anymore. He'd stopped eating them months ago; they were invariably stale, too sweet, and did very little for his energy level.

"Hi there," a girl's cheerful voice said behind him. The young nurse's eyes–when he turned around–were feline, fiercely blue and full of commotion, the kind of commotion he produced in the opposite sex. Although he was usually indifferent to his good looks, young women were not.

Full of girlish energy and barely masking her desire, she chatted him up, talking over the noise of the buses and the

1

hubbub outside on Mission street. He left a few minutes later with a mental sketch (not unlike a painter's) of her silly paper hat, her dirty blonde hair and white stockings, and the way her uniform–matte green and paper thin–hugged her narrow hips, cocked just slightly. Her voice had trailed off coquettishly, giving him plenty of room to insert the would-you-like-to-have-coffee question had he wanted to. At the very last moment, as if she understood he was getting away, she'd taken his hand and written her phone number on his palm in blue ink. *Judy 924-5166.* Then she gave him a *big* naughty-girl smile as he left.

• • •

Michael Boon smiled fatuously at him in front of the Green Street Victorian where their writing group met. The driver's-side window came down silently on the lawyer's sleek new Porsche Boxster. "Well, *some*body has to buy these babies, right?" Boon said, as if they'd been having a conversation. "Keep the Krauts busy. Otherwise, they'll march off and steal Denmark again or something." Boon gave Martin another look. It was the same satisfied look he had when the young lawyer told people he'd bought Yahoo at twenty-five dollars a share, or a cute salesgirl at Victoria's Secret that he'd take two of whatever she was sporting under that dress, and could he have a look at the merchandise. As Martin approached the car window, the Boxster's dials pulsated as if generated by Boon's own self-importance rather than the motor. Martin felt something jab him in the stomach and realized it was nothing more than petty jealousy. He felt it again and was surprised. He'd thought he was immune to the Green Man. "You want to race?" Martin said, hefting his skateboard in the mist. It sounded pathetic even to him. *I suppose it's all* *right to be jealous,* he thought to himself. *I mean, who wouldn't be?* It had taken him a hard thirty minutes of skateboarding to get across town, and he felt suddenly ridiculous and infantile holding a skateboard at his age. Six years at the University of California at Berkeley and he'd managed to become a minimum-wage restaurant coolie.

At twenty-eight, however, Michael Boon, Esq., had, like Charlemagne, conquered every god damn thing in sight. Unlike most of the young people Martin knew in town (who lived in tiny shared apartments, frantic about next month's rent), Michael already owned a four bedroom apartment on Nob Hill, filled with paintings and antiques, replete with a black granite Euro-style kitchen, a "play room" bristling with arcade video games and *all* the accoutrements of Gen-X success. He kept a 40-ft. sailboat at the marina and a house on the beach at Bolinas for the weekends. When he tired of all that, there was always his father's place at Lake Tahoe. He dated class-one girls, who were not only ravishing but accomplished—lawyers-doctors-Indian-chief types—trading them with other first tier San Francisco playboys like baseball cards in a junior high school lunch room. "I just bought it. What do you think?" he said. "Eight cylinders, baby."

"Are you going to drive it or fuck it?" Martin asked sarcastically. He'd always tried to get up to speed with Michael and act a little more the "alpha male" than he really felt like. Michael brought out the frat boy in all his male friends, and Martin was no exception.

"Very funny."

The fact that the two had ended up best friends always struck Martin as ironic, given how different they were as people. They were complete opposites, even down to the kind of novels they tried to write. Michael's novels were copies of all the bad lawyer thrillers he'd read while in college; they weren't bad, but there was nothing honest about them. They were full of chases, coeds who answered their door in lingerie, and evil real-estate developers with dope on the coed's past life as a loose woman and, of course, the "Young Lawyer" who stands between the coed and alloyed evil. Martin always thought of them as good-bad novels. Martin, on the other hand, wrote about people who lived on the fringes of society and were on the verge of some crime of passion which would change them forever. His style was serious and terse, and his heroes were all driven, sensitive types who had chips on their shoulders and something to prove, all rendered in a bleak-is-beautiful style.

"Get in, I want to talk. Where *were* you yesterday? I waited over an hour for you at the Black Cat," Michael said. Martin slid into the passenger's seat. The car's interior smelled of aftershave and new leather. "I was worried about you," Michael said, looking at him. "Why don't you get a *phone* for god's sake?" Martin didn't bother answering because Michael already knew the answer to the question. He couldn't afford the $24-a-month-plus-extras bill, much less a cell phone. Part-time dishwashers weren't part of the wired world. The windshield began to steam up. Michael reached over, studied the dash, and flipped one of the cool-looking switches. Martin looked at his friend, who was physically imposing compared to him. Boon was technically an American but had lived in England most of his life and had a slight English accent that he felt gave him an edge in the circles he aspired to.

"What? Me? I'm fine. Why?" Martin said. The heater blasted them and the windshield cleared quickly. Martin could see the fog-tarnished streetlight outside the building where their group had met for years now. The apartment upstairs had become a kind of temple for him. The one place in the world he felt he truly belonged; at least, when he was in it.

"Didn't you hear what I said? What happened to you yesterday?"

"I thought you were joking," Martin said. He had no recollection of their lunch date at all.

"No. I'm not joking. We had a date for lunch," Michael said. "Don't you *remember?*" Martin spun the front wheels of his skateboard and then stopped quickly, afraid that it would splatter dirt in the new car. He'd been working so hard lately on trying to finish his novel that he'd become absentminded, forgetting to shower and even eat much. Several weeks had gone by during which he'd done nothing but write and wash dishes in the restaurant where he worked. And, of course, he'd come to their group meetings, faithfully, on Friday nights. The meetings were the highlight of his week, his contact with his girlfriend and with what he jokingly referred to as the "art world."

"Jesus. Sorry. I must have completely forgotten. But it was a "blood" day, and afterwards I can forget my name sometimes," he said. "I had to sell twice this week." He couldn't remember having made a date and felt embarrassed by his lapse. "Are you sure we had a date, Mike?"

"Forget it. You artist types! It's all right. We can talk *now*, before we go in," Michael said, relaxing slightly. He took his large hands off the steering wheel.

"Sure," Martin said.

Michael turned in his seat and looked at him the way he would a difficult client. The light from the streetlight caught his handsome and determined face.

"Martin, I've been meaning to talk to you about Kevin."

"I was afraid of that. I know what you're going to say, and I don't want to take sides," Martin said quickly.

5

"You have to. . . . You and I are the unofficial leaders of the group. We started it. We have to be the ones who do something," Michael said.

"Was there an election?" Martin asked, joking.

Michael laid his head back against the headrest. His face was in the shadows, but Martin could still make out the bigger man's matinee-idol profile. He reminded everyone of a young Claude Van Damm. Martin knew he'd abused their friendship on several occasions, going to Michael in desperation to borrow money when he was broke, which was often lately. It wasn't fair, but he'd done it more than he liked to admit. *If I give up selling blood, I'll have to borrow more.* He didn't feel it was right to argue with him now about Kevin. He turned to look at the single light in the doorway across the sidewalk. He hated having to borrow money but he had no choice. Writing meant everything to him, even more than his self-respect. "What is it you want to do?" Martin asked.

"It can't go on like this. I've talked to everyone else about it, but they won't do anything but complain. I think we should ask Kevin to leave the group. I'm tired of getting calls at the office. Everyone is calling *me* about it," Michael said. "It's up to us to act."

"That seems harsh," Martin said, shocked that it was coming to this finally. Kevin had changed, and not for the better. He'd become overly critical and overbearing at times, it was true, but had it come to this? Kicking him out of the group? After all, he was one of the old guard too.

"It's for his *own* good, Martin," he heard Michael say. Martin looked straight ahead into the descending fog, whirling and endless, bathed in light by the solitary street lamp. The fog was getting thicker by the moment and gaining mass. "He's become disruptive," Michael said. "He says cruel things to people about their work—*to their faces.*" For a moment, the light in the doorway almost disappeared behind the fog.

"But throwing him out seems too much," Martin said, without really thinking. He felt the grime from the wheel of his skateboard on his fingers and wiped them quickly off on his jeans.

"Well, what do you suggest we do? It can't go on like it has," Michael said.

"Why not? Why does everything have to be perfect?" Martin said defensively. "So he's hard to get along with sometimes. So what? He has reason. He's trying to finish his last year of medical school. I can't imagine the pressures."

"No offense, Martin, but that's the problem with you liberal types. Manners *do* matter." Martin touched the dashboard of the car, trying to comprehend Michael's life. Did he really know what problems were? From what he knew of Michael's past, it had been one long successful party, beginning with the fancy prep school and culminating at Stanford Law. "Look, I know you're empathizing with Kevin because you've hit a rough patch yourself. But what's happening with Kevin is too much for us to bear. He's going to destroy the group if we don't *do* something, and we can't let that happen," Michael said. He gripped the steering wheel as if he were preparing for a fight. Martin knew he was right, but he couldn't help being sympathetic to Kevin's problems now that he had so many of his own. Only the desire to finish his novel had kept him going lately. He'd been running on fumes, hoping to see a filling station up ahead. He realized, too, that there was a small piece of him that was giving up hope. He had to fight every day to keep going. It was as if, slowly but surely, the lights in the house were dimming; there were rooms he couldn't use now because they were completely dark. He

7

sensed the "Big Man," artistic failure, lurking like a criminal behind him.

"Would you throw *me* out, too? If I cracked up?" Martin turned and looked at his friend. He meant it. The idea that he, too, could slip over the edge was a very real possibility. His situation actually had become desperate. He read all the time in the paper about artists killing themselves in fits of desperation, depression and disappointment. God knows, he'd had plenty of those dark moments, when the walls of his tiny apartment seemed to move to within an inch of his face.

"Don't be ridiculous, old boy. *You're* fine. It's just a rough patch. I keep telling you that. You *will* make it. You've been working so hard on that book that you've neglected to make much money. I'll loan you all the money you need to finish. And besides, you'll sell it. I'm sure of it."

"Michael, you won't say anything to anyone about my having to borrow so much from you, will you? And I'm keeping records. I'll pay it all back some day when I make it. I swear to God." He made a rough calculation. It was over five-thousand dollars he owed him now. *How could he repay so much?*

"Of course not. It's our secret." Michael put his hand on Martin's shoulder. "Look, I can't park here–I have to move. Are you with me on this?"

"I suppose so. But let's give him *one* more chance. Everyone should get one more chance," Martin said. It was something his mother had always said and he'd loved her for it. They agreed that they would give Kevin one last chance. Martin got out of the car, relieved that there would be no scene, because tonight he had good news for everyone, and he didn't want to spoil it.

TWO

Along the way up the stairs to the flat were black and white photographs of famous writers: James Baldwin, Hemingway, Plath. Four years ago, Martin thought, climbing past Lorca's photo, everyone in the group had been so eager and energetic. They had all just completed graduate schools or prestigious writing programs. He and Michael had met at City Lights, Ferlinghetti's famous bookstore, and formed this group of young, ambitious and talented writers, each one positive at the start about his or her shining future as an American novelist. At year two, the group had been reduced to six writers. All the poseurs left when they'd instituted something called "the brutal rule." The rule simply said you couldn't show up unless you *actually* had written some fiction during the week. Now, just a few years later, the group's giddy naïveté was spent, people were changing and there were rifts among them. And too, Martin suspected, time was passing too quickly. They were all—except Betsy Austin, their baby—looking at the redoubtable year number thirty approaching quickly. Thirty, the ultimate sucker punch. He had nothing to show for his years of hard work but dog-eared, unsold manuscripts, whose only use now were as doorstops.

Sybaritic in feel, and smelling sweetly of marijuana, there were two distinguishing features to Betsy Austin's huge poorly-lit living room: it belonged to a very rich girl and it was unkempt. Betsy was no housekeeper. Facing him at the top of the stairs was a Delacroix; a *real* one. As if to imitate the corrupt feel of the harem scene in the painting, the room's plush sofas were draped with boudoir-red fabric and purple North African throw pillows. Martin knew, slipping off his jacket, that the flat legitimized the feeling in fundamentalist quarters that living in San Francisco was somehow morally dangerous and—at the bottom of it—sexual and perverted.

There was a lot of furniture, "artistic" lamps, and a small Jackson Pollack on loan from Betsy's mother, who'd carried it with her on the plane once from New York as if it were a souvenir. As soon as he'd walked into the apartment the first evening, he surmised Austin came from the kind of family you meet on the pages of *Town and Country,* and he'd been right. As it turned out, Betsy had never had one job since he'd met her. She wrote full time and, unlike the rest of them, *never* talked about money, which was a sure sign she had plenty of it. She would dash off to New York or Aspen or some exotic locale as readily as she would go across town. She would return from these trips, suntanned and ready for another run at bohemia.

Under a large serigraph of the *Follies Berger,* Cindy Wang, beautiful and uncharacteristically tall for a Chinese girl and dressed in Vietcong-style black pajamas, sat alone in the cavernous smoky room, rolling a joint.

"It's Wonder Boy," she said laconically, looking up. She'd nicknamed him Wonder Boy the first day they'd met, and he'd never fully comprehended the significance of the name. Trying to roll a joint, she went back to concentrating on the Zigzags and a plastic bag of weed balanced on her lap. She looked up again with a bitch-princess look as he approached. "Or is it *Mr.* Wonder Boy?"

Cindy Wang was their bomb. She'd been to Harvard and had a nervous breakdown in the middle of a PhD program in computer science and been hospitalized in an institution called, ironically, Sound Mountain. Her stay had cleaned her parents out financially. With Prozac, she'd been able to return to school and finish her degree. She'd decided, upon coming home—to the Wang family's horror—that she wanted to be a writer, not a computer scientist, and she stopped taking her medications. She told Martin once during their one-time fling, not bragging, that she'd never gotten anything less than an A during her *entire* academic career. *Never.* Over the four years he'd known her, she'd rebuilt herself, brick by brick, from a demure, Asian knockout genius, with lots of psychological problems who barely spoke, into a two-fisted, coke-snorting, gin-drinking novelist with lots of problems who did speak. It was remarkable how the problems hadn't changed along with her career.

"You may have been to Harvard, but you can't roll joints worth shit," he said, flopping down on the couch beside her. "Now at Cal, baby, we learned how to roll a joint properly."

She gave have him a long sideways glance, stuck the joint in her mouth and extracted it, saliva-wet; she lit it with the strike-anywhere match she had stuck behind her ear.

"Hey, I got a new job, Wonder Boy," she spoke between prolonged hits, the joint sputtering loudly. During their fling, he'd been astounded by her libido and appetites. Oddly, they'd ended up good friends and not lovers. Martin figured he was too safety-conscious in bed for her taste.

"Great," Martin said. "Where?" Cindy looked at him a moment, holding smoke, then exhaled energetically, shooting the weed smoke in his face. She'd had a least fifty jobs since they'd met.

"On Broadway. . . . Dancing at the Flesh Factory for frat boys and propeller-heads from Intel with Gumby-sized penises," she said, matter-of-factly, rubbing a saliva-soaked finger on the run. Martin could see the joint was ruined already.

"Come on. You can see their faces, but *not* their size," Martin said. He had a logical streak.

"After *I* get on stage, babe, you can," she said with pride, handing him the joint. Martin, nonplussed, didn't know how to answer that. It was probably true, he thought—inhaling for all he was worth before the joint fell apart—but he knew Cindy's family would be appalled if they found out what she was doing. (They ran a well known fruit stand in Chinatown.) He passed the joint back. She took another hit and spoke in little bursts without exhaling. "Pays great. . . . Best job. . . . think I ever . . . had," she said, then exhaled all at once. "You should hear the girls talk about the customers, Wonder Boy. Jesus, Martin, they really *hate* men, and that's the naked truth."

"Does everything go?" he asked with nonchalance. He signaled for the joint. "Or are there tassels and bangles, like in the movie *Lenny?*" He tried to make light of it. He figured it really wasn't as easy as she was making out. She hit him on the shoulder playfully, as beautiful as ever. "Everything goes but Cindy," she said. "I can get you a discount coupon for drinks if you come in on Monday nights. Some girls bend over and show their . . . you know . . . but I won't do it. You got to draw the line somewhere, right? As an artist, I draw it there," she said again, as if she'd given it a lot of thought, like a daunting calculus problem. Dignity and its square root. . . "Every night, the barker on the street shouts 'Ladies and gentlemen. . . . Dazzling degradation and fabulous filth.' Good alliteration or what?" she enthused.

Martin picked up the joint and got the last hit out of it, letting the smoke pour out his nose; it burned a little. The joint disintegrated into paper and ash; he let it drop into an amoeba-shaped ashtray, a little depressed at the thought that his friend was stripping for money.

"I like it," he said. He rolled his skateboard under the coffee table, stoned now.

"Yeah, he's, like, better than Wordsworth. This is Big Sur dope. I buy it from one of the girls at work. I tell you this stuff puts the oh-boy in orgasm," she said proudly as she rolled her eyes up into her head.

She turned and reached over the top of the camel-backed couch and turned up the volume on the radio, searching the dial for some rock and roll. "Want to see my act?" she said, her slender back to him, the small of it exposed, erotic and brown. He remembered he could practically encircle his hands around her waist when they had made love, and the color of her nipples, like burnt paper. The music, *Turn The Beat Around*, boomed suddenly. She began to dance, Sixties-A-Go-Go style, as if she were climbing a pole, fists clenched. She mouthed the words to the song: *Love to hear percussion. . .* Martin watched her breasts beat rhythmically against the silk.

Artists have to eat too, he thought, watching her. *Stripping couldn't be any worse than writing for TV.* He watched her boy's hips writhe with a terrifying energy that seemed to say everything there was to say about Ms. Cindy Wang. *Remind me not to get too high an IQ,* he thought. She stopped dancing when the commercial came on, a dopey look on her pretty excited face. "You know I was in love with you for about a week," she said completely out of the blue, coming out from behind her stripper persona. The old pre-crazed Cindy was back for a moment, talking like a schoolgirl. "I *was*, Martin!" She moved her long, silky hair out of her brown eyes. "Didn't you know?"

"I'm *still* in love with you," he said, joking.

"Yeah, right. Bullshit," she said, the hardened Cindy back again suddenly.

"Where's Betsy?" he said, trying to change the subject.

"She's on the phone in the kitchen. I think she's talking to Virginia."

They both heard the front door slam. In a moment, Virginia Winston crested the stairs with her backpack on and her cell phone up and running. Virginia had a way of seeming to be in motion even when she was standing still. She waved from across the room as if she were miles away. She was their best writer, he thought, smiling back. She had dropped out of NYU film school and gone to Africa for a few years with the Peace Corps where she'd started writing just to get her mind off the awful weather and huge chiggers. She'd told him she'd decided she wanted to be a novelist because she liked the actual *feel* of writing in longhand with a fountain pen on pads of paper. She'd come to San Francisco because it seemed the right place to start out as an artist. He had expected their affair would probably crash and burn because they were both too selfish and obsessed with writing, but she was fun and passionate about everything from restaurants to the Rosenburgs, and perhaps, most importantly, he could talk to her about his work. They spent a lot of time in bed talking about books and reading the *Chronicle's* Sunday *Book Review,* which was always good for a laugh.

Virginia stopped for a moment at the top of the stairs and looked at them both while listening to her phone, her skin very white against her short black hair. Athletic and thin, she was wearing high lumberjack-style boots with bright yellow laces, a holdover from that summer's hitch as a firefighter in the Sierras. Her backpack was wet, her black hair glossy.

"I'm in your damn living room," she said. She winked, out of breath, a devil-made-me-do-it look on her young face. She closed up her phone and ran the rest of the way across the room to give Martin a big kiss. He felt her tongue slide into his mouth, and then she was gone, having kissed and run. She pulled Cindy with her by the hand into the kitchen to huddle with Betsy Austin about something. The taste of her kiss was smoky and sweet from the Indian cigarettes she smoked. The flavor stayed with him as he crossed the room. He had to admit he liked everything about her, he thought happily.

Betsy and Virginia sat across from each other at a beautiful antique kitchen table. Cindy sat on the green granite counter by the sink and poured herself two-fingers of gin from a pint bottle of *Gilbey's* she'd brought with her. Martin thought of joining her in a drink but decided he better not. His writing heroes, Hemingway and Faulkner, had been drunks, and he was afraid of becoming a cliché.

Betsy, her blonde hair in a short ponytail, turned to Martin. "We're talking about Kevin. What do you think?" she said with her girl-next-door enthusiasm. "Should we ask Kevin to leave? He hasn't read anything in weeks and weeks. And he says such awful things to people. Virginia has been sticking up for him for an hour on the phone." Betsy, a petite, perfect size 0 blond, was only twenty-five and the youngest member of the group. She had been to Smith College and won an important literary award for an earnest schoolgirl poem about the women's soccer team. She'd even gotten to read her prize-winning poem on NPR. She wrote earnest Quinlin-style novels about brave, young single mothers, who were intrinsically goodhearted and believed their fair-minded goodness would win in the end (after you married the right man, pre-

15

ferably a software tycoon, or an Ivy Leaguer). She seemed the most confident of her impending literary stardom despite all the rejection letters she received. Her optimism was based, Martin thought, on the simple fact that she was so blonde, darling, thin, and rich that the world couldn't say no to her *forever.*

"Kevin deserves a break. He's a great writer. Great artists aren't always *nice* people," Virginia said. Martin could tell the argument was getting serious.

"He's crazy! And creepy. . . . Billy Bob Thornton creepy," Betsy said quickly, twisting her ponytail. The two girls were literary opposites–like Michael and himself–but they had a roaring friendship nonetheless.

"Blondie's right. Screw him," Cindy said. She let the heels of her worn Vans bounce against the cabinet door for effect.

"And he's no genius writer either." They heard the front door open and close. Martin stepped out of the kitchen so he could see who it was. Kevin Fitzgerald was coming up the stairs followed by Michael. Kevin looked up at Martin but he didn't return Martin's nod of hello. His blue eyes were steely. They must have had words, Martin thought.

A reserved and laconic Southerner, Kevin was very slight, with an almost girlish body. Plain-looking, he had a school-marmish quality, made worse by his doctor's icy intellect and Baptist psychology, which made him, at bottom, oddly naive. He had come to San Francisco to study at UC Medical School. Once a charming rural kid, each year of his residency had changed him. He'd become more and more distant, more and more superior. His novels were about doctors, of course, young ones, who entertained complex issues of science and ontology but whose intellectual gifts went unappreciated by the world, even though their brilliance was blinding. In less than a year now they would have to call him "doctor." Martin shuddered at the thought. He respected Kevin's intellectual prowess, but couldn't say he liked him anymore.

Virginia got up and came to the kitchen door. "Hi sweetie," she said. She and Kevin were close. Martin hadn't pried but he supposed they'd probably been lovers. (He prided himself on what he imagined to be his "adult" attitudes concerning sexual relations: don't ask, don't tell.) Kevin gave her a surprising smile that made him seem suddenly like the old kid from Memphis for a moment. At the top of the stairs, the two traded a "European" kiss, their arms thrown around one another. Michael, holding back, shot Martin a look from the bottom of the stairs. Martin wondered what he'd said to Kevin.

THREE

Virginia's Indian "bidis" produced a sweet, clove-like smell not too different than incense. The stiff blue smoke hugged the walls around her side of the room, the tendrils illuminated by a Craftsman-style lamp next to her. Michael was sitting directly across from Martin on the couch with Cindy. Drinking wine out of a paper cup, jacket off, Michael wore "power" suspenders decorated with dollar signs. He'd smoked some weed and it had softened his expression. Their eyes met and it was clear to Martin that Michael had given Kevin some kind of ultimatum despite what he'd promised him in the car. Martin glanced back at Kevin. His clothes were very clean and very square and did nothing to diminish the stamp that said "poor white Southerner." He dressed in chinos and white shirts usually, like the Memphis clerk his father had been. His red hair, almost orange, had been kept very short lately. *There's something different about him tonight*, Martin thought. Something he couldn't quite place.

Michael casually brought up the annual literary prize being offered by City Lights Books for best novel. The prize was a contract with the store's small press.

"I didn't come here to talk about ridiculous prizes," Kevin said, cutting him off. He'd worked on losing his accent, but it was still there, marking him as a country boy. Virginia had told him that Kevin had admitted to her that his family had been dirt poor after his father was killed in a robbery. They'd been forced to leave Memphis and move to a small backwoods town in Arkansas. His mother started talking in tongues on Sundays at a Pentecostal church, forcing Kevin and his brother to follow her into the netherworld of midnight tent revivals and hate groups dying to thrash anyone who didn't love God or hate the Jews, niggers, spics and homos enough. Fortunately for him, he won all sorts of scholarships. "I came to hear people read their work. The brutal rule," he said. "That's my rule." *And it's mine too,* Martin thought. That rule had kept them all working hard on their books, despite the constant shower of banalities and worldly responsibilities that interfere with writing novels.

"My rule is to drink two glasses of wine before you make love or write," Virginia said, breaking the tension. Everyone but Kevin laughed. The relaxed stoned feeling in the room had been spoilt now.

"It's Cindy's turn," Martin said, clearing his throat and trying to get the group under control. "Cindy's going to read first tonight," he said calmly. All eyes turned to Wang's expectant face, almost hidden by her long black hair. She and Betsy were trying the hardest to be popular novelists and had no pretensions to the art novel, unlike Martin. But it seemed the harder she tried, and the more she dissipated, the weaker her work became.

"I have the mother of all horror novels here. You white people will have to make an appointment with my social secretary when I sell this thing for seven figures," she informed them jokingly as she slipped out a new chapter from her messenger bag. She put on her glasses and started to read.

Cindy read with passion, slumped forward in her usual place next to Michael. The novel, a horror epic, was about a Sierra town under attack from some *thing*. Martin couldn't remember now *what* exactly. The story had changed many times, and had lost much of its visceral punch because she was forcing it to be scary. She'd captured the isolated town's beauty, but somehow the story had all been frittered away. The writing was too thin. You couldn't blame her, Martin thought, after all, she was dancing naked to keep a roof over her head these days. It *had* to be humiliating, and it *had* to make you want to sell something *fast*. Betsy shot a glance at him. Martin looked down at his worn high tops to avoid her eyes. She'd been giving him *those* kinds of looks lately, as if she were charging down field and he were the goal.

Cindy's novel, he decided, was a disaster. *Cindy must know it too,* he thought. Cindy was too damn smart *not* to know. He could tell by the expressionless faces and obvious lack of enthusiasm that they didn't like this chapter. If your work was good, everyone took on a look of rapture, and you felt it, almost like a religious experience. Right now everyone just looked bored. He glanced at his watch furtively. It was after twelve o'clock. He wished Cindy's novel were better. He wished she didn't drink so much. He would make some suggestions tonight on how she could fix her chapter. He wanted her to succeed. Dancing naked was the last straw. Someone had to succeed soon or it was going to kill him, he decided, trying to concentrate on her words. *We can't all stay wannabes.*

Determined to help, Martin made several pointed suggestions to try to straighten out some of Cindy's problems, such as stop killing people and start developing the characters. She took the criticism surprisingly well and even made notes as Martin dug into her work, sometimes brutally. The others in the group echoed his thoughts, and Virginia had some ideas on how to punch up the writing. He felt respect for Cindy; despite everything, she really wanted to grow as a writer. That hadn't changed about her. It seemed that the group was getting down to business and back to normal, and it made him happy in a way he hadn't been for months.

"Well, Martin, what do you have for us tonight?" Cindy asked, looking at him. "We have to have pages. Pages, Wonder Boy. The brutal rule," she said, slipping off her glasses. Betsy, Michael, Virginia and Kevin were all looking at him now.

"I've finished!" Martin said, theatrically holding up his manuscript.

"Jesus! Why didn't you tell us?" Michael said, coming alive. He'd been rather subdued all evening since Kevin had lashed out at him.

"And what's the theme of this opus? It's been pretty light on ideas," Kevin said with a slow drawl, the country singer twang of his voice making him sound even more ominous. Martin looked a little shocked. The question had taken him completely by surprise. He wasn't sure what to say. He'd been so excited about just *finishing* the damn thing.

"I'm not really sure, I guess it's about how your life is colored by the past, and the way the past holds on to you. The way it trammels us and makes us repeat our mistakes. Yes. That's the theme: the power of the past on our lives. I'll put that in the query letter I send out," he said, the surprised look still on his face.

"I don't think anyone should write a novel without a theme clearly in mind from the outset," Kevin said pompously. His accent became even more pronounced when he was being critical. "You have to be Apollonian from the start."

Martin looked at him. *Oh fuck you,* he thought. *Apollonian, Jesus. . . .* He wanted to ask him what the hell was the matter with him; what had happened to his humanity?

"It's a mistake. To do otherwise is just self-indulgence," Kevin said from his corner. He continued attacking him. Martin glanced at Michael who had an I-told-you-so smile

21

on his face. "Even what's his name, the ordnance person–" Kevin said off-handedly. "That thriller writer who looks like a Margaret Thatcher impersonator. He wears big glasses. . . . *Love's Mercenaries.*"

"Kominsky," Martin said.

"Yes, even that syphilitic imbecile has *some* kind of theme. War is good, I suppose," Kevin said.

"Oh, yes. Yes, Kominsky's novels are full of ontological themes, Kevin," Virginia said, putting out a cigarette and deciding to wade in. She was the only one who was not intimidated by Kevin's ugly moods or his rapier intellect. "For example, just the other day, I heard he was lecturing on the subject of how to be a *complete* fucking right-wing hack, and get rich doing it," she said. "Kevin could you *please, please* take that stick out of your ass, dear, and give Martin a break." Everyone looked at Kevin and then burst out laughing.

"Oh shut up, everyone, and let Martin finish telling us the news," Betsy said, smiling at him as if he were made of chocolate.

"I've been working night and day to finish by my thirtieth birthday," Martin said.

"I hope you left plenty of white on the page," Kevin said dryly. "They don't like too much print on a page in New York. That's what I read somewhere, anyway. And maybe you should tell them that it's a *group* effort. No, maybe you should tell them you've stolen all my best ideas," he said. "What's the title?"

Betsy looked at Martin and then at the others in open-mouthed astonishment.

Virginia nervously opened up another package of cigarettes. There was a look of real shock on her face now, too. Kevin had gone too far this time.

"I think it's time for a break, don't you?" Virginia said in a quiet voice.

"Oh, fuck you, Kevin. You pompous redneck *asshole!* Why don't you go back to butt-fucking your cousin in Hayseed Hollow!" Cindy said. "If I were a man, I'd knock the crap out of you. I swear to God!" She got up and stormed from the room heading for the bathroom. No one said a word for a moment. They heard a door slam.

"I want to read after the break," Kevin said, ignoring Cindy completely. He stood up stiffly. "I have a new chapter done," he said. He handed out a copy to each of them. He stopped in front of Martin. Martin looked up and saw that clinical and confident look in the young man's eye. *He really doesn't like me.*

"You didn't answer my question. What's the title?" Kevin said, handing him the pages.

"The Burning Bay," Martin said.

Martin stood up and went to the too-bright kitchen. There was a cardboard box of wine and paper cups. He picked one up and poured himself a drink. The wine had been put near the heater vent and was warm and tasted like chemicals. Betsy came into the kitchen and looked at him. They had been trading looks now for weeks. It was obvious she wanted to, as the advice columns euphemistically put it, "take their relationship to a different level." He took a swallow of warm wine, watching her over the edge of the paper cup. *Why now,* he wondered. He supposed Virginia hadn't told her yet that they were seeing each other up on that "higher level."

"What are we going to do?" Betsy said. "I mean, *really.* That was so unfair, what he said to you."

"I don't know," Martin said. "I don't think he means anything by it, really."

23

Martin finished his drink and crushed the paper cup. He didn't care about Kevin's problems. He felt insulted but didn't want to admit it. He threw the paper cup in the overflowing garbage bag in the corner. *Fuck him. Cindy's right,* he thought. The wadded cup fell off the top of the pile and onto the floor making a hollow sound. He went and picked it up.

"We have to do something about it. Michael says we should," she said. "I think he should be asked to leave. That's what I think. I've been saying it for a month now," she whispered. She gave him a profound look that had more to do with a different subject altogether. The thought of making love to her crossed his mind and then left just as quickly.

"Fine with me," Martin said. He was through protecting him.

"I can't take this . . . this *atmosphere* anymore," Betsy said. "Why can't we just get along like we used to?"

"You sound like Rodney King," Cindy said from the kitchen doorway. She walked past them and poured herself another shot of gin. "Fuck him. I never liked him," she said. "I wish someone would punch him out."

• • •

Two months later, stinking from the heat of a hotel kitchen where he worked as a part-time dishwasher, Martin tore open a letter from a famous agent at the William Morris Agency who had picked his manuscript off the "slush pile" and loved it. "Dear Martin, We're pleased to tell you that your novel, *The Burning Bay,* has sold to Jupiter House. I would have called but, as you do not have a telephone, I am sending this notice by mail. Congratulations. Contract to follow." Nothing in his life would be the same afterwards. He quit washing dishes that very night.

FOUR

Paul Kline waded through a sideshow of street "artists" on Post Street selling gaudy jewelry from shabby little card tables to shorts-wearing tourists. He rounded the corner onto Maiden Lane where, in the sudden quiet, an army of yellow Cinzano umbrellas were tilting this way and that under the cool April sun. The outdoor cafés were packed at noon, filled with bohos and office types doing lunch, and lots of pretty young women showing bare tawny midriffs. Kline walked past the cell phone chatter, his aviator-style sunglasses hiding clear blue eyes that caught each and every pretty girl.

Breeze-block solid, with gray highlighting his close-cut blond hair, he was forty, Jewish, and ruggedly handsome. His years spent overseas in the Marine Corps had cut lines into his middle-aged face, but they only served to make him more attractive to most women. His intense masculinity was perpetually at odds with his intelligence. Neither one had ever got the upper hand, and he had needed both to survive combat. A first impression of him was of a man whose switches had all been taped to the "high" position. Because he was sexually needy, the women he'd met since coming home thought he ran too hot. His seeming indifference to status and money made a lot of the men think he ran too cold. When he looked at you though, his energy was palpable, like a hand on your shoulder. He could be understanding when others found it too expensive to be.

Like the character in Edith Pief's soldier's anthem, *Non je ne Regrette Rien,* Kline knew he was vulnerable to regrets. He had to fight them off every day; every sunny day. He knew he was being pulled downhill towards some kind of emotional La Brea Tar Pit where, if he weren't careful, he'd be emulsified forever by anxiety and middle age. He didn't want that. *If I could just write about my experiences; get them down on paper, maybe I could put it all behind me and pull myself out of this slide…Write it down. Get it on paper. That's all I want to do now.* Yet, every time he'd tried to begin to write, he'd been unable to get past a few painful and inadequate pages. *Is it possible to headfake yourself?* he had wondered. He wished, more than anything in his life now, that he could be less worldweary and feel whole again, like those young unspoiled faces looking at him as he passed the gauntlet of tables.

A young, shabbily-dressed man, in his twenties and pony-tailed, stood up from a café table to greet Kline. The two had met at a bookstore where the young man worked–Green Apple Books–a cavernous known haunt of the city's intelligentsia. Would-be writers, like Kline, came to be physicked by the tattered atmosphere of stacked scholarship and decaying novels. Kline bought hard-core things like *Wittgenstein in Vienna* or Hannah Arendt on the Dreyfus Affair, or obscure novels by Latin Americans like *Los De Abajo,* or poetry by Sor Juana De La Cruz; books with which the young man was unfamiliar until Kline brought them to the counter. The two had struck up an egghead's friendship, which can be similar to that of dope fiends, because the next book, like the next high, is the only thing that matters.

Kline spoke animatedly during lunch, and the young man listened closely, noticing the way he could lose himself in a discussion about books. Kline demolished his huge roast beef sandwich; only bits of bloodstained bread were left on the greasy white plate. Kline was saying how he'd read *Madam Bovary* while stationed at Guantánamo (his voice slightly nasal with a San Francisco accent) and how much he'd enjoyed it because it was so lonely at the base, as there were no women there (except fellow female officers, or enlisted women–who were off limits to officers).

He said he could imagine how Emma Bovary must have felt, isolated and depressed in that French country town, and that sex could make you feel connected to the world even if you really weren't. *Why was Emma Bovary always portrayed as a bitch?* Kline went on to discuss the language in Hemingway's short stories and how language had the power to move people. *The Snows of Kiliminjaro* had been the best damn thing he'd ever read. Kline was an intellectual Gatling gun, spraying the younger man full on with ideas and opinions. But when the young man mentioned he was reading about the Dreyfus Affair at Kline's suggestion, Kline's face lost its animation. They talked about their both being Jewish for a moment, then dropped it as if they were cheating on a test and the teacher had walked into the room. The young man decided to change the subject and give Kline the good news, the reason he'd asked Kline to meet him for lunch.

"I got you into that writers' group I told you about!" the young man announced as the dessert arrived. He'd meant the news to be a big surprise. The young man put a fork into his slice of cake, waiting to see what Kline would say, sure that he would be happy. A pretty waitress passed between the tables, and Kline turned to watch her move. Kline had forgotten all about the request he'd made before he'd gone to Europe on vacation. "You know, that *writers'* group you were pestering me about. I spoke to Virginia Winston when she came into the bookstore, and they have a space. You have to've *started* a novel before you can go, though, man.

They're real serious about *that*. But I told her I had a friend who I know has a great novel in him, and I really *believe* that, Paul. She told me she bought my recommendation and that you can join if you want to." The young man took out a scrap of paper with a telephone number on it and slid it across the small tabletop toward Kline. "I hope this is the *start* of that novel."

Kline picked up the bill and they said good-bye. His friend disappeared into the crowd, well lunched, content with life and thinking he'd done his good deed for the week. Kline turned and made his way down the alley that had emptied somewhat. His cell phone rang.

"It's Michael Boon at Rosenthal and Fleishman. Can you come up to the office, Paul?" Boon's law firm and several others were keeping Kline's life very comfortable since he'd left the military by employing him as an investigator. Kline's former Stanford classmates had all gone on to law school and now were in a position to hire him. The Jewish community in San Francisco—despite its having assimilated in so many ways—still stuck together tightly, behind the scenes, with their own "good old boy" network. Kline had been, since he was a child, the community's poster boy because of his parents' tragic history; and now he was even more so because of his sterling military career. They were proud that one of their own was a decorated American military man. Someone had asked him at a party the night before why he didn't go to Israel to fight? He'd told them to go themselves.

"I'm in your neighborhood. I could come up right away," Kline said.

"Wonderful."

And that's the way the case would start, simply and without much ado, except perhaps the noisy colorful lane seemed to narrow just a little as Kline thought about how he'd stood at the gates of Dachau–the camp where his mother and father had been held by the Nazis–unable to enter. The ten year Marine veteran of several wars was stopped cold by an empty blanched field, with nothing aimed at him except history's immobilized face and a few hoary wooden buildings which were the most frightening things he'd ever seen in his life. He turned away from Union Square and walked back in the direction he'd come, past the café. He glanced at the tables as he walked by, but couldn't spot the pretty waitress he'd made eye contact with earlier. Since he'd come home, he'd done nothing but chase women, and he wasn't getting tired of it. He had decided long ago that sex was *his* drug of choice. He wondered why the French call it *le petit mort.*

As it turned out, both men had been to the same party given by the firm the night before. The young lawyer was imposing in a blue pinstriped power suit, life-long privilege written all over his good looks. He had blond hair in a parted-on-the-side Ivy League cut. Kline's physical antithesis, the young lawyer had one of those Protestant faces that was accustomed to viewing the world from a safe high place. They spoke briefly about the party the night before, which had been given by Boon's boss at the firm, a childhood friend of Kline's. Boon smiled tightly, aware that Kline was well connected with the senior partners of the firm. Kline sat down across from him. Boon asked if he wanted anything to drink. Kline turned the offer down. There was silence for just a moment. Kline felt as if he were being measured inch by inch while Boon looked him over, finally reaching for a file on his desk.

"Here's the case, Paul. The firm has an important client. Our client's daughter died years ago, leaving a son. Our client had the boy, their grandchild, adopted. They've paid the grandchild's way all along, until he graduated from college. Now our client wants to give him his legacy. We want you to go over and explain the situation to the grandson. He doesn't know he was adopted, so it means breaking the news." Boon stood up and handed the file over his huge messy desk. "His name is Martin Anderson. As it turns out, I know him. He's a good friend of mine, and the senior man on the case didn't think it would be appropriate for me to do it myself. He said I should call you." Kline spotted an unfinished lunch pushed to one side of the desk as he took the file. The firm has been in charge of the kid's trust since the beginning, Boon explained.

Kline took the file and glanced at a photograph of a young boy, maybe five or six, professionally done. He supposed it was the "sales" photo taken years ago, the one that was sent to would-be parents. "He lives up on Lombard Street," Boon said, sitting down again. His chair made a funny deflating sound as he sat back down. "He just bought the place."

"Then he must not need the money," Kline said, judging from the tony address. "What does he do? Software?"

"He gets it whether he needs the money or not," Boon said officiously. "He's a writer—novels. He's just had one published, his first. He's very good. The firm did a thorough vetting of him to make sure there was no drug problem or anything else in his background. Our client didn't want to feed any bad habits. That's how they lost his mother from what I've heard. We had Levine do a complete background check on Martin. No drugs as far as he could tell, but I could have told them that. Martin is very hard working. He hardly even drinks, but the client insisted on having him checked out. You were out of town, or I would have had you do it," Boon said quickly. Kline looked up from the file.

"Levine is a good man," Kline said. He felt a pang of jealousy without even knowing Martin Anderson because Anderson had become at a young age what Kline wanted to be—a novelist.

"How much does he get?" Kline asked.

"Over a hundred million dollars," Boon said casually. Kline looked up from the file.

"Jesus. . . . Big time family then?" Kline said wistfully.

"Let's just say that they're rich as Croesus. It's going to be quite a shock to Martin. It might ruin him as a writer," Boon said. He seemed to begrudge the kid his inheritance, Kline thought. He looked past Boon out the window onto Maiden Lane. Kline wondered why the well-to-do always begrudge good fortune when it happens to ordinary people. The lawyer gave him a quick smile, signaling the meeting was over. Kline didn't move.

"Shouldn't a social worker give him this news?" Kline asked, closing the file.

"We don't employee social workers, Paul. We're a law firm," Boon said coolly, as if he were explaining the facts of life to a child.

"This kind of news could be a shock," Kline said. "Psychologically."

"That kind of money would shock anyone, old man," Boon said, misunderstanding him completely. "We were hoping you could review the file and contact Martin as soon as possible. Give him the ground rules he has to sign off on. It's all in the letter to him, signed by one of the senior partners who knows the family. The family wants to remain anonymous for the time being." Kline stood up. "And Paul, as I said, Martin and I are good friends. It's a fluke I got the case. I don't want to jeopardize our friendship. I would appreciate it if you didn't tell him that I knew just yet."

31

"Sure. Why didn't Levine finish up the case?" Kline asked. Boon's secretary buzzed and said he had a call he had to take. The lawyer looked up from his phone, his hand shooting up in a not-now fashion. Kline left the office. He thought he knew the answer to his question anyway. Levine had told him once that he and his wife had adopted their two daughters. Kline understood.

• • •

All big "Indie" and chain bookstores seemed the same to him now—the magazine racks, the coffee bar, the manager's blasé seen-'em-all handshake. *Oprah Club Meets Here*, the banner said that was hung over the entrance outside the store. "This bookstore is very important," his PR girl said as if she could read his mind, pulling the parking brake on their rental car. Martin imagined there would be plenty of well-dressed "Oprah" people there.

His PR person was a short blonde buxom girl from New Jersey with big hips, who seemed like a character out of the poem *The Wild Party*, by March. "Monty's is on the *New York Times'* list. They report *directly* to the *Times*. If you want to *stay* on the list, you *have* to sell a lot of books here," she said knowingly, like a drill sergeant talking to a stupid recruit who can't get it right. Plain, she was the type who was greatly improved with make-up and underwear that controlled her zaftig figure. He'd taken to calling her Wild Party behind her back. "Or you'll end up in the mid-list," she added threateningly, popping up her sunglasses onto her forehead and poking at her Palm Pilot. She'd told him the moment they met in New York that she'd "done" Clancy's Soviet Tour.

"Right," Martin said dully. He wanted to say that the Oprah types scared him a little but didn't bother. He'd gotten down to one-word answers with her. "Mid-list oblivion," as a famous female mystery author had referred to it, taking him aside at a bookstore in Delaware, her face frozen with self-importance, nursing a diet coke. "What*ever* you do–don't stand for it. We have to fight it!" she'd said. He thought she was drunk and never did figure out exactly what "mid-list oblivion" meant.

Wild Party told him that if he were *really* successful his publisher might give him *two* PR people for the next tour. "You need two to control the crowds," she explained. "Stephen King has to have *four*."

This particular giant independent bookstore was somewhere near Scottsdale, Arizona. There seemed to be no architectural features to any of the buildings in Arizona whatsoever except for the signs. He longed for the cold fog and calm bay of home, real landmarks, hills and good restaurants. He spotted the usual logos–The Gap, Victoria's Secret, Starbucks– slapped on the buildings. "If there's a Bloomingdale's," Wild Party said, still studying her Palm Pilot, "Then we're in Tuscany." They both laughed and he decided she wasn't that bad.

At first the crowds queuing up at bookstores for his signature had been thrilling and very flattering. Book tours–how different they were than how he'd imagined they would be! He'd thought the trip across America would be full of intimate gatherings with his fans and intelligent conversations. Instead, he'd been asked the same three questions for the last four weeks: Where do you get your ideas? Are you in the book? Is this going to be a series? Out of genuine respect for the people who came, he conscientiously answered them as if he'd heard them all for the first time. His sudden celebrity, born with his novel's spectacular success (it had been mentioned on Oprah *twice*) was overwhelming him with the last thing he'd expected–boredom.

Monty's Books was as big as any chain store, and he knew exactly what it would be like before he walked in–a queer mix of belt-and-suspenders conformity and hippie chic. There would be two kinds of books piled up near the front, waist high. If there *was* a Bloomingdale's in the mall, both would be about Tuscany, or if novels, they'd be by foreigners, usually young Indian women whose novels were about their struggle to have an orgasm *and* keep a rich husband in Delhi (recipes included). He'd learned from weeks on the tour that the "Indies"–suburban or otherwise–hated the chain stores, which they considered to be the capitalist antichrist. In either case, the coffee bars were interesting messy places with sticky tables where people tried to survive the quiet desperation surrounding them.

Before he got out of the car, Wild Party handed him a FedEx package. "I forgot to give this to you. It was sent to Denver but missed us twice. I had it forwarded." He opened the package. It was a beautiful and expensive coffee table book of photographs of San Francisco's Coit Tower. He turned to the first page and saw a note in Michael's handwriting: *We're all thinking of you and very proud. Here's something from home. Thought you'd get a kick out of this. See you soon!* The page had been signed by everyone in the group: Michael, Virginia, Cindy, Betsy, even Kevin, which surprised him.

The room they had at Monty's for book signings was warm and airless. They'd arrived early, so he took a seat in the empty room and leafed through the book on Coit Tower. When he looked up sometime later, there was a crowd of people staring at him expectantly. They all, god bless them, were buying his novel and wanted it signed. He closed the book on Coit Tower and smiled at the crowd. He heard the manager mention Oprah several times during the introduction. It was about then he usually went on automatic pilot. Twice, while he was giving his spiel, he glanced down at the book Michael had sent. There was something compelling him to stare at the picture of Coit Tower's brooding nighttime photo on the cover. He'd grown up with the landmark and, until this moment, had never thought much about the place. Suddenly, the tower seemed important for some reason.

That evening, after two drinks alone in the desultory bar of his hotel in Phoenix, he'd gone to his room and fallen asleep watching Larry King. He'd had a nightmare, the dreamscape resembling scenes from *The Cabinet of Doctor Caligari.* In the nightmare he was a small boy, abandoned at Coit Tower by a young blonde girl whose face was concealed from him. The dream was vivid, full of cinematic detail and profoundly disturbing. He awoke upset and off balance. Even Wild Party noticed the difference in him when she came to his door at eight the next morning to remind him that they were flying to San Francisco for the tour's big finale.

FIVE

At the top of Coit Tower, through the signature arched openings that ring the observation deck, Martin watched the San Francisco Bay waters around Alcatraz turn choppy, the water's surface changing with each sharp gust of wind—taupe, marine blue, matte green-gray. Standing close to him, a blowzy tourist in her fifties with dyed red hair, wearing a yellow windbreaker with the words *Sunnyside Tours* on the back, yelled again, arms over her head. She was waving madly to someone six stories below her on the circular parking lot. Martin suddenly realized that he had no idea how long he'd been standing there staring at the Bay.

"HONEY! HONEY!" the woman's grating voice, sharpened by the wind, seemed to slap him physically. He pushed his way through the crowd to the edge of the observation deck to get the hell away from her. He could hear the maddening whirr and click of every sort of camera. A family of Arabs hunkered down facing into the wind. They had their picture snapped by a stranger.

The observation deck that afternoon was packed with tourists from every corner of the world who were there for the popular end-of-the-day spectacle. The skyline west of the tower was magnificent, with its yellowish shell-colored buildings glued to the hillside like some child's handicraft. His cell phone rang. Afraid it was Wild Party, he didn't answer. The woman, to his left now, yelled again. He turned, agitated by her voice. He forced himself to ignore her and look out on the red angry sunset that was sweeping over the water like a fire.

Looking out on the city, he remembered walking out of his book signing on Market Street. He'd been frightened by the line of people, all with the same anxious expression—a mix of wonder and the need to identify with him. Depleted, he had nothing left to give them. A man in his forties had asked him to sign his book. "Can you write something *special* for me?" He stared at the balding man for a moment. "You know— something really *unique!*" the man said, pushing his book across to him. He'd put down his pen, stood up and walked away. Wild Party had chased after him running out of the store, catching him on the sidewalk to ask what he thought he was doing. Shocked, she told him that there were still "fans" waiting in line for his signature. Martin had looked at her blankly and simply hailed a cab and left.

The stinging June wind whipped at his T-shirt, making the material crack like a flag. He read a dirty bronze plaque on the face of the rampart wall that surrounded the deck. "*Coit Tower was built in 1933 at the top of 284 foot high Telegraph Hill with funds left to the city by Lillie Hitchcock Coit, an eccentric San Francisco pioneer and philanthropist.*" He glanced at his watch. He'd left the bookstore hours ago now. There were several hours since then that he just couldn't account for. He looked out at the diminishing skyline without a clue as to where he'd been all afternoon.

He leaned over the rampart. Coins, tossed by the tourists, sat sparkling on an outside ledge below him, catching his eye, as he tried to recall where he'd been. He forced himself to stare down at the parking lot below with its small cars, the plinth with a statue of Christopher Columbus and the little white figures that were people. The view, vertiginous like a tunnel, made him slightly sick. The scene on the parking lot seemed to move even further away suddenly and without any warning. He had an urgent and overwhelming and irrational desire to throw himself off the tower, to dive toward the parking lot head first, to die there on the steps below. He fought back the bizarre feeling, pulling himself back, terrified and confused. The wind snapping at his open coat, he tried to get hold of himself.

He looked again at his watch to make sure. *Yes, three hours gone.* Where had he been? Had he been there at the tower all that time? What was happening to him? He turned again to the plaque, forcing himself to read the words as if they held the answer. "*Coit Tower was built in 1933 at the top of 284 ft high. . . .*"

"Martin, are you all right?" It was Michael's voice. Martin turned, amazed and relieved to see his friend after all these weeks.

"How did you know I was here?" Martin said, throwing his arms around him, hugging him excitedly.

"You asked me to meet you here!" Letting him go, Michael looked at him, surprised. "Are you all right? You said it was an emergency; I came right away. Your tour person has been calling my office looking for you. What are you doing *here* of all places?" Boon asked. Martin looked at his friend, who was wearing an elegant dark overcoat, glad to see someone he knew after all these weeks of being on the road with strangers.

"I don't know exactly. God, it's so good to see you!" Martin said.

"Martin, are you sure you're all right?"

"No, of course not! I've been eating at Denny's for six weeks!"

"What the hell are you doing *here?* Your person said you were supposed to be signing books somewhere. She was very upset that you ran out on the signing," Michael said.

"I can't explain it. I've never felt like this before. I felt trapped in the bookstore. I had to get out of there," he confessed. The woman who had been yelling earlier pushed by Martin and maneuvered herself to the edge of the deck in front of them. Martin could see the dark roots of her dyed hair. Her hand shot up as she waved to a Lilliputian figure below. They tried to move away from her.

"Trapped? What do you mean?" Michael said.

"I don't know, really. Nothing? Everything? I felt like throwing myself off just now. That's what I mean." Michael looked at him.

"I think you should see a doctor, Martin."

"Why?"

"Because I just do. You're obviously under a lot of stress. Look at you. Have you gotten any sleep at all? You look awful. I have a good friend, a psychiatrist. Why don't you see her? I'll give her a call. She's very good at these things," Boon said with a reassuring smile. "Obviously, you've been under way too much pressure since all the hoopla started with the book. You've been on Oprah, no less, for godsake!" Michael had the Englishman's brio when he spoke. It always seemed to be eleven A.M. in Michael's world, even now.

"All right. All right, I will. If you think I should." He persuaded Michael to call his PR person and make excuses for him. Martin promised he would make the evening signing at "M" is for Mystery on the Peninsula. There was to be a party at the store, and everyone from the writing group was coming.

"I have a surprise for you." Michael dug in his overcoat pocket and came out with a set of keys. "I couldn't get the apartment you wanted, but there was another not far from here that I got for you. It's yours. The deal closed while you were away," Boon said. Martin had turned his business affairs over to Michael as soon as the money from the book started rolling in. He had been overwhelmed by the amounts pouring in from foreign sales. Never good with money, he'd let Michael handle it for him. He'd asked Boon to buy an apartment he'd seen before he left on the tour. "You trust my judgment, don't you?" Michael said, looking at him.

"Of course I do," Martin said.

"I had to bid in a hurry. The real estate market has been insane. I tried to call you. I think it's everything you wanted and more," Boon said. "And, I got a good price." He handed the keys over.

"Thank you." Martin clutched the keys. He broke down suddenly. "It's just so good to be home. I hated being away. I hated shaking hands with people I don't know. Over and over, the same questions."

"I thought it would be exciting," Boon said. "One always thinks these things would be."

"Can I afford it? The apartment?" Martin said, pulling himself together.

"Yes, you can afford it." Boon smiled. "You're not rich yet, but you're getting close, Martin. Money won't be a problem anymore."

"There's been a movie offer," Martin said, turning toward the view. "My agent called me this morning."

"I know. You told him to call me, too. We discussed it."

"Should I take it? They want me to work on the script. I'm not sure I can write a script. I've never even read one."

"Of course you can" Michael said. "They're going to pay you a *fortune.*"

"How's everyone been?" Martin said. He wanted to change the subject. The idea of the movie only seemed to make him feel worse.

"Fine. They miss you. Everyone is very proud of you. You're all we talk about now. You're living the dream for us all," Michael said.

"I'll be there Friday. Just like before. I've been looking forward to it. Nothing is going to change."

"Good," Michael said. "You're our star now. You can't drop us. I'll call my friend and make an appointment for you." Martin looked at him blankly. "The doctor."

"Yes. Yes. Of course," Martin said. Michael told him he had to go back to the office but made him promise he would show up for the party that evening. He was sorry when Michael left. He felt completely alone.

He wanted to leave the tower but somehow couldn't bring himself to go. He waited, wondering why not as the sun flat-lined. He waited until the hordes of tourists thinned out to just a few hearty teenage Goths, their long dyed-black hair blowing about in the wind. Their pale young faces were ghost-like, their black clothes both dramatic and childish. One of the kids looked at Martin carefully, then decided it was safe and lit a joint. Martin watched the city turn on its lights and move into those sweet minor keys of twilight that he had always loved so much. *Home sweet home,* he thought. He forgot completely about his date on the Peninsula. He spoke to himself. *No more glad-handing people I don't even know. No more questions about where I get my ideas. How am I supposed to answer?* One more signing and then it would be over, he told himself. He felt better now. Seeing Michael again had helped. A good night's rest in his own bed and he would be fine. Everything would be fine.

One of the Goths came toward him across the now deserted deck. The kid had pimples and wore lipstick, a la Marilyn Manson, and some kind of make-up that made his skin appear even more bloodless. He was hideous and ridiculous all at once. The kid held the joint out to him. Martin couldn't stop looking at the boy's ugly face. He refused the joint. One of the other Goths turned on a ghetto blaster behind him. The music was strangely familiar. Martin turned from the view to see where the music was coming from, then turned back and saw the kid's pale face only a few inches from his. The kid's eyes were red and intent from the dope. His lips were wet.

"White bird must fly or she will die," the kid said holding the joint out towards him. Martin looked at him panic-stricken.

"What did you say?" He heard the sound of his own voice over the wind.

"White bird must fly or she will die," the kid repeated the words from the sixties classic playing behind them.

"Leave me alone," Martin said. He grabbed the kid by the shirt and threw him violently against the wall, almost sending him over the rampart. The kid screamed, barely managing to stop himself from going over the side.

"Who are you?" Martin said, holding him by the throat against the wall.

"Hey man, don't be an *asshole.*" The kid, terrified, stared up at him wide-eyed, the wind whipping his long hair. Martin dragged him further over the edge of the rampart so that his shoulders were out in space. The boy struggled frantically, kicking out and screaming.

Martin looked down at the ugly face; he was suddenly blinded by bits of his nightmare from the night before–the young pretty blonde girl, the car, and himself as a child standing in the parking lot. He heard the scream and saw the young blonde woman wearing a white dress with orange polka dots fall from the top of the tower. For a moment, it was as if she were floating above him, held by the blue sky. Then quickly, she plummeted to the ground as he watched helplessly. She hit the concrete steps and was covered immediately by a crowd of horrified tourists, their shoes splattered with her blood. The hallucination played in the milky-soft Zepruder-like colors of an eight-millimeter film, with a close-up at the end of blood-encrusted Pat Boone-style saddle shoes.

"Stop that fucking music!" Martin screamed. The ghetto blaster went silent, leaving only the sound of the wind. Martin dragged the boy back from the edge and let him go. He stepped back as the kid fell onto the deck in a heap, stunned, his black hair over his pale face. The joint he'd dropped spun about the deck like a firecracker, the wind making sparks fly and tumble around the kid's black motorcycle boots.

"You're fucking *crazy,* man! *Asshole! Jesus!*" the kid said. "You're fucking nuts."

Martin, frightened by his outburst, ran down the interior stairway of the tower, listening to his own footsteps echo on the cold unpainted concrete walls.

He stopped suddenly on the stairs. A blonde—dressed like the one in his dream—stood in the stairwell below him. She turned to look up at him. He wasn't sure if she was real or not. He decided she couldn't be.

"Who are you?" Martin said.

"Martin?" She turned around and ran down the winding stairwell and disappeared. He ran after her, but when he got to the bottom of the stairs and through the heavy metal fire door, she was gone. He rushed into the lobby, sure that he would see her. By the stairway door, a security guard in a blue uniform looked at him, barely awake.

"Did you see a woman? A blonde woman?" Martin asked, frantically scanning the empty lobby. The guard shook his head.

"No sir," The guard had a thick Latin accent.

"You had to have seen her! You had to! She ran out from the stairs . . . just now!" Martin turned to point at the stairs behind him and saw on the wall before him the painted image of the girl in the polka dot dress he'd just seen. The painted figure was part of a large mural, one of many gracing the tower's walls. He walked slowly towards the mural, stunned and unable, he thought, to tell the difference now between fantasy and reality.

SIX

He would have never foreseen that success would make him sick like this. Martin closed his eyes for a moment and rubbed them. He opened them again and looked at the pretty doctor. Only six months had passed since he'd sold his novel, and already it seemed like such a distant event. He'd felt desperately tired all the time from the Zoloft she'd prescribed, which, as far as he could tell, hadn't seemed to be doing him a damned bit of good, so he'd stopped taking it. When he'd been on the "meds," as she called them, he'd felt like a grinning monster or an on-the-edge psychopath.

He liked the fact that the doctor sat at a desk and that she was very beautiful and that she wore a blue business suit (there was something sincere about that color), and he was comforted that outside it was a perfect spring day with a powder-blue sky. Hope seemed to linger in the empty cloud-less space outside. He turned to look out the window again. He stared out onto Market Street below. He wanted to tell the doctor what had happened up at Coit Tower on his first day back from the book tour–that he'd seen the girl in his dream on the stairs–but he was afraid to. It frightened him to think about it. He was afraid she would have him committed if he told her that a girl in a mural had spoken to him.

Despite his problems, the view below was intensely beautiful to him. It was not just people, or just buildings, or even sky, but rather a glorious moving whole, like a painting with all the shading and details and spirit of a canvas by Coro. He watched a cable car glide silently on its tracks ten stories below. In his mind, he heard the bell the conductor would ring at each stop; he envied the people on the street who were free to enjoy life's small pleasures, like a cable car bell on a spring afternoon in a beautiful city. He felt trapped by his recurring nightmare. Night and day now, his life was a shambles; he was unable to enjoy anything anymore. He was barely able to hold onto his relationship with Virginia.

"You said you received a present while you were on your tour, a book about Coit Tower. You said that it upset you," Dr. Elders said.

"Yes." He stepped closer to the window and rested his forehead on the glass.

"Why do you think the book upset you?"

"I don't *know* why, but that's what happened. Maybe it wasn't the book at all. Maybe it was just the stress of the book tour. There's a speed to success that I don't like. You never really know where you are or what to expect. And it's all happened so fast."

"You said you began to lose track of time once you got home from the tour." The doctor had a nice quiet voice, womanly and sonorous, that made her questions easy to take.

"Yes."

"What happens?"

"Mostly, I end up at Coit Tower at the strangest times. I don't remember where I've been. I just find myself standing up at the top of the tower looking out at the view," he said blankly. Then suddenly, "I know where you're going, doctor. The patient crosses the room, *stunned,* and says the two must be connected–the book and the interludes," he said, trying to joke about it. He sat down in one of the comfortable leather chairs across from her and was immediately swallowed up by it. He tried to remember the name of Van Gogh's doctor for some unknown reason.

He'd assumed the first time he'd come here that she must be very successful from the look of her consulting room with the oiled-wood paneling, the tones dark and confident, all very sober. There was a John Marin watercolor on the wall that had to be worth a fortune. If he were writing the scene, he would have put her in a different kind of office, he thought, more feminine and youthful. The office seemed slightly presumptuous for a pretty young woman fresh out of medical school. The furniture was leather and oversized and masculine in the extreme. She'd told him that first day that it was her father's office (he was a psychiatrist, too), and that he was letting her use it until her practice grew and she could afford her own.

Elders looked at him, a half-smile on her pretty freckled face. She reminded him of the character in *Ann of Green Gables,* not a psychiatrist. If he were writing about her, he would have said she was pretty in a girlish way, but sophisticated, her intelligence leading her severe beauty. Tall, she had a mass of golden tight curls that cascaded around her slight shoulders. Sunlight streamed into the office as she smiled at him. It played with her hair, and he felt there was something there, in that confident intelligent smile, something he knew intimately. Perhaps one of his girlfriends from the past had it too—*or was it something else?* She was tall like he was. Her skin, for a blonde, was dark. But the freckles were her real beauty mark; there was a shower of them across her face, glorious, like an afternoon rainstorm. They made her especially beautiful, he thought. Imperfections can cap a beauty as well as ruin it.

"Tell me about the dream," she said.

"How's life treating *you?*" he asked, not answering her question.

"*I'm* supposed to be asking the questions," she said.

"Yes. Of course you are," he said. "Ask away then," he said. "Fire at will."

"You haven't told me what happens in the dream," she said. "Only that you're a child. What else?" He looked across the desk at her. He was wearing a black turtleneck and black jeans. He'd taken to dressing better now that he had money. He looked at her pearl necklace and again got a funny feeling about her cherubic face. *Weren't psychiatrists supposed to be old and covered with dandruff?* Van Gogh's doctor's name came to mind—*Gachet. Now there was a worthless and pompous shit. If he'd been any good. . . .*

"I don't like to think about it," he said. He stood up and walked back across the room to the windows.

"You have to face it sometime, Martin," Elders said. Her tone was that of a governess who's caught her favorite charge lying about some trifle. He thought that it *did* seem unfair. *She* wasn't the one suffering a recurring nightmare that was ruining *her* life, after all. She jotted something down on her note pad. He turned and noticed how delicate her hands were. There was a tape recorder on, something he found intrusive. He glanced at the tiny machine on her desk.

"Why do I have to face it? Aren't some things best avoided? *Why* do we have to dig until it hurts?" he said, tapping the window. "It seems you might push someone over the edge if you do that. I think it's all very Protestant, that attitude. I think we should just leave some things alone. Sleeping dogs and all that. . . . I've stopped taking the medication," he said. He waited for her reaction, afraid of what she would say. He'd threatened as much on the phone with her and she'd argued strongly against it.

"What would we talk about then?" Elders asked. She smiled that charming clever smile again, and he thought it suited her face all right. She was beautiful, but he'd known plenty of beautiful women. There was something else about her that interested him, something about the *way* she looked at him in that sun-drenched office holding late afternoon close. She ignored his confession about the medication. He relaxed. What, he wondered. *What was it? I suppose she's just a nice woman and I'm grateful for her kindness. I'm grateful to get the attention.* "Aren't you going to warn me again about taking my meds? Tell me all the risks I run if I don't?"

"You aren't a child. I already told you what you can expect," she said. "You're asking for trouble. Do you want to talk about it?"

"Why don't we talk about the—World Trade Organization—or, better yet, my new apartment! It's very grand, my new place. I've spent a fortune remodeling it," he said. It had given him enormous pleasure to spend his book money in a wanton way. "In fact, it's right at the top of Lombard Street. I have a wonderful view of Coit Tower," he said. She was studying him carefully now.

"Martin. Please tell me what happens in the dream after you get to the tower. I can't help you unless you open up. Why do you always stop there with the car parking?" she spoke in such a nice way, he thought. If he'd had a sister (and he'd always wanted one), then he would have wanted one just like her.

There was nothing clinical about Susan Elders, and he'd found his first visit to be such a relief. They'd simply talked like people who sit next to each other on a plane and find they are from the same old neighborhood or that they both sell the same kind of widget. It had been a wonderful unexpected delight just to talk about whatever came into his tired mind. He'd worried he was going to be trapped by some clinical sixty-year old snob in a terribly comfortable chair and be forced to talk about himself in agonizing detail. Instead, their first visit had seemed more like a platonic date. He'd ended up telling her all about his college days at Berkeley.

"You told me last week. . . ." She turned back to her notebook. He saw that she kept a whole library of notebooks behind her desk stacked very neatly. He imagined that all those twisted wire-bound books represented twisted-up people like himself, each one a small catalog of unhappiness. "'I think if I make a clean breast of the dream, it might stop',", she read back to him his own words from her notes. She flipped back to the present, the pages moving quickly under her fingers. *God damned capable woman, with all that hair, and those legs.* "Don't be afraid, Martin," she said. "I can help if you let me in. We can talk about your medication later, just tell me about the dream. It's obviously key."

"I'm afraid I'm going mad." There, he'd said it. He'd been thinking it for weeks now and he'd finally told her. A weight he had carried fell from his shoulders, and he felt better for a moment. "And then what will happen to me? I suppose I won't be able to write anymore. I suppose I'll be put on even more drugs and be wheeled around smelly corridors in some frightening institution called "Haven's Court" or something like that. My friends will send me long consoling letters that I'll drool on and be unable to read or even want to read. What do people *do* all day in those places, *anyway?*"

"That's not going to happen," Elders said. "I promise you. I won't let it happen." She moved the golden locks from her face. "I can't give you the courage to do this, if that's what you think. *You* have to supply your own. Martin, tell me the dream from start to finish, and I'll help you get well. I promise you." They looked at each other for a moment. He stood up again, drawn to the big window across the room and its view of the city. The familiar scene below on Market Street made him feel better. He got right up to the glass again and looked down the ten stories. He checked for any courage he might have summoned up on the way across the room. No, that horrible fear was still lodged where it had been since he'd seen the girl on the steps, at the pit of his being. He looked down on the busy street below. *I'm going mad. It's true.*

"I'm a child. I see someone die at Coit Tower. That's what the dream is about," he said quietly. He turned away from the window and looked at that angelic face staring at him with the blonde curls dangling against the dark blue jacket. "The dream always begins on the road to Coit Tower." She began to take notes as he spoke, but he decided he wouldn't tell her any more than that. How could he tell her and not expect her to think he was a lunatic?

SEVEN

There was a noisy clatter of iron weights in the cavernous mirrored weight room of the down-at-the-heels gym on Broadway near Columbus. Kline studied himself in the mirror. The expression on his face was already fierce and it was still early in the morning. He wore a green worn-out sweatshirt that had been cut at the armpits, and his biceps, huge and swollen from exercise, hung like raw meat from the sweatshirt's openings. The muscles of his arms and legs were mapped with veins. Over the years, he'd worked his body into a kind of crushing machine, and he was proud that he was the antithesis of the 1940's emaciated shtetl Jew. He looked like the last man in the world you'd want to pick on. He called Martin Anderson's number on his cell phone in the locker room before he got dressed and left a message saying who he was and that he planned on stopping by that morning. He knew he was about to put the young man's life through an emotional shredder. But it had to be done, and he'd decided this morning to get it over with.

There are some buildings in San Francisco that seem to encapsulate everything glamorous and chic about the city. 404 Lombard was that kind of building. Only a few blocks from Kline's office on Washington Square, it was the last building on the street before the road headed up to Coit Tower. Six stories high, painted green and facing the bay, it flew a huge American flag that was blowing in the breeze that morning as Kline walked up the driveway. In the sixties, someone had gotten the bright idea of installing an outdoor glass elevator.

"My name is Paul Kline. I'm here to see Mr. Anderson. Could you ring him, please." He had to speak up over the loud noise of a gardener's leaf blower. The doorman, a Latin kid in mufti, towered over Kline and must have weighed three hundred pounds. He wore a heavy gold crucifix the size of an index finger and seemed more like a bouncer than a doorman. Kline supposed the building was full of rich young people who didn't hold to hide-bound lifestyles for themselves or conventional uniforms for their doormen. The doorman called Anderson on the house phone nearby and came back to say he would come down to meet Kline in the lobby.

The elevator doors opened a few moments later, and Martin Anderson emerged, dressed in a white T-shirt and jeans. He was very young, blond, and extremely good looking, Kline thought, but Anderson seemed somehow unimpressed with himself. The detective felt a pang of jealousy and was surprised. It was an emotion he usually never felt, but he felt it now, and it was strong. The kid had managed to accomplish something that seemed impossible for him to do, no matter how hard he tried. The doorman turned to Anderson and said something Kline didn't hear. The detective tried to look *official.* He even smiled, trying to put Anderson at ease, when he looked at him.

"I thought I paid everyone I owed money," Anderson said half-jokingly as he walked up to Kline. "The doorman said you looked like a bill collector. Don't worry. I'll pay up. You're the last one, I hope." They shook hands. Kline was embarrassed that they'd taken him for a bill collector. Anderson held his door keys in the palm of his hand, obviously on the defensive. "Believe it or not, I used to run when I saw you people," he said.

"I'm not here for that reason, Mr. Anderson. Could I have a minute of your time? I promise it won't take long. I left a message on your answering machine this morning." Kline got one of his cards out and handed it to him.

"I'm sorry, but I haven't checked my messages yet." Martin took the card Private Detective Paul Kline. "Sounds like the movies," he said.

"Yeah. I'm full of mystery," Kline said. Anderson took a good look at him and smiled.

"Mr. Kline, what can I do for you?" Anderson softened a little.

"I have some news to give you," Kline said. He didn't see any reason not to get right to it.

"You really *are* mysterious. What kind of news?" Anderson asked still smiling.

"It boils down to money," Kline said. "Someone has given you a legacy." Anderson looked at him carefully and shut up for a moment.

"Well, Mr. Kline, in that case, why don't you follow me up to my apartment?" he said. Kline followed him into the small glass elevator and waited for the door to close. The elevator moved soundlessly. They seemed to be hanging on the edge of a cliff, the city and bay spread out below them, as the elevator climbed. Anderson jangled his keys and turned to look at the detective, half-smiling, obviously not believing any of it. Kline noticed that the kid's hand was shaking slightly and he was surprised.

"So who died? Both my parents are already dead. I don't have any brothers or sisters. No rich uncles. So what is this *really* about, Mr. Kline?" He looked down at Kline, studying him hard.

Kline only smiled. The elevator door slid open and he followed the kid out into a wide hallway with beautiful carpeting. "You are *very* mysterious, Mr. Kline." Kline followed him down the hall. Anderson used his key and held the apartment door for him.

The apartment took Kline by surprise. It was so spectacular that you'd expect a Hollywood goddess to come slinking casually out with a cocktail shaker. The view was dramatic—sky, rough-looking islands and water. You could see Alcatraz, Angel Island and the East Bay. Anderson went into the kitchen, which was across a huge living room with bleached hardwood floors that sparkled in the sunlight. The apartment looked like it had just been completely remodeled, everything in pristine condition. There were ceiling-to-floor windows across the width of the apartment designed to take full advantage of the view, and very little furniture in the living room. Kline, like everyone who walked into the place for the first time, was drawn to the windows. He noticed a backpack purse on the floor next to a library-style brown leather couch. Anderson came back from the kitchen. Kline hadn't even noticed he'd left the room, he was so taken by the apartment and view.

"You want a cup of coffee?" Anderson asked. Kline turned from the view.

"No thanks. Nice place. No, it's a fantastic place. I've never seen anything like it," Kline said. "And I grew up here."

"Thanks. I used to live south of Market in a trash-barrel-sized place with more cockroaches than a Mexican jail. I liked *it,* too, believe it or not. I kind of miss it, actually. That's why I thought you were a bill collector. They used to follow me like pilot fish. Now, what is it you want to tell me, or is it give me?" Anderson said. Kline went over to the couch and sat down. He didn't take any pleasure in turning people's lives upside down and he wanted to get it over with.

"I have a check for you for a million dollars from the estate of your birthmother. Your birthmother's family has hired the law firm I work for to tell you that you were adopted when you were five years old and to see that you get this money. Your birthmother's family wants you to know that if you want to–and *only* if you want to–you can ultimately be reunited with your family. Or, if you choose, you can just take the money and not follow up. You get one million dollars for the next several years, and you get the rest in a lump sum when you are thirty-five years old. It adds up to over a hundred million dollars. It's up to you," Kline said. "You get the money whether you decide to see your birth family or not."

"Is this some kind of joke?" Anderson said. He looked like he'd been punched.

"No." Kline said. "It's not a joke, Mr. Anderson. I have some documents I'd like to leave with you. You don't have to decide anything today, of course. Look them over and call me."

"There's been some kind of mistake. My parents would have told me if I were adopted," Anderson said.

"The law firm that hired me is very careful," Kline said. He got up and handed Anderson the file he'd taken from his briefcase. Kline heard a door close, and then he saw her for the first time. A girl glanced at Kline as she went down the hall. He really only saw her for an instant. He just saw her short black wet hair–and her legs. He saw her white thigh flick at him through the robe, but that was enough. He'd never forget her. Anderson must have noticed the look on his face.

"I don't want the money," Anderson said. "And I don't want to know the family. *If* it's true." Kline tried to recover from the girl who had radiated something powerful and splendid and profoundly sexual.

"That's your right," Kline said.

"I don't want anything to do with this," Anderson said. He went back into the kitchen, visibly upset. Kline sat down and waited, hoping the girl would reappear. He figured she was dressing and would come out eventually, and then he'd get another look at her. Sometimes in life you want just one more look to make sure of what you've seen. Kline was torn between wanting to see the girl again and wanting to be sensitive to Anderson, who looked like he'd been shot. He put his briefcase on the coffee table and opened it. The latches flicked open. He didn't hear anything coming from the kitchen. It was unnervingly quiet and so he decided to check. Kline pushed open the kitchen door and saw that Anderson had poured himself a cup of coffee and was sitting at a wooden table. There was a laptop in front of him, but it wasn't opened. The table was messy, covered with reference books and writing pads and a juice jar with pens stuck in it. Anderson seemed to have forgotten that Kline was there. He looked up at the detective in a way that wasn't good. He was pale.

"Why didn't my parents tell me?" Anderson asked.

"That was part of the deal. It was a private placement with a private adoption agency. They weren't supposed to tell you. They received money on a monthly basis even after you turned eighteen. Your birthmother's family wanted it this way," Kline told him.

"Why tell me now?"

"To be honest with you, I don't know," Kline said. The girl came into the kitchen then. She'd put on a black miniskirt and a white blouse. Her hair was wet and curly. Kline tried not to stare. She was taller than he was, and it wasn't that she was so beautiful, it was that she was so impressive in her bearing. He watched her bend over and put on her black shoes, first one, then the other. It wasn't really fair to be that sexy, Kline thought to himself. *Not fair at all.* He felt himself go haywire with those chemicals that rush through men and are unstoppable.

"Virginia, this is Mr. Kline," Anderson said. Anderson seemed to try and snap out of it for her benefit. "Virginia Winston. . . . Mr. Kline."

"Hi." The girl, in her late twenties, Kline guessed, put her hand out. Kline shook it. "Are you a cop?" she said. She had a whisky voice, and it was the last thing he would have expected, looking at her.

"No," Kline said. He looked at her full on for the first time. Kline noticed her eyes, they were blue and set wide apart. The effect on her beauty was dramatic.

"He's a detective." Anderson said. "Like one of yours."

"Fiction writer," she said, shaking Kline's hand, trying to explain their shorthand. She smiled. "My guy kind of looks like you. Only he's a cop," she said. "I couldn't sell that book, so I switched to romances. I can't sell those either, though," she said sheepishly.

"She didn't do too well at crime fiction," Martin said. Virginia shot him a hot-eyed glance and then smiled. Kline noticed she had a tattoo on her shoulder—a small sun, yellow with blue rays.

"No day job?" Kline said, staring at the tattoo.

"You even sound like my guy," she said. "Only my guy's a little—"

"Taller," Kline interjected.

"Just a little." She smiled at him and then looked at Anderson suddenly. "O.K. Martin, I've got to go to work. I'll see you *soon,* I hope." She turned around. "Nice meeting you, Mr. Kline," she said, looking back at him over her shoulder as she left the kitchen. He heard her steps in the living room and then the front door close. He wanted to say "beautiful girl" but stopped himself.

"Take your time to decide what you want to do," Kline said instead.

"Are we finished? I've got to get back to work."

"I'm sorry," Kline said coming out of his reverie. "I'll leave the file with you then."

"No, *I'm* sorry, Mr. Kline," Anderson said quickly. "I didn't mean to be rude. It's been a rough couple of weeks. I apologize. I haven't been myself lately. I've been working too hard, on a movie script of all things. It's been a strain. I apologize."

"Forget it," Kline said. They shook hands. Kline heard a dog barking next door.

"New neighbor," Anderson said. "The dog seems to bark all the time. It's not what you'd want to hear after paying nine-hundred thousand dollars for an apartment."

Kline said he would let himself out. He stopped one last time to look at the view. He realized that Anderson and the girl might be members of the writing group that had offered him a place. His friend had said the girl's name was Virginia. In the elevator Kline felt suddenly keyed up, the way you get in combat after someone shoots at you and you just want to shoot back. For the rest of the day, all he could think of was that white flick of her thigh.

EIGHT

Psychologically bombed out, Martin turned off the water in the shower and did nothing for a moment. For the first time in a week, he didn't hear the damn dog barking. He'd gone next door on several occasions and tried to talk to the neighbors about it, but they seemed never to be at home. He'd complained to the doorman, but there was nothing he could do about it. Every time he sat down to work, the dog started to bark, ruining his morning. He relished the unexpected silence.

He'd brought a cheap clock into the shower with him. He looked at its wet face. The phone in the bathroom began to ring. He slid the glass door open and grabbed a towel. He glanced at the pretentious white phone hanging on the wall across from him. *How ridiculous to talk to people in a bathroom,* he thought, snapping out of his stupor. The phone had been his decorator's idea. He decided to take the call in his bedroom and made for it straight away.

He finally admitted to himself as he walked down the hall that his life had gotten even worse since he'd heard he was adopted—the repeating nightmare, the lost hours, the hallucinations (he was seeing the blonde girl *every*where now). He felt trapped. The doctor had warned him that if he didn't get back on his medication she wouldn't be responsible. *Maybe she's right.*

The phones rang throughout the apartment as he made his way quickly down the grand hallway, a towel around his flat waist. He picked up the extension in the bedroom, killing the insipid ring.

"Martin, old boy. It's Henry Fisher. I've been over the first fifty pages of the script you sent down. I like them *very* much, *but–*" Martin heard the famous movie director's voice. The director tended to call at odd times, either very early in the morning or late at night. God knew what kind of hours the man kept. Martin glanced at one of the many clocks on the table. He'd begun to carry them around the apartment with him since his interludes had become more frequent. All the clocks said it was after five o'clock, but he wasn't sure if it was A.M. or P.M. He glanced out the windows and guessed it was afternoon but wasn't sure. Was it dawn or dusk? The sky was streaked with bloated crepuscular clouds and it was raining. He remembered now that he'd come straight home from Coit Tower. Or had he?

Hearing Fisher's voice made him want to hang up immediately. There was always a "but" with Hollywood people. A shiver ran down his back as he watched water drip onto the floor in the stale light of the bedroom. He'd done three different versions of the script for the producers so far, and they *still* weren't satisfied. Each rewrite had been like going to a dentist who insisted on going through your nostril to clean your teeth. He regretted now getting involved with Hollywood, but the money had been so fabulous he couldn't say no. Only a fool turns down that kind of money. Michael had urged him not to give up on the project. (He was relying more and more on Boon's advice now, it seemed, and was glad he had it, given his state of mind.)

Fisher, in his breathless cell phone-ese, told him he had made *reams* of notes. "I'll be up there at end of next week, how's that? Hope you'll be *ready* for me. We'll fix this thing once and for all!" Martin hadn't thought his script was broken in the first place. He moved his wet feet on the wooden floor and tried to think of something to say to the man. His mind was a total blank.

"Yes. I'll be ready," Martin lied. *How can I be ready? I'm barely sane.* The little puddle of water grew under him. In his mind, he felt like he was talking to the warden in the Death House. *"Yes, I'm ready. Let's go."* He could feel the priest slip up *alongside and ask him if he wanted to confess anything else. "Guilty. Yes, Padre, I'm guilty of sticking to my novel."* The two of them stop in the Death Row corridor. The guard's sour face (who looked an awful lot like Syd Fields, the screenplay guru whose insipid books he'd been forced to study) looked at him like he'd missed the whole point. *"Was I wrong, Padre?"* One of the other guards smirked and yanked him forward. It seemed even the guards knew better.

The director raced on about his star's bizarre behavior during a meeting at Kate Mantilini's, a famous industry lunch place on Wilshire Boulevard that Martin had been taken to several times while in L.A. Martin, barely listening, picked up a few words. "Narcissistic little shit. . . . Wrong table to start with. . . . He wouldn't eat at that table. . . . I should have known. . . . Just got up and left. . . . Went and sat with some bitch from development at Fox. . . ."

Fisher rang off after what seemed like hours. Martin put down the phone and glanced up. Shivering terribly, he tried not to, but then gave in, and went over to the big picture window to gaze again at Coit Tower. *"I want to thank the members of the Academy and most of all that narcissistic little shit for starring in my narcissistic little movie. . . ."*

He walked to the other side of the bedroom and lifted his leather jacket from the loveseat. He fished in the pocket and found it, a ticket to Coit Tower. "Admit one," it said. He walked over to a crystal bowl and threw the ticket in with the rest.

The bowl was overflowing with green tickets. "Admit one," he said out loud. He'd stopped counting how many times he had gone to the top of Coit Tower since he'd gotten back from his book tour.

He heard music coming from somewhere suddenly. It was the same song he'd heard that day at the Tower, "White Bird," the one the Goths had been playing. It grew louder. He ran out to the living room and checked the stereo but it wasn't on. He looked down the hallway, still shivering from the cold. The lights on the stereo suddenly turned on and he backed away. *"White bird must fly or she will die."* Music began to blare from *his* CD system now. He ran out of the living room and down the hall. The music stopped suddenly. Frightened, he went into his bedroom and sat on the bed for a moment. In front of him, in the semi-dark room, he saw that his closet door was slightly ajar. He remembered having closed it earlier. He stood up and pulled the door open completely and looked into the dark closet. He felt for the light switch and snapped it on. He dropped the clock he'd been carrying. He heard it crash on the floor. He saw a dog, a miniature collie, hanging dead at the back of the huge walk-in closet, its face twisted, eyes sad, protruding and staring at him. The dog was hanging from a belt around its broken neck, its hind legs dangling grotesquely beneath it. A horrible long string of saliva hung from its open mouth. The music he'd heard before started up again in the living room, very loud. The clock had rolled to the back of the closet and stopped against the full-length mirror facing him. Martin saw himself, naked, in the mirror's reflection. He backed out of the closet, terrified. He saw the dog kick once, silently, horribly, and he screamed.

• • •

One of the policemen had given him a bathrobe to wear. They hadn't let him dress. "I've told you what happened," Martin said to the men who were standing in his living room. "I've told you five or six times already." He looked at Michael, who'd come over immediately when he'd called him in a panic. Boon had gotten there just after the police. The police had been through the apartment very carefully. "The dog was in the closet. It was dead. I'm sure of it," Martin said. "I *saw* it. I *know* I did." They were all looking at him. Martin looked down at his hands. They were shaking. "I want to take a Valium," he told the police lieutenant.

"Not just yet," Lt. Cross said. The lieutenant had arrived after the two uniformed policemen. One, a hulking lesbian with a butch cut, had already been to the closet and found nothing. The lieutenant was a middle-aged Irishman pushing fifty, forty pounds overweight with thinning gray hair, and not much of that, combed straight back. He had what Martin thought of as a "heart attack face"–slightly puffy, bug-eyed and round. Martin decided that the lieutenant probably had a drinking problem. Cross's one swipe at fashion was an out-of-date cop's mustache that he'd worn since the seventies. Otherwise, the man was sloppily dressed and, having slid down that muddy hill to middle age, was stuck there now.

"I'd like my client to get some rest," Michael said. "He's obviously been through a great deal today. He's ill and suffering from delusions."

"We can't have people making false reports to the police," Cross said. "And if there *was* a crime committed, we have to get to the bottom of it."

"Well, obviously there has been no crime committed. My client is suffering from delusions. There is no dog in the closet, is there?" Michael said. "Or anywhere else." He reached forward and put his hand on Martin's knee. "He's under psychiatric care. I'm sorry it came to this, Lieutenant. If he made a false report it was only because of his state of mind."

"Yes, I know. You've told me that several times already," Cross said dismissively.

"I'm not crazy if that's what you all think," Martin said. "I'm telling you there was a dog in there." Cross looked at Martin as if he were a fool, or worse.

"But there is no dog, is there?" Cross said. "There isn't *anything* in the closet. I should charge you for making a false report."

"I don't care what you do. There was a *dog* hanging in my closet. I guess I brought it here and killed it," Martin said, looking up at Cross, angry and defiant now.

"I don't believe a word of it," said Cross. The two uniformed cops nodded in agreement. "Go ahead, go get that medication. . . .You need it," the lieutenant said. Martin got up and walked down the hallway. He stopped in front of his bedroom door. The closet had been ransacked. His shoes had been taken out by the police and were lying scattered on the wooden floor. There were bits of glass everywhere from the clock he'd dropped. All his clothes were heaped in a pile on the bed. He heard the front door close and hoped the police had gone. Michael came down the hall after him.

"I've convinced them that you had an episode. What an appalling shit that man is. . . ." Michael said. "But it's over now."

"Thank you, Michael. Thank you for coming. God, what's happening to me? Maybe the doctor was right. Maybe I shouldn't have stopped taking the Zoloft."

65

"I think we should call Susan and let her know what's going on with you," Boon said.

Michael put his arm around his shoulder. "It was so real, Michael. You can't believe how real it was. I thought maybe I'd killed it. It was horrible. Would you call Dr. Elders for me, please?" From the bathroom, uncapping the Valium bottle, he heard Boon talking to Elders' answering service. Martin wanted to tell him about the music that he'd heard but was afraid he would think he'd gone over the edge entirely.

"It's Michael. When you get this message, please call me at Martin Anderson's. He's had a nasty interlude." Martin shook three yellow Valium out from the container into his palm. He wanted to sleep and he knew three would put him out for hours.

"I think one is enough, Martin. Don't you? You want to be able to tell the doctor exactly what happened when she calls back." Michael was looking at him, still holding his cell phone.

"It's all gone to shit, hasn't it?" Martin said looking at his friend in the mirror.

"Not at all, old boy. Not at all." But Boon wasn't smiling now.

NINE

It was still in Kline's office at that time of day. There was a lull in the street noise between three and four in the afternoon when North Beach seemed to slow down. He was sitting at his desk in the small one-room office, staring at his computer but not able to concentrate. Instead, oddly volitionless, he was recalling, for the hundredth time, the details of his train trip back to Paris from Germany the month before, how relieved he was when the train had crossed the border back into France, the greens and blues of the French countryside, tender-looking and somehow feminine. *"I'll never come back to Germany,"* he'd said to himself, alone in the train's compartment. *"Never."*

The silence in his office was broken by the slam of a door down the hall, then footsteps falling away. His office door rattled sympathetically. Someone laughed, he heard a woman's voice, then a man's. The sounds—footsteps, laughter, doors—mixed in the hallway, with its cold marble floors and high ceilings acting as a kind of amplifier made of stone and wood. The building was old-fashioned and he liked it that way. He had grown up with parents who were much older than all his friends' parents. Old-fashioned things were familial to him. He stood up and went to the tall Victorian windows, still angry with himself for his failure to walk into Dachau, where his parents had first met.

Going to Germany had opened up feelings in him he couldn't shut out now, he realized. *You have to remember to forget. Forget that place.* He looked out over the stunted pines that ringed Washington Square just below his office on the third floor. At four o'clock, the intimate square, with its green space and park benches filled with tourists clutching maps and cameras, was as far from Dachau's sad necropolis as you could get. (He'd always thought "sad" a useless word until he approached the camp's gate.)

Outside his window, the well-scrubbed tourists and office workers shared park benches with blue-faced Chinese winos and the young riffraff of North Beach. It all seemed so innocent and peaceful and ordinary. But, he'd learned from his parents, years ago, that what seemed ordinary could suddenly turn sinister.

Ironically, like his parents, he felt he was a victim of the camp, too. He knew his mother and father conceived him in hopes a child would change everything for them. His birth had been his parents' grasp for normalcy as they struggled to become assimilated Americans despite their fumbling accents.

Newspapers had been pored over for clues about the future. *Was there another Hitler out there?* Soul-less linoleum squares were washed on hands and knees every Monday by his mother long after she could have paid someone to do it. Their house became an important bulwark against the outside world's ugliness and violence. His mother sought to protect them from the chaos with red plastic buckets of "Mr. Clean" or by using a gray vacuum cleaner late at night. The riots and assassinations that occurred during his childhood had made the vacuum run hot, its noisy motor a reminder that a second knock could come at anytime.

Only A's on his report card had been acceptable to her; anything less made his mother cry as if he'd stolen something.

So he'd gotten A's. He'd done everything right. He'd done everything right all the way through Stanford. And then he did the unexplainable–he joined the Marine Corps and became a soldier.

When his father died, the rabbi who performed the service, a rotund and affable young man, buried number 136599, Max Kline, victim of the twentieth century's excited and noisy parade of vicious imbeciles and mass murderers, all promising a better world. Max Kline had hung on to the barbed wire of life as long as he could and then suddenly dropped off without so much as a good-bye. *When you see God, papa, tell him you're pissed off.*

When the phone rang, he was grateful to be pulled from his melancholia. He'd tried again that morning to start a novel and failed. His failures weren't helping his mood. Somehow, writing had become the only good reason for living. His computer was malevolent and uncaring about his need to purge himself creatively. Nothing happened. He just couldn't write. He was just another middle-aged man holding onto a young man's dream, he decided, picking up the phone.

"Kline here." He always sounded colder on the phone than he meant to.

"Paul, it's Martin Anderson."

"Yes?" *An odd case*, Kline thought to himself, *very odd.*

"I'd like the report. I'm at the bar in Moose's next door. Can I come up?" Anderson asked.

"Sure, come on up," Kline said

Anderson had come to his office the week before with a simple request. "Follow me and write down everything I do. I'll be back in a week for the report. I think I may be going mad." Anderson had told him about seeing the strangled dog in his closet and how it had disappeared by the time the police came. Kline couldn't remember anyone ever asking to *be* followed before. He remembered once that one of his men had shot a dog in Somalia and how it had shocked everyone in the platoon, more than when they killed the enemy. He couldn't see the kid killing anything, much less strangling a dog.

He hadn't been surprised to see Anderson again, but he had been surprised when Anderson wanted to hire him. Kline smiled, part envy, part interest in the case. He'd seen Martin's dark-haired girlfriend again when he'd followed him. He'd thought about her since the day they'd met in Anderson's apartment weeks before. There had been something about her. Maybe it was her waist or the lift of her bosom. With women it was the details. One would mark itself on you and then you were interested. He couldn't get her out of his mind. He'd tried all his usual tricks and she'd stuck there like some microbe his immune system couldn't overcome. *I'm too old for her,* he told himself. He got up from the desk and went to the file cabinet.

Kline heard the knock on his office door, which he habitually kept locked. It wasn't soft and polite like most people's, it was loud, almost desperate. The moment he went for the latch, some very profound instinct warned him. *It's going to turn out badly,* Kline thought, looking at Anderson's fresh youthful face standing in front of him when he opened the door. The feeling had never let him down.

Anderson was carrying a Day-Runner, looking like a college student late for class. They shook hands. "Paul. Did you do it *exactly* the way I told you, by the half hour?" Kline closed the door. "Is it what I thought? Coit Tower?" Anderson asked as if he were talking to himself, unable to wait another moment for the answer.

"Yes, I have it all here," Kline said. He handed him the report. "We did exactly as you asked. I followed you sometimes and sometimes it was someone I use. But every half hour, whoever it was made a note of your location and the time of day," Kline said. Martin nodded and started to read the file Kline had handed him. Anderson went to the library table Kline had in the corner and spread his own Day-Runner out, then put Kline's notes next to it. He turned the pages, quickly glancing from one set of notes to the other. Kline noticed the kid hadn't shaved and looked the worse for wear.

"Is it what you were expecting?" Kline asked finally from the other side of the office. The small office, like its owner, was clean and sparse, and felt slightly cloisterish, as if Kline lived there. There was something terribly personal about the room's emptiness.

"Yes, it's what I expected," Martin said, looking at him. "Come here. I'll show you." Intrigued, Kline went across the office and looked at Anderson's notes. "I go to Coit Tower, you see? Monday at two o'clock, that's what you report. But here, on mine there's nothing. It's blank. No entry in my book." Anderson tapped his finger down on the spot. The nail was chewed, Kline noticed.

"I see," Kline said. Anderson had been keeping track of himself, too. Kline could see the young man's notes in long-hand in his Day-Runner. The previous Monday showed a blank page in Anderson's book. Kline's report had him at Coit Tower for over two hours that afternoon.

"You like Coit Tower?" Kline said. Martin didn't answer at first. He seemed to be debating something. He lifted his hand from the desk.

"I think I've gone mad," Anderson said matter-of-factly. "That's why I hired you. To prove it. I've been missing chunks of time, even before you came to tell me the news about my parents, but it's gotten worse since then. I guessed at what

71

was going on, but I had to be absolutely sure." Kline looked at him. "I am now."

"I'm not sure I understand," Kline said.

"I don't remember *any* of this," Martin touched Kline's file. The detective looked at him a moment. Kline had a talisman, a small tiny plastic revolver he kept on a key chain in his pocket. He'd bought it the day he joined the Marine Corps. He felt his fingers surround it as he looked at Anderson.

"You need a doctor, not a detective," Kline said. Martin looked at the man. The detective was the kind of man who said what was on his mind. The remark wasn't meant as an insult, Anderson could see that. Kline was just blunt. It was reassuring.

"What do I do at the tower?" Anderson asked. Kline felt suddenly sorry for him. There was something pathetic in Anderson's blue eyes. He was frantic like he'd been the day he'd come to the office the first time—not obviously, but frantic nonetheless. He displayed the quiet angst the detective had grown up with and knew so well.

Kline went and sat down at his desk. There was a moment as he drew on his memory from his new executive chair.

"You stand out in the parking lot first," Kline said. "That's what interested me about it. You go to the same pay-to-view binoculars and wait. You seem to study the tower from just that same spot each time. You never deviate from that."

"Do I meet anyone? See anyone else?"

"No. Never."

"And the blonde girl I told you to keep an eye out for?"

"I saw her twice in the lobby, like you said, by the elevator," Kline said. "You'll see I've noted it." Anderson looked down at Kline's report.

"Did you follow her like I asked?"

"Yes."

"And?"

"It's always crowded in there when she appears. Then, somehow, when I try to get close to her, she goes toward the stairs. I lost her twice in the stairwell. There are all kinds of passages in there," Kline said.

"Is that all I do?"

"No. You wait, like I said, maybe a half hour, and then you look at your watch and go up the steps and into the building. You look at the murals for a while, one in particular, the one by Albro that has the girl in it that looks like the blonde girl that follows you. At least she's dressed like the one in the mural, with the polka dot dress and all, but her straw hat always manages to keep me from getting a good look at her face.

"Am I crazy?"

"You don't *act* crazy, I can tell you that. You seem kind of. . . . Well, I hate to say it but, *happy,*" Kline told him.

"Happy?"

"Yes. I'd say so. I've followed plenty of unhappy people. I should know."

"Then what?"

"You go up to the top of the tower to the observation deck. Sometimes you take the stairs, sometimes you take the elevator. Mostly, you take the stairs. I could have killed you. It's two hundred and thirty seven steps up there, you know. You did it *twice* one day. I'd already been on the Stairmaster that day," Kline said, trying to joke.

"Yes, I know how many steps there are. What do I do—up at the top?"

"You do what the tourists do. You gaze out on the city. Never from the same spot. You move around."

"That's it?"

"No, sometimes you tell things to people. You tell them about the tower. You act like a kind of guide. That seems to make you very happy. People seem to like it. You know a lot about the place. You're a regular expert," Kline said.

"Well, at least I'm *enjoying myself!*" Martin said, perplexed. Kline didn't answer. He swiveled in his chair. The phone rang and Kline let the answering machine pick it up. Kline glanced at the phone then back at Martin.

"I enjoyed following you. It was different. I've been doing a lot of boxcar cases lately." Kline decided to let the call go.

"Boxcar?" Martin said.

"Big corporate searches for discovery purposes. You have to move the paper with a forklift. It was fun to play the gumshoe for a change."

"Is there anything else? Do I take anyone with me?"

"No. You've always been alone. No, that's about it, except for the ordinary things everyone does—go to the supermarket, barbershop, that kind of stuff. Oh, by the way, I saw your book at Borders the other day," Kline said, changing the subject. "Are you famous yet?"

"I guess I am," Martin said. "If being on Oprah qualifies."

"What's it like?" Kline asked.

"What? Being on Oprah or being famous?"

"Being a writer? Do you like it?"

"It's a lot like being a detective, I would think."

"How so?"

"Well, you have to put up with a lot of bullshit then wait for the money in the mail." They both laughed at the joke.

"Is that a writers' group you go to on Fridays?" Kline said. "I've thought about writing. I want to write up some of my experiences in the Marine Corps." He looked away out the window as he said it. He didn't have the nerve to mention he'd been invited to join.

"The girl I described," Anderson said, changing the subject abruptly. "She looked just like the girl in the mural? She wears the same dress and hat, right?"

"Yes. Exactly like the mural. It's kind of strange," Kline said. "If you're having interludes, you should see a doctor. But you haven't imagined the blonde. I saw her, too. People can react very strangely when they find out they've been adopted. I've heard there can be any number of psychological ramifications," Kline said. "But the blonde is no hallucination."

"So you mean I have good reason to go crazy." Anderson stopped talking and moved towards the window. "Look!" Kline stood up and looked out the window. There was a young girl out on Washington Square dressed like the girl in the mural. It was the same blonde that Kline had seen at Coit Tower.

"That's her, isn't it?" Anderson said.

"Yes. That's her. That means you aren't crazy, doesn't it?" Kline said. The girl crossed the square below them. They watched her disappear into the traffic on Columbus Avenue. "Have you decided what you're going to do about the money?" Kline asked. Martin turned from the window. "They haven't heard from you yet."

"I'll take it. Tell them I want it."

"There's something I should tell you," Kline said.

"What?"

"I've been invited to join your writing group."

Martin looked at him for a moment. "Do you want to be a writer?"

"Very much," Kline said. The tables had turned. All of a sudden, Kline realized he was giving something away about himself that gave Anderson power over him. Until now, he had held all the emotional cards.

"Join then," Martin said.

"Okay. Thanks. I thought I should tell you, seeing that, well–"

"You won't tell them about all this. . . ."

"No, of course not," Kline said.

TEN

Kline parked the Cadillac he'd inherited from his father and walked down the dark foggy street to the building where the writing group met. He went up to the door and hesitated. Nervous, he tried to look through the glass on the front door, but there was nothing to see but his own reflection. He knocked, and then rang the buzzer. He'd brought a bottle of wine. He looked down at it stupidly as he waited for the door to open. He was late. Having been afraid to come, he'd driven around the neighborhood for over an hour trying to get his courage up. A young woman, very blonde and petite, came to the door, shoeless and with a keen smile.

"Paul? Hi! I'm Betsy Austin." They shook hands. "Martin said you might be coming tonight."

"Yes. Sorry I'm late. I had trouble parking," Kline lied sheepishly.

He felt slightly relieved as he followed her up the flight of stairs. There were photos on the wall of famous writers. The one of Plath caught his eye. Upstairs, Kline could make out in the lamplight a huge living room decorated like a millionaire's exotic crash pad. Everyone in the room was in their late twenties and good-looking, it seemed. Kline wondered if he shouldn't go back home, back to his apartment where he could lie to himself about his talent, back to where there were no cutie-pies with naked midriffs. They were all looking at him now as he stepped into the room. He was forty, had two wars marked on his face, and it all seemed so stupid now. He was twenty years too late.

"This is Paul," Austin said in her kindergarten teacher tone. Kline looked at a beautiful Chinese girl across the room dressed in all black, then at the other faces that were measuring him. They wore clothes that marked them as the hip and the young and the daring. *I'm too old*, he thought. *Good God. This is all wrong.* He was only forty, but he felt like he might as well be a hundred. He wondered what in God's name he'd been thinking as he surveyed their pulchritude. Had he known they were *all* going to be his junior by a generation, he wouldn't have come. He felt silly. Virginia came up to him and took the wine bottle out of his hand. He let her tug it away. There are some women that you only think about in one way. She wasn't the prettiest one, she was just the one that made you think that one way. He was suddenly sure of why he'd come, and it had nothing to do with art. He didn't care about the rest of them or what they thought of him suddenly.

"In vino veritas," Virginia said. "I'll go open it. If I don't like it, you can't join." She smiled quickly, putting him at ease.

"That's Virginia. Don't let her scare you. She's a loose literary cannon," Boon said as he stepped out of the kitchen. "Sit down, old man." The two men traded a look. Kline was surprised to see the young lawyer. He was the last person he would have expected to see in a writers' group. "We were just discussing Hemingway. What do you think of him?" Boon asked before Kline could get his balance. "People say he's making a comeback."

"He's my favorite author," Kline said quickly. Boon made no attempt to acknowledge their knowing each other.

"Oh shit, he's one of *those* white guys," the Chinese girl said. She looked horribly disappointed. Kline tried to smile, not sure what he'd said wrong. Virginia came back into the room with the wine and a stack of nested paper cups.

"Let me introduce everyone," she said. "That's Michael by the kitchen, the one with the big ass. That's Betsy Austin, and she's *not* gay. That's Cindy. She just posed for *Penthouse. Really!*" Virginia turned and looked at the slight redheaded young man who was just now turning around. He'd been tearing pieces of paper and throwing them into the flames of the fireplace. "That's Rainer Rilke. . . . Just kidding. That's Kevin Fitzgerald, soon to be a medical doctor, a.k.a. God Almighty. I'm Virginia. I don't bite. I'm not a lesbian either, in case you were wondering. Isn't that what everyone wonders these days? I write romance novels. What do you write? You look like you might write cheap crime fiction or artistic pornography." She handed him an empty cup. Like Boon, he wondered why she acted as if they hadn't met before. "Welcome to our little group," she said. "I'm letting it *breathe,*" she said, nodding to the bottle. The redhead was giving him an appraising look that was anything but friendly, Kline thought. He watched Virginia fill his cup with the wine and was glad he'd come if it meant he could look at her all night.

Tattoos, seen and unseen, flashed now and then as the young people moved about the room during the break. The unseen ones were only hinted at, their blue-black marks riding at the edges of underwear like sexual icebergs. The sense of raw energy and nervousness that belongs to the young and to the artist filled the room, that desire to be brutal but fair all at once, on canvas, on paper, in music, to judge the world and find it lacking. It was everything Kline had hoped to find and feared because it made him feel inadequate.

They listened to Virginia read first from her sex-rammed romance novel that had shocked him a little. He couldn't imagine her selling it to anyone. She'd turned the whole form on its head, taking the love story and the sex seriously. Kline thought he'd been forgotten, until the break when Cindy came and sat next to him, plopping down like a teenager visiting Mars. "First thing you have to do is learn to smoke dope," Cindy said. "Otherwise you can't join." Kline looked at the pretty girl, not sure whether she was joking or not.

"Okay," he replied.

"Good." He supposed Cindy was looking at him like a kid does a natural history exhibit of "Early Man." He smiled but she didn't crack. Her pretty face was stern. Instead, she handed him an unlit joint.

"Which end?" he said, trying to joke.

"Either one. Do you have the glands for real fiction? Not that *GQ* crap like 'How I wrestled alligators', or shit like that. We don't care if you wrestled alligators or not. We don't care about Montana chic fishing and fucking novels. Is that what you write? Fishing and fucking novels? Like Jim Harrison's 'Ode to the special white male's burden?' 'Where's my dick' novels? Or are you just a stupid-ass mystery *wallah* with nothing to say and fourteen boring ways to say it? Maybe something fresh, like an alcoholic detective with Lyme disease."

"Maybe he's the *New Yorker* magazine professor type," Kevin said from behind Kline.

"You mean like Saul Bellows," Cindy said. "Run, asshole, run, books? Very profound . . . for one percent of the fucking population."

"Don't mind our Cindy. I have a whip in the car if she gets out of hand," Boon said from across the room, obviously enjoying the literary hazing. They were all looking at him now as if they'd just realized he was in the room.

"I don't know how to fish," Kline said.

"What *do* you know how to do?" Cindy said.

"I know how to set up ambushes and kill zones. I know how to storm beaches and call in air strikes, that kind of stuff." She looked at him wide-eyed.

"We've all tested positive for the art virus," Cindy said finally. "Still want to sleep with us?"

"I think he just wants to corn-hole the bestseller list," Virginia said. "I'm afraid there are only a few holes and they're all taken," she said.

"I write thrillers, Kline. Don't let them scare you off. I've seen people run right down those stairs and out of here, never to return," Boon said. "They're a pack of Bolsheviks. I've said so for years. Especially Virginia. She's a veritable Nikita Khrushchev."

"And one black-flag anarchist," Martin chimed in.

Kline could feel their stares, waiting to see if he'd panic under fire. *First night in the barracks,* he told himself. He picked up the Bic lighter and snapped it on. "So this is marijuana. I've heard about it." The lighter made a tiny flame in his hand. A Muni bus rolled by outside and shook the building. He took the joint from Cindy and lit it.

"Like it?" Cindy said, still looking at him. He smoked half the joint then handed it back to her. Martin called Cindy back to her end of the room. It was her turn to read.

The more Kline studied the scene through the lamplight, and his own deep breathing, the more the kids in the room reminded him of those magazine ads that posed young models as drug addicts collapsed in the corner of some fancy apartment. After all, they were appropriately young, thin, and chic. The late hour, the dope, the comfortable furniture and the spotlighted paintings made the room seem more interesting than it might have been in the full light of day, but he liked it.

Kline stared at Virginia sitting in the smoke of the impromptu temple. He could have sworn that he saw several arms waving from her body, like Shiva, the Hindu goddess of creation/destruction. He realized he was stoned and that she was speaking to him.

"We have only one rule; the brutal rule," she said. Cindy was unpacking her manuscript.

"What?" said Kline, sitting up.

"You have to bring something new to read every other week. Something new you've written. That's the only rule. *You* have to read next time." He looked around him.

"Horny man, burning bright, in the forest of the night," Fitzgerald said in his drawl. "He's *obviously* come here to get laid." Kline saw that Fitzgerald was still wearing his scrubs from the hospital. "Tell *Homo erectus* to go away. We don't want any," he said.

"Fuck off, Kevin. I say he stays. I'll sleep with him. . . ." Cindy said, putting on her glasses. "I'll fuck him until he changes his mind about everything he ever believed about America."

"It's settled then, you can join," Boon said. "You get Cindy, a month's supply of raw meat, and a box of paper. Congratulations."

ELEVEN

Wearing only his running shorts–he never dressed before noon when working–Martin heard his answering machine click on a few moments after he booted up his laptop at the kitchen table. His new stockbroker's voice (another friend of Michael's) filled the sun-dappled kitchen. "Hey buddy! Listen to this. . . ." The overly-earnest male voice went on about some Internet IPO, bowling.com, he *had* to buy this morning, right now, or all Western Civilization would come to a halt.

He had an office in his new apartment, but he was used to writing at kitchen tables since he'd been in college and now couldn't get out of the habit. The apartment's fancy office seemed frivolous and he couldn't bring himself to use it. He wrote in the kitchen, in part, so he could be near the coffee maker. He heard the answering machine click on again and stopped typing.

"This is the chance of your lifetime," a familiar voice said. "You know how many writers would take it up the *ass* to work on this picture? *Do you?* Now I want that script by next Friday, you lazy s.o.b., and I want it *right* this time. And I keep *telling* you I want those two girls *kissing* in a pool, *naked, on the screen.* I want the big lesbian love scene! And I'm going to tell that lame putz faggot director I hired the same *thing.* . . ." The answering machine cut off Marvin Weinstein, the producer who'd bought the motion picture rights to his novel. Like David O. Selznick, Weinstein, a human gargoyle, was always leaving messages or sending him vapid memos by fax about what he wanted in the script. The memos invariably were full of contradictions and spelling mistakes. Ham-fisted and stupid, Weinstein was the personification of everything base and ugly in Hollywood. He had described himself when they first met as an "entertainment genius."

Martin looked across the kitchen. The book, the script, the money, the fact that a famous actor might star in the movie, *none* of it was that important to him anymore. *What is?* he wondered, staring at the answering machine. He knew the answer instinctively. He had to get new material for the group. The brutal rule, now *that* was important to him. Writing a new novel would help him hang onto his sanity. It was the only hope. *If I'm not careful, I'll turn into one of* them—*the walking banal of Rodeo Drive.*

Three new pages into a first chapter, he heard a noise in the hallway. It had been unusually quiet all morning, no dog barking from the next door apartment. Apparently, the dog was alive and well, as he'd heard the barking every day since his bizarre hallucination.

Just after ten A.M., he looked up through the open kitchen door and down the sunlit hallway and saw the door to his bedroom open. Frightened, his heart began to pound as he watched. He had thought he was alone in the apartment.

Virginia stepped out of the bedroom. She stood naked in the doorway. The sunlight caught her black pubic hair. The sight of her stunned him, he didn't remember bringing her home. The beating of his heart was very loud in his ears. His fingers hovered over the keyboard.

"Good morning, Martin." He was too shocked to answer. "Cat got your tongue?" Virginia said. Her words seemed to rush around him. He stood up and walked out of the kitchen.

"No, I'm sorry. . . . I just–"

84

"You just bed 'em and forget about them? Is that it?" she said.

"No. No, of course not." Appalled with himself and frightened because he couldn't remember inviting her back here after the group meeting the night before, he turned and looked back at the kitchen and his work table trying to remember what had happened last night. He wracked his brain, but it was a blank. He remembered leaving Green Street alone. He was sure of it. Seeing Kline at their group had brought all his problems back to him, the whole mess of his adoption.

The sun intensified coming through a skylight in the ceiling of the hallway. The sun suddenly highlighted her skin when the clouds passed above. There was something ethereal and fey about her standing in the sunlight like some kind of Irish goddess who'd run from the glade straight to him. He was staring at her and felt ashamed of himself for not remembering anything about last night.

"Would you please stop acting weird, Martin?! Are you stoned? What's wrong with you? *Do* something normal! You're scaring me."

"Sorry. I'm just surprised. I thought you'd gone home already," he lied. He wanted to tell her that he didn't remember a thing about last night after he left the group, but he couldn't bring himself to. "Let me get you a robe." He walked down the hallway towards her. The closer he got, the more beautiful she looked, all flat waist and breasts. The Mexican sun—blue and yellow—tattooed on her right shoulder was bold and terribly sexy. He looked beyond her to the door of the bedroom closet and turned around immediately. The sight of the closet still frightened him.

"I'll make coffee," she said, watching him. She reached out and touched his shoulder as he walked by. He felt her hand on his T-shirt and stopped. It was an odd touch, immediately soothing. She turned to him and took him in her arms and they kissed. His arms reached around her. Her skin was warmed by the sun. She pushed herself into him, molding her body to his, kissing his eyes, touching his hair.

"I'm in love with you. Do you care? Probably not," she said. "I'd do anything for you. Like last night. Anything. When you came to my place, I was so glad to see you!" She kissed him again. He didn't know what to say or do. He thought that he was in love with her, but now it seemed absurd, and even dangerous, her being there. She was kissing his face. Her lips traced a circle on his unshaven cheek. Nervous, he pulled away a little too abruptly. She let go of him, surprised. He walked into his bedroom and to the closet. He forced himself to open it, his hands shaking now. He took a robe from a hanger and surveyed the room.

The curtains were closed. Everything except for the bed was tidy. The bed covers were piled into a sexual heap. He saw her clothes draped over the end of the bed. Looking at them in the semi-darkness, he tried desperately to remember anything about last night. He couldn't. *Nothing.* He crossed the room with the robe in his hand and went to the curtains and tore them open. He could see Coit Tower framed in the center of the window against a perfect cold blue sky. *He saw, for a moment, Virginia's face in ecstasy. He was doing something to her against a wall, at the tower. Her face was turned away from him against the tower wall, he was–* They'd made love. He remembered now.

"Hey, I don't have all morning. Why don't I fix us something to eat? You know what a bitch I am without coffee." He turned around. She was standing in the doorway, the hallway behind her was drenched in golden mid-morning sunlight. "I tell you what. Let's just forget breakfast," she said, as she

86

stepped into the bedroom and closed the door. He heard it click shut. Instinctively, he reached for the cord and closed the curtains again. They were plunged into a special darkness that was riddled by the light that seeped in through the crack in the curtains and cut across her marble-white nakedness dramatically. Strangely, he felt a rush of sexual adrenaline, almost as if he'd taken a hit of coke. His fear of her melted away as she came towards him.

They were both glossy and wet when she kicked off the sheet. "So what's with Coit Tower?" she said. "What does it have to do with your new book?" She rolled over in the bed and faced him. She made love like she wrote. It was always exciting with her, nothing exotic, but eroticism on top of eroticism, the way she could look at you, both smoldering and happy, all very natural. "I don't care, but it was kind of strange. Kind of big time kinky. You said you were writing something and–"

"What did I say, *exactly?*"he said. She paused for a moment and looked at him. There were dust motes floating in the air above them that had came off the blankets, raised from their frantic lovemaking. It smelled close. She looked at him, then glanced at one of the cheap wind-up clocks on the table by the bed. It was so quiet that he could hear the clocks all ticking out of sync, a maddening symphony of ticking.

"You came by my place and said, 'Hey, I'm writing something about a crazy man who takes girls up to Coit Tower and screws them.' And then you asked if I wanted to go. I thought it was kind of, well, *strange.*"

"But you went," he said. Naked, he reached out and touched the tattoo on her shoulder. The lovemaking had liberated him for a moment from his fears. He felt normal, just a man in bed with a woman. For once, he wasn't afraid of what was going to happen next.

"Yup. Silly me," she said.

"Why did you come?"

"Well, for one thing you said it was a favor only another writer could do for you, and I thought that was funny. I guess it's more fun than paying your rent. Then I saw you were serious. That you *really* wanted to, well you know—do it at Coit Tower. I thought it was harmless." She picked up one of the cheap wind-up clocks on the nightstand and looked at it. He decided that if she asked about the clocks he would tell her what had been happening to him. "I didn't realize it would be outside. Maybe I would have changed my mind if I had known. So what are you writing about?" She put the clock down. "I'm *intrigued.*" She turned to him. He noticed the tiny mole above her left breast. He instinctively put his finger on it and then touched her breast with the back of his hand, feeling the nipple move across the back of his fingers. He noticed the dark color of the mole against her white skin. "I suggested the zoo but you weren't too interested. I thought it would be more fun to screw in the monkey house," she said. He had to laugh.

"Thanks," he said.

"No problem." She reached over and held his hand.

"No, really, you are the only person I could think of, that I could go ask to—" He tried to make it seem as if he had been in control of his actions when he knew he wasn't.

"I'm sure there are scores, you're such a cutie," she said.

"No, I mean who wouldn't think I was a lunatic. *You don't,* do you?"

"No. I just think you're kinky. But, frankly, so am I." She bent down and sucked his finger as if to prove it. "I had fun. You got very excited." She spoke around the tip of his finger.

"It was interesting. I'm going to use the scene myself. Only I can't put in what we did. I always have to stop when it gets good if I want to sell." She pushed her hair out of her eyes and looked up at him. She started to read from a book in her head in an over-the-top-tone of voice.

"It was dark. Mark was upset that his first wife was getting the kids. I could feel that he needed me. He called. I waited outside in my lobby. The doorman kept looking at me. Finally, I saw Mark's car pull up outside. I rushed towards the car, not hearing or thinking anything. My heart was pounding frantically. I hoped he liked what I was wearing.

"Anyway you get the idea. A romance writer can't exactly say (she made quotation marks in the air), 'He took me up to Coit Tower, tore my hundred dollar underwear off and fucked my brains out.' I tried that and it didn't work. The rejection slip said they didn't buy soft-porn, only legitimate romances. I suppose I have to say it like this:

"He didn't want to talk. He drove up Lombard Street. The zigzagging of the street reminded me of how screwed up and twisted this whole affair had been. They were heading towards Coit Tower when he finally spoke, 'Tonight, I asked for a divorce. I told her about us. I told her you wanted to marry me. I told her that I loved you and nobody else.' She fell apart just like when her father died.

"Scratch father. Make it brother. Brothers are always dying, aren't they?" He stopped her.

"Virginia, what did we do up there?"

"*Excuse* me?"

"I mean, if you were writing it straight. If you were doing it like, well, not a romance." She moved her body against his. There was that body-hot feeling again, tinder hot. He could smell her again. She was starting to smell like pure sex. It was the smell from earlier, only thicker, riper now. He felt her hand on his chest. She looked into his eyes. Her hair was a mess yet beautiful. Her blue eyes shone in the demi-light. She started to speak, quieter now, in a tone of voice he'd never heard before; the put-on voice was gone.

"It was dark. I liked the dark. We didn't talk the whole way over there. I remember the window against my face was very cold. I remember looking out and seeing the sidewalk and houses go by. I remember my breath on the glass and the way it made a small ghost circle. I wanted to be made love to like I were made of glass. Neither one of us spoke.

"Up at the tower we stopped and parked. We got out of the car. I wanted to kiss and I tried to kiss him, but he spoke to me instead. He said he wanted to do it against the tower. It was cold. I wasn't sure we wouldn't get into trouble. He said please. There was a glossy moonlight shining on the bay. The water was black, the sky midnight blue. I put my arms around him and realized it wasn't me he was thinking of. I was just some fill-in, some stand-in, and I didn't give a shit. I thought if I did anything he asked, anything, anywhere, he would love me. It's crazy, but I've loved him from the moment I set eyes on him.

"He took me up the steps to the tower. It was locked and dark inside. He was holding my hand, leading me. We circled around to the back and had sex against the wall. He seemed to like it. I didn't. It was cold, and I hardly felt anything except the weight of him and my hands on the concrete and the way my panties got in the way.

"We sat in the car afterwards and listened to a jazz station. We talked about my work. I was in a slump. He listened. He didn't say much. He looked at me because I'd started to cry. He said he was sorry but I knew he wasn't. Not really. He liked what we'd done. I really didn't like the selfish way he'd done it."

"Is that all I said? I'm sorry?"

"That's about it. You don't have to be ashamed. You didn't do anything wrong. I went there of my own free will. You asked me. It was an art thing. I accept that. I believe in you. She wiped the tears off her face with the back of her hands. She was crying now, as she must have been there. He was shocked by what he'd done to her. "Did you get what you wanted out of it? That's all I want to know?" She moved closer to him and put her head on his chest.

"Yes," he said. He was lying but he couldn't say anything else. It would have been too horrible to tell the truth, that he was probably going mad and it hadn't meant anything to him. Nothing.

"Don't worry. I'll get you back for this. You know I'll come over some night and say come on let's go make love on the bar at Kuleto's or something, and I'll make you do it on the bar. You'll see." She hit him on the shoulder.

"Yeah, it's an art thing," he said. He tried to joke but kept holding onto her.

"Damn right. Do you ever get tired of it?" she said suddenly. She reached up and touched his face tenderly. It was that soul-healing touch again that always took him by surprise.

"Of what?" he asked.

"Of not being like other people. Are there times when you'd just like to see the world, I don't know, like a civilian, instead of *always* transposing it into prose. I tire of it. I'm tired of being afraid to open the mail because I know that it's a rejection letter before I even open the envelope. I'm tired of not having a husband and kids, a normal family life. And I'm scared about the future. Really scared. One day, I might not be able to write at all. I'm almost thirty. In ten years, it will all be over. I know it. You won't want me. Nobody will want me. I'll eat cat food and walk around the streets in pink house shoes, my face old. Homeless, maybe. That's what I fear most of all. Homelessness. Lovelessness. Ugliness. Being alone," she said. She moved up on him as if by making love again she could forestall the future she saw so clearly in front of her. As they were making love, the dog started to bark from the next apartment. The whole time they were doing it—her on top of him—he watched the closet door, not feeling anything, fixated on the dog's metallic bark.

TWELVE

Broadway had a sexual junkyard feel to it, with the blistering neon signs and tawdry six-foot high photos of cavorting girls plastered on its storefronts *(Garden of Eden–Adam And Eve–Swim Suit Edition)*. The effect was as erotic as chalk. The legendary street was packed with tourists and cap-wearing college boys from Cal in "posses" who were thirsty for a little silicon.

Passing the Black Cat, the college boys glowered at the urban types sitting at the bar. All sporting the same driven faces, the college kids were openly hostile to the sophisticated clientele of the restaurant and bar. Twice, since Martin had sat down next to Cindy at the bar, a kid had screamed obscenities as he passed, set off, Martin supposed, by his own mis-firing testosterone. "It's not our fault you can't get laid!" a painter friend of Martin's yelled back without looking up from his drink.

Cindy had spoken with her Harvard-girl's manner on the phone–proof that she wasn't high–saying it was a matter of life and death that they meet. Martin had been holed up with Fisher, the Hollywood director, all day at the Hotel Union Square working on the screenplay based on his novel when she'd called him. He'd agreed to meet her at the Black Cat before she went to work.

Cindy, wearing her black glasses, was reading aloud from the dog-eared pages of a manuscript she'd found in her messenger bag at Betsy's. Martin watched her face in the bar's mirror as she read to him. She had that keen expression he'd seen before that verged on sexual excitement, her long bangs covering her eyes as she read. She was wearing black pants and shoes and a white T-shirt so he could see the firmness of her small breasts press against her look-at-my-nipples bra.

"Okay. . . ." Martin said dryly when she finished reading.

"Well, it's about some one killing *me.* How would that make *you* feel?" She threw her tiny green drink-sword on the bar in mock disgust.

"Flattered," Martin said. He caught the bartender's eye and ordered another glass of wine. He was slightly wired. He and Fisher had taken some speed when they had run out of ideas. Martin tried a little and found he liked the drug. It made him feel confident. Fisher had proceeded to run at the mouth for the next several hours with mostly stupid ideas and Hollywood stories.

"Where did you get this manuscript?" Martin asked.

"You ought to know. You put these pages in my bag at the last meeting. It's *yours,"* she said emphatically

"It's hardly my *style,"* Martin said, a little surprised. He felt slightly flushed from the drug and the alcohol. He wasn't used to either. He held the wine glass and looked across the bar into the mirror that looked like framed mercury, the two of them centered in the frame, like young, wet, human blots.

"Oh, *come on,* Martin. It's yours. Why don't you admit it? I *like* it. Are you ashamed because it's some kind of cheap crime story? Who cares? Don't be a snob, Martin."

"I did *not* write that!"

"You're such a snob. You really are!" she said. "I think it's a thrilling side of you. Really, Martin, you're a pulp guy at heart!" She took a drink and bent over the pages, completely enthralled with what she imagined was his sell-out work.

"It's got your . . . I don't know. . . your emotionless emotions and odd sensibility," she said looking up. You have that damn feminine/masculine voice. It's fucking androgynous. I try and copy it sometimes but I can't. What do the crime writers call this style?"

"It's a procedural," Martin said.

"That's it! I know you wrote it. Come on, 'fess up. You even know the *lingo*." She elbowed him like a longshoreman. "You're Elmore Leonard incarnate. Why deny it, stupid? Did you forget about the note?" She took a half sheet of paper from the manuscript box and waved it at him.

Dear Cindy,
> *What do you think? Let me know.*
> —*M.*

"Sorry to disappoint you, but I didn't write that note either," he said. "Anyone could have written it. It's in that old-fashioned first person tough-guy speak *anyone* who has ever seen *Double Indemnity* or read Jim Thompson even *once* could have written. Listen." He took a page from the stationery box on the bar and began to read. He read it with some B-movie flair just for the fun of it.

Cindy put her martini down on the bar. "Well? It's good, isn't it? And I'm flattered that you used my name for the dead girl. Anyway, it's very compelling. I care about this man and his predicament. Is he guilty? Is he innocent? You're probably tired of that arty stuff you've been writing."

"I can tell you, honestly, I *didn't* write it," he said.

And then suddenly it dawned on him that he *could* have written it. The manuscript could be one more manifestation of his mounting insanity.

95

"Go ahead. Read some more," he said quietly. Cindy smiled at him.

"Ah ha! You see!" She took a fresh page out of the box and read. He listened more carefully now, but the words were flat. He heard a dozen phrases he would have never let stand. She leaned in close to him, and he could smell her as she read to him. She had a wonderful late night smell of body odor and perfume that smacked of sex. She stopped. "Oh, I hope you killed me off, you know, in the *French* way. . . ." She put the page down, reached over and kissed him on the mouth.

"It's been too long since I've done *this,*" she whispered. Cindy was purring now and had barely moved her lips from his. He swore he felt a slight electrical charge pass between them. She was just like a cat. He could feel the puffs of breath from her lips as she cooed, "I want you to *fuck* me to death." She kissed him again. This time he felt her tongue slide into his mouth and fill it up, tasting of vermouth. The bartender, a weightlifter type with a chipmunk face from steroid abuse, coughed on purpose.

"Would either one of you like another?"

"No thanks," Martin said.

"I'll have a double," Cindy said. "I can't *believe* I kissed you. Now what?"

"I suppose we'll have to get married," he said, trying to make light of it.

"Which bar do you work in?" Martin asked her, changing the subject. He turned and looked out the Black Cat's clean windows.

"It's right next door," Cindy said.

"God, I hope I don't end up having to do that. I've got no ass at all," he said, trying to joke. But Cindy didn't laugh as the unintended implication of the remark sank through her. She knew that she had "ended up" badly.

She reached over and held his hand earnestly. "I want to get straight. Clean up. Stop dancing. Do you think I can?" she asked urgently. He didn't know how to respond. He watched her expression in the mirror. His remark had hurt her. He saw it in her face. It was the strangest look he'd ever seen. She looked away from him for a moment out onto semi-deserted Broadway with its bright emptiness. There was a sudden sense of lassitude as if they were waiting for the *answer*. They stared into the mirror for perhaps a minute, and she studied herself resolutely. Then she looked down on the page in front of her and read the rest of the chapter to him, as if nothing had happened.

THIRTEEN

Blue cigarette smoke hung in the air around Virginia as she read to them, a *bidi* sitting in the ashtray next to her. It seemed that things might just finally be getting back to normal, Martin thought, listening to Virginia read. The living room and everyone in it had a timeless quality. He wanted more than anything now to return to the life he'd had before he was published. He realized how happy he'd been then, free from the world's nasty grip, free of nightmares and interludes, and free from the pressures of success.

He'd said goodbye to Fisher, Hollywood and script work forever. Both high on speed (Fisher seemed incapable of working without using drugs), they had fought bitterly about the script the night before. Fisher had threatened to bring in another "professional" scriptwriter if Martin didn't change the ending. He had stormed out, leaving Fisher standing slack-jawed in the middle of his enormous suite, not believing anyone would walk out on him and the lucre he represented.

The group was listening intently to Virginia as she read from her chair in a corner of the room. The reading was going well. There was an electric feeling in the air because the work was both damn good and shocking.

Virginia was reading from her first really serious novel—neither crime nor romance. Martin could see that she was nervous about its reception. She was wearing platform tennis shoes and velour multi-colored pants. Her whisky voice was mellifluous and sexy, drumming on the words. The story was about a love affair between two writers, and their writing group. Stunned, no one had spoken a word since she'd started reading. She told the story about the group's first meeting here in this very room several years before. She'd gotten it all down–their excitement, their youth, their beauty and the sexual attractions.

He watched Cindy listen; her face like the surface of some snowy lake, still, intrigued by what she was hearing. Virginia described a character based on Kevin. The narrator (who was obviously Virginia) and the character were having an affair. The young man had just come to the big city from Atlanta; they'd met at a bookstore. The shy young man lost himself in Sunday morning sex in what Martin recognized as Virginia's apartment in the Mission. The young man she was in love with was brilliant, confused and angry about being from a poor Southern family, angry at being thought of as a redneck every time he opened his mouth. In the novel, the girl does everything she can to understand him and to appreciate what he can be. She is both his lover and mentor.

"I can't believe what you're saying," Kevin blurted out suddenly; his voice was very sharp and angry. Martin looked at him. Virginia tried to keep going. Kevin jumped up off of his chair, incensed at seeing himself portrayed as the young man and not liking it. Virginia finally stopped reading as he got near her. Kline got up and stood between him and Virginia.

"That's enough!" Kline said. The detective said it with such finality and in such a cold piercing tone that it shocked everyone in the room. Kline made a motion for Michael, who'd stood up too, to stand back. The detective turned and faced Kevin full on. Kline's body seemed to grow in front of Martin's eyes.

"That's enough, you have to leave. That's it," Kline said. "Leave or I'll knock the crap out of you."

Kevin turned and looked to Michael for help. "Are you going to let some *outsider* talk to me like that?"

"He's right," Martin said, trying to help. Kevin turned towards Martin now.

"Shut up, you *shit*. You're jealous of me. You've been jealous of me since the day I got here, you fucking dilettante," Kevin said, turning on Martin.

"I think it's the other way around, isn't it?" Martin said.

"Stop it, Kevin!" Virginia said. "What's wrong with you?" She turned and looked at Kline. "Leave him alone. He's my friend. You don't have the right." Kline looked at Martin for support. He was taken aback and obviously hurt that Virginia was defending Kevin.

"Let us handle this. We know him best," Martin said to Kline. Kline backed off, but not without first giving Kevin a withering look. Kevin walked across the room and stood in front of him. "You're jealous and you don't have the balls to throw me out," Kevin said, his accent becoming more pronounced. He had the vicious drawl of a barn-burning Klan type. There was a bit of saliva stuck on Kevin's open mouth. Martin realized he was suddenly frightened of him. He forced himself to stand up and face him. "Please leave if you care anything about the people here—" Martin said. Virginia crossed the room and put her arm around Kevin.

The phone started to ring in the kitchen. Betsy Austin got up and went to answer it. She kept her eyes on the living room as she picked up the phone on the wall by the kitchen door. Kevin pushed Virginia back, almost knocking her down, and sprang towards Martin. Kline jumped him from behind. He slipped his big arms over Kevin's neck and got him in a chokehold. Martin watched as Kevin winced with pain, his face turning bright red. The look on Kline's face was frightening. It looked like he wanted to hurt him.

"You prick," Kline said as he ratcheted his arm tighter under Kevin's throat, lifting him up. Kevin, feet off the ground now, stopped struggling and suddenly blacked out, slumping forward. Kline dropped him at his feet. After Kevin hit the floor, there was a complete and sickening silence.

"Martin. It's for you. It's the police," Betsy said, breaking the silence.

"Well, that was fast," Virginia said. She held a cigarette in her trembling hand. Kline went and put his arm around her. Virginia shook it off angrily and went to Kevin to try to help him up. Betsy, still holding the phone, had a strange look on her face as she watched Virginia help Kevin off the floor. Kevin, coming to, was gasping for breath like a little boy in a schoolyard fight.

"Tell him I'll call him back. Get a number," Martin said mechanically. He couldn't move.

"I did. He said he'd rather hold," Betsy said.

"Please. Take him outside," Cindy said, looking at Martin. Her face was pale. She was frightened too.

Martin climbed back up the stairs two at a time. Michael and he had taken Kevin outside to the corner to talk. Michael had stayed outside with Kevin. He must have felt somehow responsible, Martin thought. Martin didn't give a damn. He hoped he never saw Kevin again. He heard his own breathing as he ran back up the stairs to the kitchen and picked up the phone that had been left hanging.

"Martin Anderson speaking,"

"Mr. Anderson, It's Lt. Cross."

"Yes?"

"Mr. Anderson, do you know a Henry Fisher?"

"Yes?"

"When was the last time you saw him?"

"Yesterday, why?"

"Because someone's beaten him up pretty badly. We think you're one of the last people to have seen him before he was attacked." For a moment, Martin thought someone was playing a joke on him.

"I'm sorry. Could you repeat that?" Martin said.

"I said Mr. Fisher was badly beaten. He may not live." There was another long silence. "Mr. Anderson, I would like to ask you some questions as soon as possible."

"Beaten up? What do you mean?"

"Mr. Fisher was assaulted in his room at the Hotel Union Square sometime early this morning. We found a movie script with your name on it. He had this number and another with your name and address in the room with him. I tried the other number and no one answered. I thought I'd try this one. Where are you?" Martin was trying to force himself to take a breath. It was as if, on exhaling, someone had grabbed him around the solar plexus and wasn't allowing him to inhale now. "Where are you?" Cross said. Martin hung up. He didn't know exactly why he hung up but he did. It was as if he had no control of his arm. The phone suddenly started to ring again; he backed away from it.

"What's going on, Martin?" He bumped into Betsy. He turned to look at her. "What do they want? Aren't you going to *answer?*" She started to reach for the phone.

"No! Don't! Don't answer," he said. She ignored him and reached for the phone.

"Don't be silly, Martin." She lifted the receiver. "Yes? I'm afraid he's gone. No, I don't know where he went. Of course. The address here is 1122 Green Street. Yes, I'll tell him." Austin hung up the phone and turned to look at him. "He says that you should call the Hall of Justice and ask for Lt.

Cross as soon as possible. I told him you'd left. I don't think he believed me. What's wrong, Martin?"

"Someone's been attacked and they think I had something to do with it."

"Who?"

"The director I was working with—someone's beaten him up," he said. Martin turned around. Virginia was standing in the doorway, her manuscript pages clutched against her chest. He didn't know how long she'd been standing there listening to them.

"Well, well, well. A wanted man," Virginia said. "If Betsy gave them this address, then don't you think you *should* leave?" The phone rang again. The two women looked at each other. Martin watched it ring for a moment then grabbed it.

"Hello?"

"Martin, I thought you'd left."

"Yes, lieutenant. I'm sorry. I was upset."

"We'd like you to come to the Hall of Justice now. I can send a car if you want."

"No. I'll come down right away, lieutenant. I didn't do it if that's what you're thinking. We argued but Fisher was fine when I left him."

"O.K., Martin. Just come down here and tell me what happened."

"I'm on my way," Martin said. He hung up the phone slowly. Betsy had left the kitchen already. Virginia was still standing in the doorway.

"I may have tried to kill someone," Martin said.

"Well that's the kind of mistake you can't apologize for," Virginia said.

"That's not funny," he said.

"You didn't try to kill anyone, Martin," Virginia said. "Don't be ridiculous."

"How do you know?" He looked at her carefully. He was grateful to hear her words, but he knew, in this case, he might have. He and Fisher had argued violently about the script. When Fisher had told him that he would get another writer, he'd felt humiliated and could have killed him at that moment.

"I just know you. You aren't the murdering type. It's much too spontaneous an act for someone like you. Intellectuals don't murder, unless it's in very large numbers," she said. "And for great causes." Michael came up the stairs and stopped by the kitchen door behind her.

"That was the police," Martin said. "They want to speak to me. Something about the director. Someone's beat him up." Michael looked at him. "Will you come with me?"

"Yes, if you want me to, of course," Michael said.

FOURTEEN

The waiting room at the Hall of Justice was windowless and chaotic, filled with bail bondsmen and upset girlfriends and mothers. He'd been doodling on a yellow lined pad to pass the time while they waited to see Cross. After several false starts, he'd managed to get the fluting just right on his drawing of Coit Tower. When they came for him, one of the policemen told Martin that Cross would see him. Michael stood up and said he was Martin's attorney and he wanted to be present.

Martin took the pad with him, following the policeman down the warren of wide old-fashioned hallways at the Bryant Street police headquarters.

Lt. Cross–the same policeman who'd come to his apartment a few weeks before–was waiting for him in a tiny interrogation room. They shook hands perfunctorily. Cross, standing behind a small metal desk, explained that he was going to tape their session. Martin nodded, suddenly frightened; he looked at Michael. The lawyer nodded his approval then reached across the desk and shook Cross's hand.

"Let's talk then," Cross said. Martin heard the door close behind them. He looked at the tape machine on the table. Its black plastic cover was scratched. He looked for a clock on the wall to orient himself, but didn't see one anywhere and he panicked slightly. He wanted to ask Cross exactly what day it was–he thought it was Friday–but was afraid to ask. He was afraid he'd seem guilty if he wasn't sure exactly what day it was. *Friday,* he told himself relaxing. *It's Friday night. I*

105

haven't done anything wrong. He heard the tape machine snap on.

"It's eleven o'clock on the sixth of June, and I'm going to ask you some questions, Mr. Anderson, in the presence of your attorney, about what transpired in Mr. Fisher's hotel room last night. How's that sound?" Cross said to him. "Take a seat, Mr. Anderson. Martin looked at Cross and somehow couldn't focus on the words in a normal way. He looked over at Michael, who'd gone to sit against the wall, the desk too small for the three of them. He wondered if he were having a nightmare. "Go ahead. Sit down, Martin. You said you left Mr. Fisher in his hotel room last night?"

"Yes."

"You said earlier on the phone that you two had fought."

"Yes. We did."

"What about?"

"About the script we were working on."

"A movie script?"

"Yes." Cross made a note.

"What time did you leave him?"

"I don't remember exactly. After midnight."

"Was the fight violent?"

"No. Of course not."

"But you were angry?"

"Yes. . . . Yes I was."

"Can you explain?"

"We had an difference of opinion about the script. I told him I didn't want to work on it anymore, and I left."

"You quit, is that it?"

"Yes. I suppose so." Cross put down his pen and looked at him a moment. He reached over and shut down the machine.

"I don't believe a word of it," Cross said.

"Excuse me?"

106

"I said I don't believe a word of it," Cross said. He leaned over the tape machine. His mustache was wet at the ends from the coffee he was drinking. He looked over at Boon for a moment. "Now tell me. What really happened?" Cross turned the machine back on. "Martin, did you lose your temper in the hotel room? What about the drugs we found in his room? Was that what the fight was about?" The lieutenant's words seemed to spin around the room.

"Is this really necessary?" Michael said.

"Yes, it is," Cross said.

Sitting there, Martin suddenly wasn't sure of anything, just that he was in trouble and now he knew why—Cross was certain he'd tried to kill Fisher. Martin looked at him for a long time. He could hear the sound of the tape machine turning.

"I told you already," he said. He looked across the desk at the policeman. Cross was writing something down in his notebook, holding a cup of coffee in his other hand. Martin noticed the coffee's oily surface reflected the florescent lights of the room. The room's stark walls echoed the aftermath of a thousand horrible crimes.

When the policeman looked up, Martin noticed his face was marked with tiny acne scars. The room smelled of the lieutenant's cheap aftershave and Martin's own rank body odor. He realized he was sweating profusely. Cross glanced down at his notebook again. "I've had a chat with your psychiatrist. She says that you've been having interludes, that whole chunks of the day go missing. Is that true, Martin? And don't lie. When there's a crime involved, there is no doctor-patient protection. Is there a chance you attacked Fisher and just don't remember any of it?"

For the first time, the idea of suicide crossed his mind. *I'll have to end it,* he thought automatically now, *if it's true I did it. There is a chance. I might have done it. Gone back and. . . .*

"What happened in that room?" Cross asked.

"I–I don't know."

"You don't know? You must have had a reason for attacking him."

"No. No, you don't understand. These interludes you spoke of. . . . I don't know what I do. It is possible. . . ."

"What don't I understand? What don't I understand about it, Martin? I think it's plain as day. You two had a fight and you beat him with a telephone. The phone was covered with blood. You beat him with that telephone in the room, didn't you?" Cross said. "Be a man and admit it!"

"I don't remember. I could have. Yes. But–I don't know for sure," he said. "I have to get out of here. I need my medication. Maybe I can remember if I have my medication. I stopped taking it. The doctor said if I stopped taking it bad things might happen. . . ." He was psychologically caved in and wanted out of the room now. "If I get back on my medication, maybe I will remember what happened. Michael, tell him."

"I think my client has had enough lieutenant." Boon said.

"You want a limo too, Martin?" Cross said. "Come on, just tell me what happened. Did things get out of hand? Did he get violent? Maybe he took a swing at you. Maybe it was self-defense. Just tell me the truth."

"Shut up for a second, will you? Let me think. I mean I did get angry with him when he said they were going to get another writer."

"I bet you were angry after all that work. Is that why you did it? Because they were getting another writer? Because you lost the job?"

"No. No. I didn't *do* anything. I *left.* I told him that I didn't want to work on it anymore and I didn't care what they did with my script. And then I left." Martin turned toward the wall with a large mirror across from them. He supposed, looking at the mirror, that it was two-way, so the police could watch the interrogation. Maybe there were people on the other side of it right now, a whole room full deciding whether he was guilty or not, whether he was crazy or not. He tried to remember anything about that night with Fisher. Doubts started to creep in. *I was angry.*

He remembered how Fisher had looked at him when he said he was bringing in a professional screenwriter. He'd felt sick; he'd worked so hard on the script to make it faithful to his book. Fisher had wanted a big action scene in the end and he thought it was stupid. The picture wasn't about that. But Fisher had a way of asking, leading him along, telling him that they could do an action scene that would give the audience the same ending as the book only a little more exciting. "It will be just like the book but with action." Fisher kept saying over and over. The speed making him insistent, petulant like a child.

"I'm not a killer," Martin said suddenly, looking into the mirror, at those who might be watching him.

"Okay, Martin. You're not a killer. Like I said, you were just defending yourself," Cross said.

"I'm a writer." He heard the tape machine turn off.

He felt like he was being collected and marked and pinned to one of those boxes collectors keep butterflies in.

"Can I stand?"

"Okay, Martin. Go on, get up. Take a long look at yourself in the mirror if that will make you feel better, then come back and tell me what really happened to Fisher." Martin

109

crossed the half-lit room and looked at himself in the polished metal mirror.

His skin was greasy-looking. Cross and the table with the recorder were reflected behind him in pewter colors. Michael had disappeared from view. There was a frightening closeness to the room. The scene was minimal, just the old furniture and the policeman looking down and writing in his notebook in a lazy kind of made-up-my-mind way. Then Martin looked into the mirror again and gave himself a real once-over. He saw the face of a thirty-year-old man who seemed almost a stranger looking back at him. *Am I completely psychotic?* He ran his finger through his hair and tried to get it to sit right but it wouldn't. *Did I try to kill Fisher? Did I?*

"Okay, Cinderella. You had enough?" Cross said. He spoke without looking up. Martin turned around and looked at Cross. Overweight, he could see Cross's belly hanging over his belt. There was a small dirty window above him. He could see the freeway that ran by the jail on Bryant Street. Beyond the freeway, he could see the lights of the city's cold-looking skyline. He walked back to the table, not sure whether or not he'd done it now. He heard the tape machine turn on again.

"Okay, Martin. Why did you try and kill him?

"Why don't you ask him?"

"I can't. He's in a coma. He can't talk. Half his skull is bashed in. Okay, let's start with how you met?"

Martin started to laugh then. He laughed really hard and long until it made his stomach hurt. He knew he looked guilty to the people behind the mirror. "You think this is funny, Martin?" Cross stopped writing and put down his pen.

He looked at the policeman. Talking was starting to seem ridiculous. "Look, I'm a writer. Writers are different from people like you, and there's nothing that will ever change that. We are selfish and brutal to ourselves and that's the cost of the ticket. But I didn't try and *kill* anyone," he said.

"I thought you said you might have, that you weren't sure?"

"O.K. I'm confused. Can't you *see* that? I'm ill. But the more I think about it, the more I know I didn't do it. O.K.? We argued, yes. That's life. Life isn't amphenic."

"I don't know what that means, Martin. Amphenic... whatever it was you said. I know you went to Berkeley, but why don't you tell us City College boys what that means?"

"It means life's not clean. Antiseptic. Life is about making mistakes, spilling the milk. Doing your best and wiping up the rest. I didn't try and kill anyone. GOT THAT?" There was something wrong with him, he knew that, something that was making him hostile suddenly. It felt as if his blood had been drained and replaced with rocket fuel. But he was sure now that he hadn't done anything to Fisher. He was sure of that. "What happens if he dies?" Martin said. "If he doesn't make it?"

"Then it's murder," Cross said. He reached over and shut off the tape machine.

Martin sat back and realized that he might be going to the gas chamber. It was frightening. He'd been frightened before, like in the moment before a car accident or after he'd slept with someone and the condom had broken. But he'd never been frightened like this. He saw the whole inarticulate banal machinery of the state as a stupid child in the schoolyard who had taken a great dislike to him because he was different, and now that fat kid was going to torture him for the rest of the term.

"I don't believe a word of it," Cross said.

"What?"

"I said I don't believe you. Not a word of it. Interludes, my ass. You can go for the time being," Cross said.

FIFTEEN

I knocked, but you didn't answer the buzzer," Dr. Elders said from the hallway. He hadn't really slept, at least not for long. Martin watched the doctor walk into his living room. Outside the big picture windows, a pewter colored sky appeared to have been shoved around during the night and was now, in places, marked with black and blue rain clouds. He remembered how it had poured on the way home from the police station. He remembered the excited full-speed slap of the windshield wipers as he talked with Michael about the interview, frightened he might be guilty. Frightened that Fisher might die.

The doctor's voice, very serious and professional, had woken him up from a 2-Valium stupor. He'd surfed in and out of consciousness all morning. Restful sleep—the kind he'd longed for—had been impossible. The moment he opened his eyes, all the horrible details from the night before came back to him—Kevin's choking face, his interview with Cross and the policeman's body odor, the small oppressive inter-rogation room and the way its walls seemed to lean in at different impossible angles a la Salvador Dali. He wondered if Michael had told Elders, judging from the way she was looking at him now, that he might be dangerous.

"Where's Michael? He promised to come over this morning," he said, still lying on the couch.

"He had to be in court this morning." There was an awkward silence. "He asked me to come and check in on you. He said to tell you he'd call you later. I had the doorman let me in when you didn't answer the bell. I hope that's all right," she said. "Michael is very worried about you, Martin. He said you were extremely agitated when he left you last night."

"I'm glad you came."

"The police want to speak to you again. They just called for you. I heard Cross's voice and picked up. I said you would call him back." Elders sat down across from him. She was wearing a striking orange suit. Her freckled skin was radiant. "I'm sorry about your friend Fisher. Do you want to talk about it?" she asked.

"I might have beaten him up. The police think I did. The lieutenant last night said he spoke to you."

"Yes. He called yesterday. Michael had already given him my number because of the incident with the dog. . . ."

"What did you tell him?"

"I said you were a patient."

"Did you tell them I was crazy?"

"No. Of course not."

"What did you say?"

"I said that you were having interludes, serious ones. "

"During which time I might beat people half to death?"

"What makes you think you did? Michael told me you weren't sure."

"Because I can't be sure I *didn't,* can I?"

"Cross seemed to want to help," she said. He smiled ruefully at her.

"Isn't that what the police *always* say? They want to help? I'm sorry," he closed his eyes. "I don't think they want to help at all. I think they want to put me in jail."

"Martin, these psychotic episodes you are having *are* very serious. I told you without medication the symptoms would only get worse."

"So you agree I *could* have done it and not know it. Is that it? Did Cross ask you that?"

"Yes, he did."

"And what did you say?"

"I told him it *was* possible but not likely." He let his head fall back on the arm of the couch. "I want you to go back on the Zoloft. And, this time, stay on it. I'll phone in a new prescription when I get to the hospital. I want you to try and eat some breakfast, too," she said.

"All right." He sat up. "Susan, could I really have tried to kill Fisher and not remember it? If you were going to remember *anything,* you think you'd remember trying to bash someone's head in with a telephone for god sakes." He put his face in his hands, completely enervated by the Valium and the unknown.

"I'm afraid that horrible things *can and do* happen during interludes. Cross told me they'd found drugs at the hotel. Did you take drugs at the hotel, Martin?" He nodded his head, unable to face her, embarrassed by his stupidity. "What kind?"

"Speed. . . . I thought I was supposed to avoid stepping on cracks or wash my hands compulsively—not try to kill people," he said through his fingers. He looked up at her. The look on Elder's face had changed suddenly. He saw the look of a concerned woman, not just his doctor. "You want some coffee or something?" he asked.

"No thanks. I just stopped in to see how you were. I have to get to the hospital." She glanced towards the kitchen. Martin saw there was a pile of clothes on the floor by his computer table. "How long has it been since you stopped taking your meds?" she asked, turning back to look at him.

"Two weeks. . . . No, maybe more. I flushed them down the toilet," he said. "Maybe they *should* lock me up for my own protection," Martin said, only half joking.

"Do you want to call the lieutenant back while I'm here?" she said. The idea of talking to the Cross again frightened him.

"No, I'm not ready for *that.*"

"I want you to come to the office this afternoon. I'll squeeze you in," she said, trying to joke.

"Isn't it too late?" he said. "If I've tried to kill someone, doesn't that scare you?"

"This afternoon at four," she said again. She went to the door. "I'll let myself out. I don't want you to miss this appointment, Martin. You promise you'll come?" He sat up and nodded, still ashamed about his illicit drug taking. "I want you to pick up the Zoloft this morning. What drugstore should I call?" He gave her the name of a place.

"Four o'clock sharp it is," he said. She smiled. She started to say something, then thought better of it and left. He waited a while, then climbed up from the couch and walked into the kitchen to make coffee. His laptop was open. He saw the screen saver was on. He tapped the keyboard and a page of text jumped to life on the screen:

Cross was looking at me with those beady workman's eyes. They were rat-brown and looked like they were tired of seeing me already. I was back in that interrogation room at the Hall of Justice.

"Anderson, what is it you want? I'm a busy man," Cross said. "You aren't the only psycho I got in this city."

"Turn on the machine," I said. "I want to confess." Cross was wearing one of his brighter ties. It looked like a nightmare painted on silk. "Where'd you get the tie?" I asked.

"My wife gave it to me for Christmas. It's ugly, but I got to wear it," Cross said. "Are you sure you want me to say this is a confession?" Cross asked. He reached for the button on the recorder. "You can call your lawyer if you want to."

"Yeah. It's a confession. Go ahead. I never want to see that asshole again." There was a snap from the machine. For a just a moment, I hesitated. I thought about lying again and then I knew I didn't want to lie anymore. I wanted to tell Cross the story. I wanted to tell the truth."

"This is Lieutenant Cross. It is four-fifteen on June the 6th. I am interviewing Mr. Martin Anderson. Mr. Anderson has asked me to record his confession to the charge of attempted murder. Is that correct, Mr. Anderson?"

"Yes. I tried to kill him. Fisher," I said.

"Why?"

"I walked in on him talking on the phone with the other writer. That was it. I kind of went nuts. I could see Fisher's gob moving. He was holding the phone with both hands like a faggot. He'd told the guy on the phone I was history, that they would rewrite the whole thing. He was going to fire me when he got back to L.A. That hurt, you know? It hurt really bad. Can you understand that, lieutenant? They were going to destroy my vision."

"Sure kid– Walk me through it."

"He hung up the phone while I was getting it. . . . The extension phone.

"'Martin, what are you doing here?' he said. He was looking at the phone in my hand. I don't think he understood at first.

"'I'm going to kill you,' I said. I said it just like that. The way you would say I'll have that on white bread, hold the mayo. Then he knew I'd heard the whole thing between him and the other writer."

"So you hit him?"

"Yeah, I hit him all right. I used the phone. One of those big-ass four line jobs. It was heavy. I smashed it right in his face. I felt like I should get a Kewpie doll, he fell down so fast. You should have seen the look on his face when he looked up from the floor. I guess he knew I was crazy by then. I guess he won't be changing my work now. I bet he can't even use the phone now, the way I twisted his arm until I heard it snap. He's real good at using the phone. That's all they do down there, you know. Use the phone on one another."

"So you *did* want to kill him?"

"You bet I did. I thought I *had* killed him. I beat him till he was quiet. I liked it when he was quiet. When he shut up, I picked up a lamp and beat him awhile with *that*. If he survived that beating then, man, he deserves to live," I said.

He stood up and backed away from his laptop, horrified by what he'd written. He looked down and saw a pile of bloody clothes on the floor near the phone. Without thinking, he picked them up and ran to the bathroom and threw them in the shower stall, turning on the water in a state of panic. He watched the blood begin to wash off, mixing with the hot water running over the white tiles. The bottom of the shower turned crimson. He realized, staring at the dark heap of clothes, that they were the things he'd worn at the hotel with Fisher. When the water stopped running red, he turned it off. He wiped the steamed up mirror with his palm; his frightened face appeared in front of him.

His answering machine picked up a call. He heard Virginia's voice. "Martin, pick up! Are you there? Damn it, Martin. Pick up the phone. I want to help you. I don't believe you did it. Why would you try and kill him?" He froze. "I'm at home. Call me. The police have just been here. Call me,

Martin. *Please* call me." He heard the machine beep. Frantic, and convinced now he was guilty, he turned around and looked toward the bedroom. *It was true.* He picked up the bathroom extension and dialed Virginia's number.

"It's me. I did it. It's true," he said. " I didn't want to believe it."

"What do you mean?" she said.

"I've found bloody clothes, Virginia. The clothes I wore to the hotel."

"Martin–"

He hung up the phone. It rang again almost immediately. The sound seemed to explode against the walls of the bathroom. All the extensions were ringing everywhere. He moved away from the phone on the wall. The answering machine came on again, Virginia's voice filled up the hallway behind him. He turned his back to it.

"I don't believe it," she said. "Why? Why would you want to kill Fisher? Why, Martin? Ask yourself that." He knew the answer. He was crazy. He'd been going crazy for months now. He'd snapped and attacked Fisher because he was going to ruin his screenplay. "Martin *pick up* and answer me that question. Why would you want to kill this man?" He grabbed the phone again.

"We argued. I got angry. . . . They were going to get another writer. They were going to ruin my movie . . . my work."

"Do you honestly believe you tried to kill him?"

"I don't know anymore. I tell you, I don't *know!* What difference does it make what I believe? I found the clothes for godsakes." He looked down the hall towards the kitchen. " I was with him all day in the hotel room working on the script. He didn't attack *himself,* Virginia. What other explanation is there?"

118

"Martin. You don't try and kill people because they fuck up your screenplay. You're not that kind of person."

"How can you be so *sure?* He told me he could do what he liked, that I should read my contract. He told me they *owned* me. I was very angry when I left him."

"I don't believe it because I know you. That's all." Martin took a breath.

"I've been having problems. I'm seeing a psychiatrist," he said quietly.

"What problems?"

"Problems. Problems that I was afraid to tell you about. I didn't want to scare you."

"What problems, Martin?"

"I've been losing time, having interludes, ever since I was on the book tour. The day I took you to the tower. . . . I didn't remember any of it. Maybe I am crazy. I don't know. I'm not sure of anything anymore."

"Martin, shut up. Listen to yourself. So you have problems. That doesn't make you a murderer, or we'd *all* be killing people." He heard his cell phone ring in the other room.

"Wait," Martin said.

"Martin?" He walked down the hall to the living room looking for his cell phone. He heard it ringing but couldn't see it. He finally found it on the kitchen table next to his laptop and picked it up hoping it was Michael.

"Hello, Martin." He didn't recognize the voice.

"Yes?"

"Martin?" He held the phone for a moment and began to tremble. "Come to the tower," the muffled voice said. "I'm waiting for you. I want to explain."

"Who is this?"

"I know what happened," the voice said.

119

Over the phone, Virginia heard the door slam. She called his name, but there was nothing but silence on the other end of the line.

· · ·

Martin watched the antique gold needle move to the left, marking the elevator's descent on a brass dial. Nearby, the tower's concessionaire's booth was full of last minute shoppers, the usual mix of tourists from all over the world. *Come on. Come on!* The elevator door suddenly opened. Full, it disgorged its passengers into the lobby.

"Where is she? The blonde girl," Martin asked the elevator's operator. "God damn it. The girl, where is she?" he screamed.

"Close now," the man said. "Deck close now. You come back *tomollow*."

"No. The girl. The blonde girl– Where is she?" He'd seen her on the stairs outside, waiting for him. She'd turned and run into the building. The elevator man looked at him vacantly. He was looking past Martin at someone. Martin turned around. The security guard who had been standing by the main door was coming their way. Martin grabbed the elevator man by his lapels, throwing him clear of the door, and pulled the elevator doors shut behind him. He heard pounding on the other side. He looked at the simple control lever and threw it but nothing happened. *God damn it.* He looked desperately for some kind of "on" switch near the lever but didn't see it. The pounding got louder outside the door. Then it stopped. A nightstick came through the gap in the elevator door. The guard was using it to try and pry open the doors. The black nightstick moved aggressively. Martin heard voices yelling on the other side of the door. Frantic, he spotted a toggle switch at eye level, and remembered the operator always threw it first. He toggled the switch and moved the lever forward again. The elevator started to move up. It made a slow dragging sound. The nightstick disappeared suddenly.

He threw the elevator door open at the top. He fought against the tide of tourists descending the stairs from the observation deck coming for the last elevator. He pushed by people until he stood on the deck. He spotted the blonde at the edge of the observation deck. Alone, she was looking out on the city, her back to him. Her blonde hair was down to her shoulders, lit by the strong spotlights. Her long dress was moving in the wind. She stood exactly as he'd seen her in his dream a hundred times. He ran towards her.

He grabbed the blonde and spun her around.

The girl from his dream looked at him. She had the same hat on and the same smile, and her blonde hair was blown by the wind. "It's *you*. But it *can't* be you!" Martin said. "It *can't* be."

The taxi Kline jumped into was caught in traffic near the parking lot. The queue of tour buses and taxis for the popular tourist attraction were all trying to leave at once. Virginia had called him and told him to go to Martin's apartment. She was afraid that something had happened to him. He'd taken a cab and gone to the front door of Martin's building where the doorman told him Martin had just left in a rush up Lombard going towards Coit Tower. Kline ran up the street at a trot past the stinking tour busses. Almost completely dark now, the trees were being blown around by the strong winds.

He ran up the center of the street, bus and car headlights blinding him, horns honking. He rounded the curb and looked for Martin at the pay-for-view binoculars that circled the parking lot. Crowds of tourists were being loaded back into their buses. Not seeing Martin on the parking lot, Kline turned toward the stairs. There was a crowd gathered there. People were looking up at a man hanging from the top of the tower, trying to hold on. Kline heard a scream. He saw a man's body suddenly hurtling towards them through swirls of fog. The crowd dispersed, trying to get clear of it as it crashed on the stairs. Kline crossed the parking lot and shoved people out of the way. He saw Martin, his legs twisted unnaturally, his mouth still moving, jerky-jawed in death. But he was dead already. Kline moved around the twitching body; several women were screaming. He looked up to the top of the tower, but there was nothing but dark sky.

SIXTEEN
ONE YEAR LATER

Over the years, whenever Kline's name came up, his ex-Stanford classmates supposed that it was his strange childhood that was to blame for what Kline had done. For middle-class Jewish boys like his friends, he'd done the unthinkable. After graduating from Stanford, instead of going to law school like the rest of them, he had joined the Marine Corps. Kline had disappeared into a world that was as complete a mystery to them as the dark side of the moon. The Marines represented the Protestant, or even worse, the Southern Baptist poor-white anti-Semitic bastion, the Cossack side of American culture that they instinctively feared. Ironically, Kline's friends blamed his parents for his bizarre decision. Both his mother and father were strange, foreign and extremely old-fashioned. Like characters out of an Isaac Singer novel, they were silent, unhinged and afraid of just about everyone who wasn't a European Jew. Kline, even as a young boy, had been dragooned into acting as their interlocutor and protector. To them, his becoming a Marine seemed a natural, albeit shocking, extension of that role.

Kline grabbed Albert Rosenthal around the shoulders and they embraced. The two had known each other since they were in grade school. Kline had done this with his old childhood friends so many times since he'd come back to San Francisco that it had become a kind of ceremony. There was always the earthy handshake, followed by comments on how trim and fit Kline was and how his old friends weren't. The two men made their way down the hallway of the "deep pockets" San Francisco law firm. It was noontime and the offices were mostly empty.

"Are you still weightlifting and chasing blondes? Are you getting enough work from everyone? Have you gotten used to civilian life?" Rosenthal asked, genuinely concerned. To all these questions, Kline simply nodded appreciatively. He knew how lucky he was to have grown up with important men like Rosenthal, men who were making his transition into civilian life a complete success. He had more work than he knew what to do with. Thanks to his friends, he had a growing bank account for the first time in his life.

They passed Michael Boon's empty office. He'd gone to lunch, he imagined. The Anderson case seemed to reside in Boon's office with its intimate view of Maiden Lane. Kline thought about how he had gone into the case the year before one kind of man and left another. It had changed him. He'd fallen in love. The fact that Anderson had killed himself was bad, but the fact that he was left loving an unattainable woman was much worse, he thought now.

"You know we're here for you. Everyone was excited about your coming home. We're proud of you, you mensch," Rosenthal said. He stopped for a moment. "Boon. He's one of *them, a 'white sweater boy',*" Albert Rosenthal said, nodding towards Boon's empty office. It was as if they were in the schoolyard again and Rosenthal was speaking to him confidentially. "White sweater boy" was their crowd's code for Stanford WASP.

"I find it hard to relate to him. But *try* to get along with him, Paul. He's a snob, of course, but he brings a lot of Silicon Valley business into the firm. All his classmates seem to be

124

software tycoons or investment bankers. I told him to use you whenever he can. I was very firm about that. Very firm," Rosenthal said. Without really saying it, he'd said it all. "The Anderson boy's suicide was a shame," Rosenthal said as an afterthought and left it at that.

Rosenthal, in a beautiful gray pinstripe suit, leaned against his desk after he closed the door to his office. There was something tarnished and sad in his old friend's eyes, Kline noticed. It was as if the things he'd seen and done over the years had finally put him off humanity, or frightened him at least. Like him, his friend was turning gray, but Kline still saw the kid he'd known since junior high. They'd been best friends all the way through college.

"You're in the papers all the time now, Al. There's talk about you running for Congress. Is it true?" Kline said.

"It's just talk right now because I've been helping with this case against the Swiss banks. The case gets a lot of ink," Rosenthal said. "I've had good press. . . . What was that you told me once when we were at school? About your mother. . . . Didn't your mother's father. . . ."

Kline and his mother had discussed the bank accounts stolen from her family during the war only once as a child. All these years later, when a letter arrived advising them of the lawsuit, she'd begged Kline not to get involved because it all made her sick. She wanted to put the war behind her and asked him not to answer the letter. Kline had been glad; he'd run away from the Holocaust his whole life and wanted to keep it that way.

"We don't want anything from them," Kline said. "Fuck them. Is that what you wanted to see me about?"

"No. I got a call about your mother from the Wiesenthal Center in L.A. They'd like to interview her," Rosenthal said. "They have some questions." Kline started to speak, to say she'd done enough interviews, but Rosenthal put his hand up. "I promise, Paul, they won't upset her. You have my word of honor," the lawyer said. "I told them you had to be notified first and that you had to agree to it. Paul, sit down. And relax for godsake." But Kline didn't sit, and he didn't relax. He'd felt extremely protective of his mother since his father had died, and any talk about the Holocaust had always made him feel anxious.

"I told you, we. . . ."

"This has nothing to do with money, Paul. They are specifically looking for Nazis who worked at Dachau who managed to escape right after the war. Some, apparently, are here in the States. I felt obligated to give her name when they called. Paul, I hope you understand. They made assurances about their sensitivity to your mother's past. She could be of tremendous help, Paul, in identifying people. They'll be in town next week interviewing several survivors. Can I call her and ask if she would see them?" Rosenthal said. It didn't sound like he was really asking, Kline thought.

"She's very fragile. I don't know," Kline said. "Is it really necessary?" Kline looked over at Rosenthal's desk. It was very clean, a sign that his friend was no longer really practicing law and had moved into power brokering and politics.

"Paul, there aren't many people left like your mother who can help us with first hand information. She might even recognize someone if she's given a photo. We don't want to see these Nazi bastards get away with it, even if they're old men now. We owe it to the—"

"All right. . . . I'll ask her." Rosenthal came forward and put his arm on Kline's shoulder. He had a desire to back away. *Aren't they ever going to leave us alone?* He was afraid that his mother was going to be angry with him, but he couldn't refuse.

It seemed profoundly wrong not to help. He looked into Rosenthal's face.

"Thank you," Rosenthal said. "By the way, they had her name but not your father's. I told them they had both been in Dachau together as teenagers. They both got compensation from the German government, didn't they?"

"Yes," Kline said.

In the elevator later, Kline had an odd and overwhelming unexpected feeling of solidarity with Rosenthal. *We're Jews,* he thought to himself, crossing the busy lobby of the building. He walked out into the sunshine and bits of fog on Powell Street. *At the end of the day, we have to stick together.*

• • •

Kline? Is that you, Paul?" He heard her voice behind him. He hadn't seen Virginia and Boon. He'd been following the hostess to his table and missed spotting them on the café's crowded patio. But she'd seen him and grabbed his coat as he'd passed their table. He was stunned for a moment, unable to speak. He hadn't wanted to see her again. He was hoping that if he didn't, his desire for her would fade away. He was dating other women but was only able to think of *her,* even now, after so many months. He turned to look at Boon, who was wearing a light blue suit, his blond hair plastered down, and then again at Virginia, and then at the hostess, who was vexed because she'd had to stop and wait for him.

"Sit with us, Paul. *Please,*" Virginia said, smiling at him. She was wearing a floppy white hat a la Carnaby Street and a white blouse and short black skirt. She was sporting over-sized dark glasses that hid half her face.

127

"Good to see you, old man," Boon said, standing. "We were just talking about you at the office. Rosenthal was asking if I'd given you any work lately," Boon said. The young lawyer was very tanned and rested-looking, Kline thought. They were a beautiful young couple. Kline became acutely aware of his own age. He'd gotten grayer since Martin died. Virginia was speaking to the hostess, telling her he was going to sit with them. Giving up, he pulled a chair up next to her. The hostess turned and left. Suddenly, it was quiet at the table. It was Martin, of course; they hadn't seen each other since the funeral. His writer's block worsened after Martin's death, and he'd dropped out of the writing group, unable to maintain their brutal rule. It had been a great relief when he stopped going.

Virginia reached over and put her hand on his. "I'm so glad to see you again. Where *did* you go, Paul?"

"Yes. You deserted us," Boon said. Kline looked up at him. Boon was studying Kline's face. It was just a woman's hand resting on his, but Kline realized now that when he'd been with other women he didn't really feel their touch. *Not like this*, he thought, not like this magnetic feeling he felt now.

"I've been here in town," he said. "I've been O.K. I've had a lot of work, that's all."

"You look so handsome," she said. "Look at you. You look like Paul Newman." He thought she was making fun of him but she wasn't. He looked at her sheepishly. She smiled and gripped his hand harder and then let go. Kline saw there were several empty wine glasses in front of her. She had barely touched her lunch. "We were talking about what makes men handsome, weren't we, Michael?" she said. "Now, some men, like that club rat over there," she pointed out an earring-wearing kid a few tables away, "are pretty, but I never really went in for pretty. Handsome yes. Pretty no." She pretended to ogle the boy. She was drunk, Kline realized, as he watched her hold onto her wine glass. Kline looked at Boon, who shot him a not-my-fault look. The sun came out and lit the table; their umbrella was tilted the wrong way to shield them. The waitress came and took his order. He didn't feel like eating, suddenly, and ordered the first thing that came to mind.

"Do you think he's handsome or pretty?" Virginia asked the waitress, nodding towards Kline. The girl, pad in hand, leaned in and looked at Kline, getting into the spirit of the thing. The two girls were about the same age.

"Handsome," she said after an eyeful.

"Who does he look like?" Virginia said.

"Virginia, stop it!" Boon said, "You're embarrassing the poor man. *Look* at him; he's turning ghastly colors!"

"Are you turning colors, Paul?" She got closer to him and slipped her sunglasses down her nose in order to better study him. "No, he *isn't.*" The waitress had gone but Virginia didn't notice. "Who do you think you look like?" she asked, leaning in, whispering suddenly. He could smell the wine on her breath.

"I don't know. Who?" Kline said.

"Do you think Michael is pretty? Men. . . . I'm not supposed to ask men what they think of other men, am I? If Martin—" She stopped talking for a moment. "If Martin were here he would answer. He was queer like that. I don't mean *gay* of course. He wasn't like other men. Most of you are all so hung up on what's between your legs, aren't you? Oops! I've gone too far. " She made a face and pushed her sunglasses back up her nose. She looked at them both. "Oh, my. . . . So sorry."

"All right, I guess I look like Paul Newman then. If you say so," Kline said, trying to rescue her *and* prove he was Martin's match. She went on about Paul Newman and how he was a good man and his salad dressing was changing the world. Boon and Kline exchanged another look. Boon stood up.

"Listen, I've got to get back to the office. Will you see she gets home all right, Paul?"

"Of course," Kline said. He was profoundly glad he was going to be alone with her.

"He's my brick. Aren't you, Michael?" she said.

"Yes. Red and square," Boon said.

"He's always calling to be sure I'm alright. And he measures the vodka bottles in my apartment! Aren't you going to tell Paul that I'm rich now?" she said. They both turned to look at her. "Martin left me all his money and I don't want it." Boon ignored her and reached down and gave her a kiss on the cheek. She held his hand for a moment and put it against her face. "He's a saint. People don't know that about him, but he is." Michael straightened out her hat and then left them.

"Are you going to be like everyone else?" she said, watching Michael leave.

"What do you mean?" Kline said.

"Are you going to look at me *funny* if I order another drink? Like a T.V. evangelist? My friends get as preachy as Billy Graham at an orgy when they think I've had enough." She raised her hand and caught their waitress's eye. She shot Kline a look, as if he might disappoint her too. She took off her sunglasses, and he noticed that her eyes were puffy as if she'd been up all night. "I'll have another one of *these*," she said to the waitress.

"Paul, I don't believe Martin killed himself," she said matter-of-factly after the waitress left. "Michael doesn't agree . . . *at all.* He thinks Martin was crazy. He told me so. I keep telling him Martin wasn't crazy, but Michael won't listen. No one listens to me. Will you listen to me, Paul, or do you think I'm just drunk?" She had her elbows on the table and was holding her chin in her hand. Her hat had gone cockeyed again. He wanted to reach over and straighten it out the way Michael had.

"You *are* drunk," he said. "Trust me."

"I know *that,* but do you think Martin killed himself? That's what *I* want to know."

"I've thought about calling you," he said, wanting to pull her away from the subject of Martin.

"Have you? *Moi?"*

"Yes."

"Why didn't you?" she said. He shrugged his shoulders.

"Maybe you intimidate me," he said.

"You didn't answer my question about Martin. Cindy and I don't think he killed himself, you see. We just don't believe it. We don't think he wrote that awful manuscript either. Cindy did at first, but not now. And we don't think he wrote that ridiculous piece the police found on his laptop and are calling a confession." The waitress brought her another glass of wine, setting it down to the side of her. "I read in *People* magazine that Fisher can't remember anything about what happened to him. He can barely speak, but he's never said it was Martin who beat him up," she said.

"I'm afraid you've lost me," Kline said. "What manuscript?" She stared at him a moment, then slid the wine glass in front of her.

"The one Cindy has. The one Martin said he didn't write. *That* one." He didn't know what she was talking about and decided that she was too high to make any sense.

"I wish he were alive right now so we could laugh about people thinking he killed himself. It's funny and ironic. We used to sit in bed and talk about the ironies of life. The big ones, the ones that take your breath away. Like when the Indians were kind to the English when they first landed at Plymouth Rock and kept them alive that winter. When really they'd been much better off if they hadn't. Or when, for example, you fall in love with someone and then they die on you. That's an irony, isn't it, Paul? People use that word incorrectly now-a-days, don't you think?" she said.

SEVENTEEN

I wasn't really shocked when we found Martin's will. He left everything to her," Boon said to Kline. "We found it by accident at his apartment. It almost got thrown out by mistake. Can you imagine?"

Sitting in his impressive executive's chair behind his desk, Boon was speaking to him differently now. They shared a history, Kline realized—the group, Martin's suicide, a concern for Virginia's well being. It was almost as if they were friends. "What do you think of her state of mind?" Boon asked him. He had called Kline the day after they'd run into one another at the café and asked him cryptically to stop by his office, saying he was very concerned about Virginia. "She's drunk half the time, of course. She hasn't been the same since Martin died. She won't accept what happened."

"She's depressed. Obviously," Kline said. "She told me she doesn't believe Martin killed himself."

"Yes, I know. She's tried to convince me too—on several occasions. It's preposterous, of course, and it's gone on now for *months!* It's *morbid. She won't let go of him.* I do everything I can. I'm over there all the time. She's turned Martin's apartment into a kind of shrine. It's macabre, Paul. She doesn't even sleep there. Says she can't. She goes back to her place in the Mission. It's as if she can't make up her mind about anything," Boon said, sitting back in his chair. "I hope you call her. Take her out, why don't you? She likes to be taken out to lunch. She won't listen to me about her drinking. Maybe she'll listen to you."

"She's set then? Financially speaking. Martin left her everything?" Kline asked.

"Yes, as long as she behaves herself. There *are* conditions on the trust. You're in love with her, aren't you?" Boon asked, smiling coyly. Kline looked at him surprised.

"What makes you say that?"

"The way you *looked* at her yesterday. That was a very primitive look you gave her, old boy." He swiveled from side to side gently in his chair "Yes, you looked at her like you wanted to drag her into the Forest Primeval." Kline didn't answer.

Boon leaned forward and grinned. "Everyone who joins the group falls in love with Virginia. Don't feel bad. Even Kevin, believe it or not. She makes you feel like an artist, I suppose. Not all women are capable of that," he said.

Boon's secretary came in bringing Kline a cup of coffee and handed her boss a file. Boon's office had been remodeled and made larger. Now, with its new windows, it had an even grander view of the shops on Maiden Lane. Kline could see across the narrow alley into a chic women's boutique on the second story that sold intimate apparel and skimpy dresses. A gaggle of young wealthy women had invaded the shop and were laughing about something. They were the kind of women Kline had never really understood. They seemed free from any kind of worry, as if the world was spinning just for their pleasure.

"The group isn't the same now," Boon told him, taking the file. "Everything's changed since Martin died. Betsy left for New York right after Martin's funeral. She just pulled up stakes. I think it was the shock. She's in Budapest now. I get long e-mails about the Danube." Kline looked down at his coffee cup. He reached over and put the cup and saucer on the edge of Boon's desk. *Was it so obvious how he felt about her?* He glanced again beyond Boon at the women across the alley in the shop and realized for the first time that he didn't like Boon. It was the way he'd adjusted Virginia's hat the day before. There was something proprietary about it, Kline thought.

"I can't blame her, really. It *is* very hard to believe what happened," Kline said. "Especially the part about Fisher."

"You mean Martin attacking him? Of course, it's hard to believe. The police say he and Fisher were taking amphetamines that day. Can you believe it? Martin was already in a confused state of mind. He was seeing a psychiatrist, you know," Boon said in a confidential tone. Kline looked at Boon and made eye contact for the first time since he'd sat down. "Virginia's running the group now. She's taken Martin's place as our über-leader. She's absolutely thrown herself into her writing. Then we found the will and now she's rich. Just like in the movies. It's a happy ending of sorts, I suppose."

"I never thought about wills when I was Martin's age. And I had reason to," Kline said. He picked up his coffee cup.

"Yes. Well, it was actually just a note. I have it here." Boon took it out of a file on his desk. "I've been working on his estate this morning. He must have done what we all do when we're feeling sorry for ourselves, get half-potted one Sunday night and write it out on a whim." Boon stood up and handed it to him. The will was written on yellow legal paper in longhand. "It was addressed to me, but he'd forgotten to send it. But it's signed." Kline reached over and took the note. "It's his signature. We had it checked. I was in England visiting my mother when they found it."

I leave everything to Virginia Winston of 212 Capp Street, San Francisco. I think this is best. She's a good writer. I hope this money will make it possible for her to keep writing. I know what it's like to be broke and not be able to write.

Martin Anderson

Kline handed the note back. "Bloody good thing too, or the State of California would have gotten it all," Boon said. "Did you know there are *royalties?* That novel of his is in its second printing."

"Martin's movie is doing well, I've read," Kline said. "It got a 'thumbs up'."

"I went and saw it. It's not bad. They filmed it all here in town. I can tell you it was a shock when I got the statement from the producers—big money. They had to get another director, of course." Boon glanced at the file, looking at other documents inside. "He left her six million dollars *not including* the trust," Boon said, putting the file down suddenly. Boon got a quizzical look on his face as if he couldn't believe it himself.

"Did *you* fall in love with Virginia?" Kline asked.

"Virginia? Of course. I just told you. Everyone falls in love with Virginia. It's part of becoming a writer." Kline didn't know why he asked it exactly, but he wanted to know more about anyone who had ever touched her.

"Did you ever tell Martin you'd slept with her?" Kline asked. Boon leaned forward. He looked at Kline differently. His face was suddenly animated.

"No. Why would I have? Everyone lied about who they were sleeping with. Cindy told me once she'd gone over to Martin's house the night they *first* met. Can you imagine? They barely knew each other! It didn't last, of course. Women like Virginia fall for men like Martin, not men like us. I know that, and I think you do, too." Boon stopped smiling and gave him a measured look.

"I just thought you might have mentioned it. He was your best friend," Kline said. "Michael, why did you ask me to come here? I get the impression it wasn't just to tell me how Virginia is doing."

"I want you to follow her."

"Virginia? Why?"

"She claims someone is following her. A blonde girl. I told her it's her nerves and that she's imagining it. But she insisted that I hire you to find out if it's true. And there is something else, something I haven't told her. If Martin's family gets wind that she's cracking up—and she is, you know—then she won't get the trust. It's written into the original trust document. I had to move heaven and earth to see that the family didn't contest Martin's will. He had a right to leave the income from the trust to whomever he chose, but they can fight it. And there's the clause about being in *campos mentis* and not abusing drugs that pertains to *whomever* gets the money. The drug clause would include alcohol, I'm afraid."

"Don't tell them," Kline said. "It's real simple."

"I can't. I have a duty to the family. You know that. I've done everything I could within the law to see she got Martin's money. I'm not her lawyer; in fact, I'm still Martin's executor. But I am her friend. I've told her to be careful but she isn't listening. I want you to follow her and prove to her she isn't being followed by anyone. It's all a fantasy. She trusts you. I want you to give me a report on her habits and conduct, too. I'm choosing you for the report for obvious reasons. You're the one in love with her, after all. Do I have to spell it out to you? I think the term I'd use is *social* drinker," Boon said.

137

"All right. Martin told me you practically took care of him, too. That you loaned him money," Kline said.

"I loaned Martin money so he could finish that novel. Yes, I did."

"Did you give Virginia money, too?

"She was always broke, just like the rest of them. I might have. I gave them all money at one point or another. Even Kevin." Boon stood up and turned towards the window. "Not too much, though. I don't think it's right. It fosters dependence. You know *writers.* They *always* want something from you if they think you have money. They're a little like children, artists. They don't understand how the world works. They have to come to men like us. Realists. Levelheaded types. Then we dole the world of possibilities out to them—a dollar at time," Boon said. "I think I paid for her dog or cat or something when it was run over, and I paid her rent for a few months once too. She had a detective novel she was trying to finish at the time."

The conversation stopped then. He realized how little feeling Boon had. He realized he hadn't heard Boon express any sympathy for Martin, his best friend, either. Even at the funeral he'd been acting as if it were all a kind of horrible joke, as if Martin would walk in the door of the church and everyone would have a big laugh. Then Kline had to remind himself that Martin had tried to kill someone and that wasn't Boon's fault. And it wasn't Boon's fault that Martin had jumped from Coit Tower either. And it wasn't Boon's fault that Virginia was still in love with Martin.

"Oh, there's something else. I almost forgot. Could you go by the apartment? My assistant was going through Martin's things to make sure we didn't miss anything else. She found a pistol in a drawer in his closet. God knows why he had one. It scared her to death; she won't go near the place again until someone has seen to it. Could you handle it? Just be sure it's unloaded and safe. Maybe break it down into little harmless pieces, if you would, and bring it here. I'd do it myself, but I don't know a pistol from pesto. I'm liable to shoot myself. But you know all about guns, don't you, Paul?" Michael looked up and smiled.

"Sure," Kline said. "I'll take care of it."

"You'll take the job then of following Virginia and writing up a character report I can use?"

"Yes. I'll take it," Kline said.

"Why am I not surprised? Well, good." Boon gave him a key to Martin's apartment before he left.

EIGHTEEN

He'd been concupiscent and anxious since Virginia accepted his invitation to lunch. Like all men in love facing "The Date," Kline was afraid of a *mal paso*. While waiting for her in front of Moose's, he was obsessed with his appearance; he'd fretted over what to wear. He stole nervous glances at his reflection in the restaurant's windows as he waited for her, his failed attempt to look hip reflected back to him. He was wearing a black T-shirt and jeans and concluded that he'd managed only to look like any hapless out-of-place Marine on leave.

A taxi pulled up to the curb and Virginia jumped out. She looked stunning, sporting a red top that showed a streak of talc-white midriff and black low cut sailor pants, in keeping with her bohemian city-girl style. Several heads turned as they entered the restaurant.

"I'm glad you came," he said. He took a sip of ice water.

"Thanks for the invite. I had to switch places with someone at work at the last minute. I forgot that I was on this afternoon. I almost had to cancel. . . ."

"You're still working?"

"Yes, I still work at Macy's, just in the afternoons. I *want* to. I'm like those people who win the lottery and keep their jobs. I didn't want to be alone all day. I was afraid of what I might do. . . . Anyway, I'm here now," she said. The waitress came, all starched shirt and nice manners, and took their drink orders. She saved them, he thought, from an awkward moment. Virginia ordered a Virgin Bloody Mary, then changed the order at the last moment to a gin and tonic. She glanced over at the bar several times apprehensively.

Their eyes met. He didn't want to turn away from such a direct look, but he was afraid it would scare her if she detected what he was feeling, so he looked away out to the square and its verdant afternoon scene, a patchwork of sunlight and shadows, all very complex and overlaid, like his hopes for this date. "I'm sorry about Martin," he said. "I know you cared for him."

"Should I take the money, Paul? It seems so strange to have it."

"Take it," he said. "Martin wanted you to have it." She looked at him carefully. "You won't always be young and beautiful." She smiled. "You might need it some day," he said.

"I'll take it if you promise I'll stop crying. Can you promise me that?"

"You don't have to take it," he added quickly. "I just thought I should play Dutch uncle." He was sorry he'd said the word "uncle".

"It's all that movie money, isn't it?" she said. Their drinks came and she took hers in hand immediately, like she was grabbing at a life preserver. "I think he hated the movie business. He called Fisher a supercilious dolt. I can still hear him. He had a wonderful way of capturing someone with a few words. I always wanted to hear him talk frankly about me. . . . He liked you. He said you were old-fashioned and honorable, like one of those officers in *War and Peace,*" she said.

They both looked out the picture window. The little square of green park was beautiful and sophisticated, clean and European. He knew, of course, that she was still in love with

Martin but, until that moment, he thought he could break through somehow, but now he wasn't so sure. Deflated, he listened to her order and wished that he could be Martin Anderson. He was tired of being Kline, the skirt-chasing, weight-lifting Jew, the solid Marine officer who wanted to write novels but couldn't. They talked; she seemed to be floating away on a raft of memories and gin. He watched her eat her salad and listened as she told him about writing a novel almost non-stop after Martin's death and how she had started a new writing group because she felt she owed something to the young writers coming up behind her. He almost smiled when she said "the younger writers." She hadn't a line on her face and she was already talking like a veteran.

"You want to share your years of experience, is that it?" Kline said, finally speaking.

"Almost six years. . . ." she said, putting her fork down. "That's a lot, isn't it?" She'd had a second G&T and was calmer now. He was sorry for not having realized that, in a real sense, she *was* a veteran, and that he hadn't wanted to think of her as a real novelist, a real artist, but rather as the girl of his sexual dreams, which were two different things.

"I thought I'd look into Martin's death and the attack on Fisher if you want me to," he said over coffee.

"Of course I want you to. Cindy and I want to know what *really* happened to him, Paul. We think he was murdered."

"Why?" he said

"Because there are too many things that don't make any sense," she said. "That manuscript I told you he supposedly authored, for one thing. Someone put it in Cindy's messenger bag at Betsy's just before Martin died. Cindy thought it was Martin's way of asking her to read it. Later, when she brought it up to him, Martin denied writing it, but she didn't believe him until it was too late. There's something strange and frightening about it. The person who wrote that stuff is crazy. We think it's the same person who wrote the confession, and Cindy thinks she might be able to prove it."

He was going to bring up the bloody clothes the police found in Martin's apartment but decided against it. Obviously, both girls were carrying the torch for Martin and couldn't accept the obvious. "He found out he was adopted just before he died. I thought I'd start there. Did he tell you?" Kline said.

"Are you the one who told him?"

"Yes," he said. "I told him the day I met you at his apartment." He was sorry he'd mentioned it. "I'll do what I can"

"It would mean a lot to me. Thank you. And thanks for the lunch," Virginia said. Kline paid the bill. They lingered on the street a moment, taking in the beauty of the park as they waited for a cab.

"I'd like to come back to the group and give it another try. I'm not getting anywhere alone. I left because—I don't know why really. I was horribly blocked, to be honest, and I couldn't keep up with that damn rule," he said.

"Of course you can," she said. "You should have told me. I could have helped." He put her into a cab, and afterwards, for a moment, he felt completely lost.

The nearly empty apartment was warm and smelled of floor polish. Virginia hadn't changed anything; Boon hadn't exaggerated. It was exactly the same as the first time he'd seen it. He went instinctively to the windows of the big living room. Late in the afternoon, the bay was resplendent, with a sparkling taupe sheen and bits of vanilla white to indicate there was a wind up, and maybe even a God somewhere. Alcatraz looked cold, its weather-beaten buildings ghostly and yellow-stained. He left the window and went to the kitchen. He was surprised to see Martin's laptop still there on the table, the juice jar crammed with pencils and the yellow writing pad. The laptop screen was dark.

He walked down the wide hallway to the bedroom and went to the dresser and opened the top drawer where he'd been told to look for the pistol. It was a forty-five, brand new, and still in the box. He grabbed the box and walked past the open door of the bedroom closet where Martin's leather jacket hung as if on display. He took off his own coat and tossed it on the bed and then he pulled Martin's jacket off the hanger. He slipped it on and studied himself in the mirror of the walk-in closet, enjoying his I'm-Martin fantasy, then went back out into the kitchen carrying the pistol.

He took the pistol out of the box, dropped the clip out and laid it on the table. The clip was full. He slid the action back and removed the unsafe chambered round. Holding the pistol, he realized how much he missed his old life. He missed soldiering. He missed the danger and the excitement of war. It was part of him now. It was a dirty truth, but the truth nonetheless. He picked up the pistol and aimed it at the clock on the kitchen wall. Startled by the sound of the front door opening, he turned to look behind him. Virginia was standing in the doorway looking at him.

"What are you *doing?*" she asked. Kline felt his face flush; he was embarrassed and startled. He'd been caught in a bizarre and intimate fantasy and didn't know what to say to her. She was supposed to be at work or he wouldn't have come. "Are you going to shoot yourself?" she asked, only half-joking.

"I thought you were going to work," he said.

"I was, but I couldn't face it after all. What are you doing here? And where did that come from?"

"Michael asked me to take it away." She came across the living room and looked at the pistol in his hand.

"Martin hated guns. I don't know why he would have one," she said. He didn't answer. She turned and walked into the living room and put her backpack purse down on the couch. "I've been trying to figure it out. What really happened to him. I come here sometimes and try to sort it out. . . . Martin didn't try to kill anyone," she said. She looked different than she had at the restaurant, sad, not quite high and not quite sober either.

"How can you be so sure?"

"Because I loved him, and I don't fall in love with wannabe murderers, that's why."

"We all make mistakes," he said. "What if he had problems. . . ?"

"He wasn't crazy or vicious," she said, turning on him. She walked over to the windows. "I don't want you to take the gun. I want things to stay the way they were."

"Okay. So Martin wasn't a danger to anyone, I still promised Michael I would remove it," Kline said. "Anyway, it's unsafe. It was loaded. It shouldn't be here." He didn't want to talk about Martin anymore. He turned away from her and started breaking the pistol down. When he was finished, it was in several pieces on the table, and his hands smelled of gun oil.

"Are you *pretending* to *be* him?" she asked, coming up behind him. He didn't look at her. "You're wearing his jacket."

"Yes, I suppose I am, in a silly way." He felt his face flush again. He couldn't face her. He felt like he was twelve years old again.

"Is that what you normally do when you investigate? Go to someone's house and walk around in their clothes?" *Was she glad she had found him compromised like this?* He turned and faced her, the pistol's clip in his right hand. No, he could tell from the look on her face that she didn't mean anything by it. He put the clip down and slid the coat off and placed it deliberately on the chair.

"I want very much to be a writer," he said. He looked down at the pieces of the forty-five. "But I can't seem to get there." He picked up the clip again and began slipping out the rounds with the thumb of one hand. He let them fall, catching them as they fell with his free hand. "It's stupid, I know. At *my* age. I loved being a soldier, but now I want to write. Even when I was a soldier, I wanted to write."

"You must know how strange that is," she said, watching him catch the bullets. "Those are very different things. One destroys, one creates."

"Do you think so? I suppose you're right."

"Put the jacket back on," she said suddenly. He handed the coat to her, afraid because of the way she'd said it. She took it from him. She smelled the coat, holding it with both hands. She rubbed her lips on it. "Go ahead, *be* Martin. Don't let me stand in your way." She handed the coat back and, when he took it, she kissed him on the mouth. It was unexpected. "I miss him," she said. "Will you make love to me?" She was kissing his face quickly, missing his lips sometimes. He pulled away from her, horrified.

"I love you," he said.

"I know that."

"You don't love me at all, do you?" he said.

"No, I don't. Not like you want me to," she said. She kissed him again. He felt the warm skin of her back. "But I want to make love. Take it or leave it," she said.

She'd stopped kissing him but kept holding him. Her touch was starting to creep through him like medicine that cures quickly and painlessly. "You want to make love to me, don't you?" she said.

"Yes, but not like this. You're pretending I'm. . . ."

"Why not like this? Go ahead. I want you to. You want to *fuck* me, don't you? Isn't that what you want? I can see it in your eyes." Her words struck him almost physically. He felt her arms tighten around him, felt his own hand hold hers, then felt her pull his arm back with that sweet playful tension that belongs to first-time lovemaking. She was smiling impishly. "If you . . . want to be . . . him . . . *start* with *me*. I can tell you what you want to know. I'm the expert."

He didn't let her say anything more. He kissed her and took her into the bedroom. She knew what to do about the shades. Closed, the room sank into a sweet semi-darkness. She tried to pull his shirt off but gave up suddenly and pulled her clothes off instead. He undid his pants, watching her, the belt buckle making a noise. She lay on the bed looking at him like some artist's model. It was better than any fantasy he'd had of her; she was whiter and harder and, when he got between her legs, she was just better than anything he had ever known. They made the kind of love that couples do who are strangers—grossly physical, almost harmful, unsafe lovemaking. Like the first time he walked out on the football field in high school and the ball was snapped, all the action seemed to go on at once, overwhelming him with its intensity— the sound of her white shoulders hitting the wall, her face half-climaxed, her legs locked in spasm. But there was one moment he would remember much later, the moment she looked up at him and smiled as she came, and he was sure she was thinking of Martin.

She had her naked back to him, her arms fastening her bra in silence. "You can't replace Martin. You understand that, don't you? You aren't Martin. Screwing me isn't ever going to change that. I want you to leave that gun here," she said.

147

"Why? Why don't you want me to take it?" he said.

"Why do you think?" she said. "The writer's curse. That's what Cindy calls it. Sometimes I get tired of thinking." She was speaking with her back to him, then turned her head so he could see her expression. "Don't you ever get tired of thinking, Paul? Fed up with it? I don't want to have to think anymore if I don't want to. And I don't want to have to miss him for the rest of my life either."

"I'm taking it with me," he said. "And stop it."

"What? Loving Martin?"

"The melodrama. You're too old for it. You're not in high school anymore." It was the first time he'd ever spoken to her like that, but she'd scared him. She turned around and reached for her blouse.

"Please leave," she said, her voice distant now. She walked out of the room. He heard the phone ring and Cindy's voice leaving a message as he climbed out of the bed. She was asking Virginia how the meeting with Hemingway went. He took the pistol with him when he left.

He went to his office and tried to forget what had happened, that they'd made love, that he'd been frantically happy for an hour, but couldn't. A spring storm had come in off the Pacific and it was raining hard now. The sound of the rain driven against the bay windows filled his office. When he couldn't stand it anymore, he went and got his Cadillac from the parking lot down the street and headed back up Lombard. On the way he used his cell phone to call her, ostensibly to apologize for speaking to her the way he had. She didn't answer. The rain suddenly slammed the street. He was frightened because he realized, if she did something to herself, it would be *his* fault and he wouldn't be able to live with himself. He had started it. He'd started it the day he'd walked in on Martin and destroyed his life and, he supposed, hers too. She didn't answer the phone. He parked in front of the building unsure what to do. Then he decided he would bird-dog her because he promised Michael he would, and because he just wanted to be close to her. So he waited.

She walked out of the building at dusk. It was raining softly. He'd parked up the street, so if she pulled out of the driveway in her car and went down Lombard he could follow her without being spotted. He hadn't expected her to come out on foot.

In a panic, he watched her walk straight towards him on the sidewalk. He turned on the engine and put his Cadillac into reverse slipping into one of the private parking spaces of the apartment building to his right. He ducked down behind the wheel, letting her pass by the carport, realizing that she didn't know what kind of car he drove. When he pulled back out into the street, he saw she was climbing the stairs that led up to Coit Tower, her umbrella open, wearing the same clothes she'd worn to the restaurant.

He stared for a moment as she climbed the stairs, the engine running. If he pulled up to the parking lot of the tower, there was a chance there wouldn't be a parking place. The police kept a traffic cop there during peak hours around sunset. He turned off the engine and got out of the car.

It started to rain harder suddenly, the rain pelting him in the face as he ran up the sidewalk toward the tower. The walkway turned to the left, and he had to make a choice between taking the stairs, or a tree-shrouded path, both leading to the tower. The stairs were the long way, he decided. He ran along the path, where the rain was unable to penetrate the old cypress trees that made a dense canopy over the walk. He began to run, knowing that he might be overreacting and making a fool of himself. He slowed down for a moment, and then a panic filled him again. He remembered the way Martin's body had crashed to the ground, the way it bounced horribly on the stairs, and the way his mouth had moved in death. He remembered the screams of the women in the crowd.

He went around the back of the tower and spotted Virginia through the windows. She was inside the lobby already. She walked across the lobby to the elevator. He pounded on the window from outside. She didn't hear him. He saw her in queue for the elevator along with a throng of raincoated tourists. He raced around to the stairs and into the lobby. The tourists were filing into the elevator. He got to the queue and pushed people aside, but the elevator door closed and she was gone. She'd seen him. They'd looked at each other. He'd shouted her name, everyone was staring at him now. The ticket collector stepped up and asked him if something was wrong. Kline looked at the old Chinese man for a moment. "Do you have a phone in the elevator? It's an emergency. Can you stop it?"

"No sir." The old man looked at him strangely. "Why would you want that?" He didn't answer.

"You have to stop that elevator," Kline said.

"Can't stop elevator, Mister," the old man said. Kline bolted for the stairs, afraid it was already too late.

He took the stairs two at a time. At first it was easy, but gradually his legs started to burn and cramp. The sound of his breathing filled the dank narrow concrete stairway, half bomb shelter, half medieval castle. At one point he heard the elevator rumble and could tell it was moving past him, descending. She was at the top, he told himself. He would be too late. He sped up as best he could. Near the top he started to gasp for air and could no longer feel his legs. At the top he hit the heavy metal door with both arms, opening it with a bang. A blast of cold air hit him in the face. He ran up the last few steps to the observation deck. The deck was crowded with tourists who were there for the sunset show that had been spoilt by the rain. People were holding onto umbrellas and their hats, looking disappointed. Gasping for air, he looked for Virginia as he pushed through the tightly packed crowd.

He saw her umbrella drop a few feet away as he pushed people aside. He lunged for her as she started to climb the rampart wall. He heard a scream, perhaps hers, perhaps the young girl next to them. He pulled her back from the edge, but she was still trying to fling herself over the rampart, even as he held her in his arms. The rain hit both of them hard now. People slapped by the wind were staring at them in shock as he struggled to pull her to safety. He could feel her in his arms, slight, feral, struggling. She was shouting Martin's name, screaming it over the sound of the wind.

NINETEEN

Kline took out the pieces of Martin's pistol and laid them out on the edge of Boon's desk. "Do you think you could put it back together for us?" Boon asked sheepishly. "We might *lose* something otherwise." Kline had caught Michael just as he was getting ready to leave the office. The young lawyer was dressed in black tie for the opera.

"How is she?" Kline asked. Kline reached for the barrel and fit it to the pistol's handgrip, still upset about what had happened yesterday at Coit Tower. He began to reassemble the pieces quickly.

"I spoke to her twice this afternoon. She's much better. She said she feels silly about the whole thing," Boon said, watching him.

"You should have warned me about her state of mind," Kline said, his fingers stopping for a moment.

"I would have, but I didn't know myself," Michael said. Kline picked up the clip and shoved it home; he cleared the action one last time to make certain there was no round remaining. Whole now, he laid the pistol on the edge of the desk.

"Is it safe?" Boon asked.

"It's unloaded, but they're never safe. That's the first thing they teach you in the military. I'd like to wash my hands," Kline said.

"Just across the hall."

"She can't be left alone," Kline said, coming back in a few moments. Boon, who was examining the gun, put it down. "Not for a second. She might try it again."

"Cindy's staying with her tonight. She won't be alone. And we're seeing about getting her a psychiatrist. She refuses to see Martin's," Michael said.

"Why didn't you tell me she was suicidal? There must have been signs," Kline said.

"No. Nothing. She hadn't said anything. . . . No threats. She was drinking too much, but I had no idea that she was that ill. Sit down, Paul. You're still upset. Thank God you were following her."

"You must have seen how depressed she was," Kline said, not able to let it go. He finally sat down. "You should have had the pistol removed immediately. She might have used it."

"You aren't the only one who cares for her, you know. I'm doing everything I can for her. I care about her very much. You're right. I made a stupid mistake, but I didn't realize how bad off she was."

"She's asked me to look into Martin's case," Kline said. "I thought you should know. I told her I would."

"What case?"

"The case the police have against Martin for the attack on Fisher and his subsequent suicide. She doesn't believe Martin attacked Fisher or that he killed himself. She thinks Martin was murdered. She says Cindy might be able to prove Martin didn't write the confession the police found on his laptop," Kline said.

"Why, for god's sake? Martin's *dead.* It's moot," Boon said.

"She doesn't seem to think so," Kline said. "Look, I think he did it. He got angry and beat the hell out of that director when he was high. Okay. It happens every day. But I told her I would look into it for her peace of mind. So, you know who Martin's birth family is, don't you?"

"Yes," Boon said. He picked up some files from a stack on his desk and moved them.

"Who are Martin's grandparents? I thought I'd start there," Kline said.

"Don't be ridiculous, Paul." Boon got up from his desk and turned towards the window. He looked out on Maiden Lane with his back to Kline. It was getting dark now.

"Maybe his death has something to do with the birth family. Some reason for framing Martin. Maybe some crazy member of the family didn't want him to get the trust. Who are they?" Kline asked. Boon turned around and faced him. "Help me out here."

"I can't tell you that. That's absolutely confidential. You know that. They've been clients of this firm for years. Impossible," Boon said. "Paul, I would drop this. I know Virginia. Believe me. She lives in a fantasy world. Don't you understand? Virginia can't admit she was in love with a crazy man. Don't you see? Martin *has* to become a martyr now. She can't admit what happened to him. What he became."

"Maybe. . . . But it was quite a coincidence that you got the case, you know. I mean, you must have been surprised as hell to see that Martin, one of your best friends, was the beneficiary of the trust," Kline said.

"Yes. It was a fluke, really. The family was a client of the firm long before *I* ever came to work here."

"Are they society? Is that the problem?" Kline asked. "I mean, obviously, they're rich, with the kind of money they gave Martin and the fact that they paid Martin's adoptive parents all those years—even after he'd graduated from college."

"Yes, they are socially prominent." Boon came around the desk and sat in one of his chairs. In black tie he looked like he belonged in a chic magazine advertisement for the cologne *Success.* "Look Paul, I've got a dinner date I can't miss. You want a drink before I have to go?" Kline nodded. Boon picked up the phone and called someone asking for two beers to be brought to his office. "Forget it, Paul, it's over. Let me handle it now. Virginia is entitled to Martin's trust. That's the law. Martin's birth family probably doesn't like that, I'm sure, but they've accepted it because it's legal. We've been working out the last of the details. I'll act like there's nothing wrong with her, but you have to help me. Don't approach them; it's the last thing I want given what's just happened. If they wanted to, they could put up a fight to deny Virginia the money. And now, with her suicide attempt, they might be within their rights to take the money back."

There was a knock on the office door. A young girl from the mailroom walked in with the beer and glasses. Kline could tell the mail girl was impressed with Boon. Her eyes ran over Kline, completely unimpressed. She pulled the door closed behind her again when she left.

"Now, I'm going to tell you something I shouldn't, Paul. It's as much as I can tell you, and you have to accept it as an explanation. When Martin's mother died, it was a terrible ordeal for the grandparents. Horrible. The circumstances were quite bizarre. They are very nice people. They tried to do the right thing from the start. If you bother them now, especially now that Martin has turned out to be one more tragedy, imagine how they'd feel. Don't do it Paul, for Virginia's sake, if not for theirs."

Kline looked at him. "There's one thing I don't understand. Why didn't they just take the kid in when his mother died?"

"I don't know. That was long before my time, I told you."

"Don't you think that was strange? Their own flesh and blood? "

"Paul. People do strange things every day. What do you want from me? They must have had their reasons. As I said, I don't know what the family thinks about Virginia getting all this money. Maybe there are some that don't like it. But if you make them angry, they will most certainly react. Martin is dead, Paul. Virginia has to accept that. It's as simple as that."

"All right. I'll leave it alone for Virginia's sake," Kline said. "If you think it will help."

"That a boy," Boon said. He smiled and picked up one of the beers and poured it into a glass. "Here, keep this. Consider it a gift from Martin's estate," Boon said. Michael picked the pistol up off the desk and held it out to Kline. "Please," Boon said. "What am I going to do with it?" Kline looked at it a moment; he had a weakness for pistols and decided to take it. He stuck it in his coat pocket. "What the hell was Martin doing with a loaded gun in his apartment? You see what I mean?" Boon said. "He *was* crazy for god's sake! Did you ever see the blonde? The one Virginia says is following her?"

"No," Kline said.

Michael put his glass down. "She wants to get out of town for a few weeks. I told her it was a good idea. My father has a place in Tahoe, right on the lake. I told her she could use it. Cindy's going too, so we don't have to worry. I'll check in on them on the weekends. I think it's a good idea for her to get away from the city." Darkness had crept down Maiden Lane. Kline put down his beer. Boon had stood up and was carefully picking up his files and putting them in a locked file cabinet on the other side of the office.

He knew that Boon wasn't telling him everything. He was going to start lying to Boon, he'd told himself when they shook hands. He was the kind of man you should lie to, he thought. They rode the elevator down to the street together. Boon was already at ease, sure that Virginia would "snap out of it" as he'd put it. There was a Town Car waiting for Boon at the office door. Kline caught a glimpse of a beautiful girl waiting for him in the back seat as the driver opened the door for him.

TWENTY

The familiar quiet of the San Francisco Main Library was soothing. The public library had been Kline's sanctuary as a child, his refuge from his parent's strange behavior, especially his mother who, throughout his childhood, had been distant because of her bouts of depression. Each and every book was a possible escape into a better, more rational world, a world that had nothing to do with his strange home life. He dreaded coming home after school because he was unsure what kind of mood his mother would be in. The kitchen would be dark, the living room empty, because his mother often locked herself in her bedroom until his father could persuade her to come down to dinner. By the time he was in junior high school, he would stop at the local branch library instead of going home after school, not leaving until he knew his father would be home. He used to thank the librarian when she stamped his books as if it were her house and she were letting him visit. There were many times he hadn't wanted to go home at all. He was jealous of his friends who had ordinary parents, parents who didn't jump every time someone came to the front door.

All morning, Kline searched the newspaper microfiche, starting with the San Francisco *Examiner* the year Martin was adopted, 1971. He'd promised Boon not to bother Martin's birth family for Virginia's sake and he would keep his promise. But he saw no reason why he couldn't give Virginia some

off-the-record peace of mind and some closure. He'd sworn
to her the day he'd brought her back from the tower that he
would find out what happened to Martin, although he was
certain that he'd gone off the deep end. If he could prove to
her that Martin *had* attacked Fisher, maybe she would let go
of him. Maybe she would stop loving him. And if he could
get Virginia to forget about Martin, it would be worth it. He
wanted her–that's all that really mattered to him.

Using Martin's social security number, which he'd found
in the original case file, he'd been able to get a copy of Martin's
birth certificate on-line from the City and County of San
Francisco for a fee. Martin's birthmother was Marguerite
Kolsrud. Anybody who had grown up in San Francisco in
the last fifty years and read a newspaper had heard of the
Kolsrud family. They were one of the richest and most
influential families in San Francisco, if not the entire state.
The Kolsruds went back to the "Robber Baron" days. Like
the Stanfords, they got here first and pushed the hardest.
The Kolsrud men had a reputation for being bare-knuckles
businessmen. It seemed to be genetic. There was a whole
new generation of Kolsruds staking out Cyberspace now. And
it was all happening at lightning speed, no poor ranchers or
Indians to get in the way this time.

He found mention of the Kolsrud girl's death in October of
nineteen seventy–a brief mention in Count Moro's column.
The Count was a society columnist who had written for the
Hearst paper during the sixties. Kline knew his hometown
well enough to know that if the family were rich enough, and
important enough, they could very likely have kept the news
of their daughter's death, even if it were sensational or sordid,
off the front page, but maybe not out of the gossip column,
where a sanitized version might be suggested. Halfway into

the column of October 15, 1970, he spotted the girl's name with a passing reference to her death.

> Marguerite Kolsrud was laid to rest at Our Lady of the Tabernacle after a short service at Grace Cathedral. Margaret was a great kid. I knew her since she was a child and I can say that this columnist shed more than a few tears. God bless her wonderful mother and father. . . . Robert Redford was spotted in San Francisco yesterday filming a scene. . . .

Count Moro lived on Upper Polk Street near California Street. The neighborhood was in transition, a nexus of new trendy restaurants, raunchy gay bars that catered to "chicken hawks," the teenage boys waiting obligingly out on the street for tricks, and Gen-Y skateboard shops that seemed somehow to belong in suburbia.

In the old days, in the fifties, Polk Gulch had been the first gay neighborhood in the city, way before anyone had heard of the Castro District. A street car went by on California Street on the way downtown. The conductor rang the bell for the benefit of the tourists, who were on their two-week package adventures and packed in tightly, holding onto the white grab poles. The famous plangent sound of the cable car bell had them smiling like little kids.

Kline parked and checked his address book as the streetcar swayed down the tracks on its way downtown. After making a call to one of his friends at the *Examiner,* he had learned that the Count still lived in the city and sold information now to detectives, lawyers and journalists of various types to make ends meet when anyone needed an "expert" on the city's big families.

"It's Paul Kline," Kline said into the old-fashioned tarnished brass speaker at the front door of the building. "I spoke with mister—"

"I know who you are, dear. Bernstein called and said you were coming," said a raspy, effeminate voice coming out of the speaker. The buzzer sounded and Kline pushed open the heavy front door. There were two new wicked-looking mountain bikes in the hallway. The stairs were clean. The ancient colorless runner had been worn down to practically nothing. Like so many places on Polk Street, the building housed a strange mix of immigrants, college students and the old. On the fourth floor, the door at the end of the hall cracked open. Kline heard the various security chains slide off the Count's door one by one. The door finally swung open. There was an immediate strong smell of steam heat, nail polish remover and cat box stink.

"Dear boy, dear boy, come in." Count Moro was tall and gaunt and wore pancake make-up that was white. He looked remarkably like a broken-down whore who'd gone to the stable, the kind who never fell in love with the customers. The old queen wore a caftan, lots of gold jewelry and worn women's house shoes. Due to his many years of cross-dressing, the Count had a practiced femininity that worked, and there was a soft, epicene quality to his mouth that made the cratered, jowly seventy-year old face seem younger. It almost made you want to believe in the female illusion that "she'd" been working on for forty years, Kline thought. But, in the end, at the center of the illusion were men's eyes studying him, he realized. The eyes, masculine in their gaze, and intelligent, betrayed the Count's soft-pedaled femininity.

The former popular newspaper columnist was down to a one-bedroom flat. Each move had been a step down from the little prince he'd once been. Kline noticed an oxygen bottle in the corner of the tidy living room as he was ushered in. The Count kissed him on each cheek in a European greeting, smelling slightly of old flesh and special powders. There were pictures everywhere from the bygone golden years, when he'd been a handsome twenty-something gay man who had, for mysterious reasons, been embraced by San Francisco's elites long enough for him to cop a job at the *Examiner,* the city's establishment paper since William Randolph Hearst ran it himself, perfecting yellow journalism in the process.

"Dear boy. Is it too early for drinkies?"

"It's eleven-thirty," Kline said.

"Sherry then? Before I have to visit my throne." The old man nodded to the oxygen set up in the corner of the room. "You're such a solid-looking man." The Count looked at him like a sailor on Saturday night. "Makes me think of all those years of *sin.* Is it *weights?*"

"Yeah, I work out a little," Kline said.

"How adorable. Of course, you're perfectly safe with me. I'm too old for all that nonsense *now.*" The Count crossed the living room to an end table by the oxygen tank. He lit a cigarette and hugged himself with one arm around his thin waist. He tried to take a deep breath and strike a pose. Kline got the impression that perhaps the Count, despite his moribund condition, might not be so sexually quiescent as he let on. "Is it information we're after, or love, dear?"

"Info dear," Kline winked. "But if I get real lonely, I'll come up sometime."

"Oh, dear, I told you. I'm completely incapable of the act. Age has a good mind, dear boy, but a saggy thingy. What is it you really want, Mr. Kline? And come in and sit down next to the Count. I miss young people." The old queen poured himself a sherry in a cheap water glass, and they went and sat down on a red Empire-style couch chinked with burn marks. The seat portion was matted with cat hair. The Count rubbed out his cigarette and then put on his oxygen headset and proceeded to pretend he wasn't sick.

"The Kolsrud family," Kline began.

"Yes. I know them. . . ." The Count's breathing had changed. It had become slightly strained from the effects of the oxygen.

"They had a daughter, Marguerite," Kline said.

"The hippie," the Count said through the mask. Kline nodded. "She was beautiful. I mean *really* beautiful, dear. One of those blondes us Jews run after." Kline remembered that the Count's real name was Lowenstein, that his father and grandfather had run a successful flower shop out in the Avenues. *"And* she was tall. Legs, well, they just seemed to stretch on forever. To tell you the truth, I was jealous of those legs."

"What happened to her?" Kline asked.

"She was born a Kolsrud. What more could happen to the poor girl?"

"That shouldn't have been much of a problem."

"Of *course* it was a problem, honey. They're rich as The Donald, but they're completely–" The Count leaned towards him. Kline saw where the white hair was growing out of the dye job around the ears. The cheap dye was almost orange and caked his hair like frosting. *"Jay Kolsrud was an *appalling* shit. I knew the wife, Kitty, very well. But the husband, Jay! God! He drove the girl to it, I swear."

"To what?"

"Suicide." He pulled the mask off and put it in his lap, seemingly bored with it. "Not just any suicide either, dear. Quite a grand one. Get me that package of cigarettes, will you? There, on the kitchen table. They go so well with drinkies." Kline went to the kitchen table and picked up a new package of Camels. He came back to he couch and lit a fresh one for the old man and passed it to him. The Count sucked at it as if it were the last cigarette of his life. "The family owns the Embarcadero Center, as well as Gemco Corporation. And I won't go into all the real estate. They make vending machines too. Every time someone buys anything out of one in the Western States, they get a quarter Kitty once told me. You can imagine, they've been doing it since the *thirties.* They have some kind of lock on candy and cigarette machines. That's just *some* of their businesses. Anyway, the girl went to Columbia University and came back with a boy. And I'm afraid not just *any* boy, dear. I saw him just once. He was a very big boy, a very big *Puerto Rican* boy. Beautiful, I don't mind telling you. Well, you can imagine. It wasn't exactly *Guess Who's Coming To Dinner.* I heard old Jay senior talk about the boy once at a party. It was *nigger* this and *nigger* that. Quite the Nazi, Jay Kolsrud. Kitty tried to do what she could, but you can imagine. It was Göring vs. Tinker Bell. I'm afraid it wasn't much of a fight." The oxygen or the drinking seemed to be helping animate him. He took a swipe at his makeup and then looked at his fingers.

"He disowned Marguerite. And it was complicated because I don't actually think Marguerite married the boy, but they had a child. She did her best for a while to make a go of it, but I think the drugs they were using didn't make it any easier. They were in some kind of commune on Haight Street. Everyone was in a commune then. After all, she'd never needed anything and then all of a sudden no money. Cut off, you see. It must have been a shock! Don't you think? Having it all then not having it?" The Count slipped on his mask again. "I don't like the way this feels, and it does something to my allure. . . ."

"You're still sexy, Count," Kline said.

"Oh, dear boy, you're so sweet. Why don't you visit the Count more often?" Like all the boys he'd grown up with, he'd made fun of homosexuals until his mother caught him saying something ugly once on the phone to one of his friends and told him that they'd been the first to go. She had known many at the camp. After that, things were different; they were victims, like his parents, and he couldn't make fun of them anymore.

"You said her suicide was dramatic."

"Very. She flew off of Coit Tower. I'm afraid that wasn't all. She had taken her little boy up there with her. The boy saw her jump they say. She was stoned of course. LSD, I think it was. Dreadful. No one understood how she could do it in front of the child."

"She was high?" Kline said.

"Stuffed with LSD Kitty told me. Stuffed with it."

"They kept it all out of the papers. How did they manage that?" Kline asked.

"Dear, don't be ridiculous. The rich *own* the *Examiner*. Why do you think it's still such a small town paper after *all* these years? I should know, honey. The trick to being a successful reporter is to know what the rich *really* want covered. And Jay was on the board. Marguerite's brother, Jay Jr., still is. The *Examiner* will always be a small town paper, honey."

"Is the old man still alive?"

"No, just the son. He's a tiny version of his father. Only richer."

"Marguerite's brother?"

"Yes."

"And the mother?"

"Kitty is down on the Peninsula. She put up with that Nazi for years and years. I think she left him in the seventies, *finally*. He had a bimbo he married. Bazooms out to here.

Kitty got half of *everything* and the palace they had. She had me down once to lunch and told me what she got. It was a laundry list, dear, a real laundry list of goodies. Gobs of zeros she told me. Houses everywhere–some she said she'd never even been to. Isn't that wonderful? Gobs of zeros," the Count laughed. For a moment, Kline thought he heard something youthful in that laugh until it collapsed into something else suddenly, something that wasn't youthful at all. The last sentence was wheezed out by sheer queer will power, his cheeks collapsing. "Of course, Kitty had to sleep with Jay all those years! *God,* can you imagine?" The Count wheezed, fighting for breath, " *Göring, in bed* with you?"

It took the Count several minutes to recover from the hacking. Kline got out the money and put it on the kitchen table. There were photographs of the Count around the little breakfast nook where he must have eaten alone. The photographs looked to have been taken forty years before and showed his attendance at innumerable elegant parties, captured forever in cheap drugstore frames. The young man waved forever from a long ago past.

"You can't believe how wonderful it all was," he said behind him. "The rich are always so gay." Kline turned and looked at the Count. The old man winked at him. "If you know what I mean."

"What happened to Marguerite's kid?"

"He was put up for adoption. Göring said he wouldn't raise a pickaninny. Kitty did what she could, always pulling strings and keeping track. I'm sure he's fine. Probably in Europe living the high life. When you're young you don't really need money. The irony was that he was a blond. And Jay *still* wouldn't raise him."

166

TWENTY-ONE

Two weeks later, Kline got a call from Virginia at his office telling him that she was back from Tahoe and she wanted to see him. She had a surprise she said. "I sold something. I didn't want to tell you until I could show you a copy of the book." It was late afternoon when they met for coffee at the Cafe Claude. The café was almost empty at that time of day; they were surrounded by a squadron of empty tables and stacked white metal chairs. The sun was long gone, the alley deserted. He'd wanted to go up to Tahoe to visit her but hadn't, only because Boon had said her new doctor wanted Virginia not to be reminded of the past.

An advance copy of Virginia's novel was lying on the table between them. Impressed, he picked it up and stared at the title in yellow–*Cool Mint Love,* by Virginia Winston. There was a picture on the back of her and Martin taken in Chinatown. For a moment, they didn't say a word. She had a strange look on her face–triumph that she had made it and sadness because Martin wasn't there to share her victory. He put the book down. She'd been so excited when she'd called him that they'd spoken only about the book and how happy she was with the cover and her good review in *Publishers Weekly.* On the phone he thought she sounded much better.

Kline decided, looking at her, that he would tell her what he'd learned about Martin's family and warn her that she might jeopardize getting Martin's inheritance if they kept up the investigation. He ordered a latte and then told her everything he'd learned about the case. She listened carefully to the story about Martin's birth mother. It was his opinion, he told her as a kind of coda to the story, that mental illness ran in the family. Martin was programmed to fail. Martin had cracked under the pressures of sudden success and the news of his being adopted. He'd been taking amphetamines with the director in the hotel according to the police report. The speed had pushed him over the edge.

"He shouldn't have gotten involved with drugs," Kline said. He blamed the drug taking for the attack on Fisher. "I'm sorry. I don't want to lie to you. That's what I believe." They were the last ones left outside. The alley seemed unusually still. Virginia looked at him a moment. She was smoking. She tapped her cigarette on a clean metal ashtray.

"A blonde woman has been following me," she said.

"I know. Michael told me."

"Who would do that to me? It's so cruel." Kline stared at her. Waiters were leaning chairs against the nearby table, hoping they'd leave. She looked so much better. He'd thought he could discuss the case without upsetting her, but now he was sorry he had brought it up. She wasn't better at all, really, that was obvious suddenly.

"Why is someone following me?" She fumbled with her lighter. It fell on the table.

"I don't know," he said.

"Am I crazy too? Like they say Martin was?" She picked the lighter up. "Maybe I'm seeing things. Maybe it's 'female hysteria.' Isn't that what they used to call it? Next, I'll think I'm pregnant with Martin's child! I wish we'd had a child; then I wouldn't be so alone," she said.

He didn't know what to answer. He motioned to their waiter for the bill. She picked up her cigarettes and put them in her vest pocket. Her fingers surrounded the lighter. Her hand was shaking. She tapped the cover of her book with it.

"I tried to kill myself. I'm seeing a psychiatrist who keeps telling me I'm—how does he put it—clinically depressed."

"Depression is a far cry from insanity," Kline said finally. "Most of the people in America are depressed." She stopped playing with the lighter and let it stand on the table like a toy soldier.

"There's something else. . . . I'm seeing someone else, Paul. I didn't think it was fair not to tell you after what happened the other day at Martin's." He'd been reaching for his wallet. The waiter approached. Kline took out his wallet and placed his credit card on the plastic tray without looking at the bill. He heard the sound of traffic in the distance and forced himself to take a breath, the way he had in combat whenever he got scared.

"Paul, I was never in love with you. I never said I was in love with you that day. I never led you on. I never lied to you," she said. He wanted to speak but couldn't. He fought to control himself. He fought to find some words that would keep it all together. Nothing came to mind. She reached over and tried to take his hand but he pulled it away. "You're going to find someone that loves you back, Paul," she said.

"Am I?" he said. She'd reduced him to a kind of child and he didn't like it.

"Yes. I'm sure of it. You're a wonderful man. A good man."

"Am I?" he said again stupidly. "That isn't exactly what you want to hear from someone you're in love with." Her cell phone rang and she picked it up. He saw something cross her face. She handed the phone to Kline almost immediately and he took it.

"It's Cindy. Can you meet me at Martin's? It's important!"

"All right," he said.

"In an hour," Cindy said. "Take my number." She hung up after giving him her cell phone number. Kline handed the phone back to Virginia. He wanted to ask her a million questions as he input Cindy's number in his own cell phone's speed dial but didn't. It was as if he'd been thrown out a window and was still falling.

"There's something else," he said. He slipped the phone into his pocket. "Michael says that if I bother Martin's family or if they think there is *any* kind of investigation into Martin's death, you won't get the big money. You shouldn't go around telling everyone you're being followed." He lifted his eyes and looked at her. She was crying; tears were rolling down her checks.

"I don't care. I wish Martin were here. That's all I care about. I don't even know what I'm doing anymore. I just want Martin to see this book. I want to see his face. That's all I want," she said. She reached for the book and wiped her tears. Her lighter fell and rolled on the table. She knocked it away angrily and then batted her book off the table too. He got up and picked up first the book and then the lighter. The cover was torn and scuffed. The picture of her and Martin was scratched. He stood up.

"Who is it you're seeing?" he said without thinking. "Can you tell me that?"

"It's Michael. He's been coming up to Tahoe to see me. I need him now. I need someone like him in my life, someone who really knows me. Can you understand that, Paul?" He nodded silently as if he already knew. "He wants to help me get better. We've talked about everything and why I was drinking so much. He's helping me sort it out. I can talk to him because he knew Martin. I need someone like him, someone I can lean on, someone who really knows me. I want to get over this depression. Michael says I can if I try," she said. The manic string of words all hooked onto something he couldn't understand really. But he'd felt from the first time he'd gone to the writing group that they'd all been welded together somehow and that he could never be part of that.

"He's an asshole," Kline said, and then he was desperately sorry he'd said it that way because it sounded so ugly after everything Boon had done for her. He looked across the table and wanted to apologize.

"I know everyone resents Michael because he has money and a good job. It's not his fault that he worked hard and now he's able to have things. Is that a crime? Being successful? It shouldn't be. Why is everyone so fucking jealous of him?"

"You know what he said about you. He said you and Martin were like children. That you couldn't take care of yourselves," he said vindictively. He couldn't stop himself. She looked up at him. She flattened out the torn cover of her book trying to make it right, her face wet with tears.

"He's right in a way. We couldn't. I can't. Even now, I'm not sure I can. You don't understand because you aren't an artist. We *are* like children sometimes. We live in our imaginary world with imaginary people. That's what we do. Don't you *see,* he's right? We never grew up. What we do *is* crazy, Paul. It makes you crazy, and it's childish. And some people shouldn't write novels or paint pictures, but we do it anyway. We can't help ourselves."

He pulled the Cadillac into the small parking lot in front of Martin's building. He turned off the engine and banged the steering wheel once. He thought for a moment of going to Boon's office and kicking his ass. It's what he needed, he thought. Then he said something out loud. "Why not me!" He banged the steering wheel again. He wanted her to love *him;* that's all he wanted. Just as Virginia had, so pathetically,

171

wanted Martin there to see her novel. And neither was going to ever happen.

He looked out on the bay, peeking through the thin cypress trees. The water was a hard gray color and choppy. He realized that he had nothing, now. He was almost forty-one years old and he had nothing. His life was as empty as the wind. The idea of going back to his old desperate, hopeless, loveless life frightened him and made him sick. His Spartan apartment, with its bachelor's mess and no pictures on the walls after two years, had a dirty clinging emptiness about it that spoke volumes about all his life's mistakes and his resultant loneliness. He envied Martin again. He envied the fact that he was dead and didn't have to feel anything. He realized, looking up at Coit Tower to his right, that his whole life had been a mistake, a kind of horrible joke culminating here in middle age without any rhyme or reason.

Walking toward the building, he noticed the outside elevator moving and Cindy waving to him from inside it as the glass cage ran up the building's exterior. Kline glanced toward Martin's penthouse apartment. He saw the blonde girl, the same blonde he'd seen following Martin, in one of the windows. The girl turned from the window. She was talking on the phone. He realized she was standing, not in Martin's apartment, but in the apartment immediately next door.

The blonde put down the phone and walked across the room until she disappeared from view. He glanced back, looking for the elevator. It had stopped two floors down from the top floor. His eyes scanned the top floor windows again for the blonde. For a moment, all the windows were empty. Suddenly, he saw the blonde walk by the window in Martin's bedroom. It seemed impossible. He stared for a moment and everything suddenly fell into place. Obviously, there was a connection between the two apartments. He turned and waved his arms wildly and screamed Cindy's name as the elevator started up again moving toward the top floor, but she couldn't hear him.

He started to jog across the parking lot, fear now replacing the confusion of seconds ago. He ran past the front of the building and down the driveway to the garage level. The metal gate that separated the underground parking from the driveway was closed. He looked helplessly through the gate at the parked cars inside. He could hear the elevator motor from somewhere inside the garage. He thought he might be able to stop the elevator manually if he could just get past the gate. He shook the gate's metal fabric in frustration. The elevator motor stopped suddenly. He took out his cell phone and dialed Cindy's number hoping she'd answer.

"Hello," Cindy answered, the line full of static.

"It's me, Kline. Don't go into that apartment."

"Why? It's too late. I'm here, inside. Get up here, Kline. I have to talk to you."

"Are you near the door?" Kline said

"Yes."

"There's a button to open the gate to the garage. Do you see it? By the speaker, I think. Push it."

"Kline, why don't you just come through the front. . . ."

"Push the fucking button and get out of there!" He moved away from the gate, hoping to Christ she'd listen. The gate shuddered and started to move up.

"All right, Kline. Jesus, what's wrong?" Cindy said.

"There's someone in the apartment."

"I don't see anyone," she said.

"Just get the hell out."

"No one is–. Who the fuck are you, bitch! *Kline!*"

"Just *leave* for Christ's sake!" He ran across the garage toward the stairs.

The hallway on Martin's floor was empty; the door to Martin's apartment stood half open. Breathing hard from running up the six flights of stairs, he'd taken out the door key Boon had given him, but put it back in his pocket when he saw the door was open. He called Cindy's name as he pushed the door open further. He stood in the doorway for a moment and then bent down to grab his backup pistol from the ankle holster on his right leg. He didn't see the door coming back at him, fast. The force of the blow caught him on the side of the head as he bent down. The solid core door knocked him back across the hallway and into the wall. The hammerless 38 revolver, partially withdrawn from his ankle holster, tumbled down the hallway and hit the elevator door.

The elevator doors opened. Cindy stepped out clutching Martin's laptop. She picked up Kline's gun. "There's some crazy bitch in there. She tried to kill me. I pepper sprayed the bitch," she said breathlessly, holding the gun, still excited.

"Take that gun and get out," Kline said. He was having trouble seeing her. "If you see her, *shoot* her. Understand?"

"She's still in there. I hid in the elevator. You're bleeding, Kline." Cindy came towards him with his pistol pointed at the floor.

"I said get out! Shoot her if you see her again. Now go, get out of here." She retreated back into the elevator. He watched the elevator door close in front of her.

He got to his knees slowly and waited a moment. The bright pattern on the carpet was moving as if it were an image on a screen. He staggered to his feet. The walls of the hallway spun violently as he rose, one knee at a time; he walked through the open apartment door, unable to really protect himself, still groggy from the blow to the head. He glanced around the empty living room. The room seemed to rotate wildly, as if he were on an amusement park ride. He walked into the kitchen. There was a mess on the floor, forks and knives scattered everywhere. The kitchen table was over-turned. Martin's writing things were scattered over the floor along with everything else. He walked back out into the living room. He stopped and wiped his face and felt with his fingers where his scalp was cut, the blood running down into his eyes.

He walked down the hallway toward Martin's bedroom, reaching his arm out to the wall for support, his legs wobbly, his vision foggy. The bedroom door in front of him twisted and turned as if it were alive. He stopped and tried to pull himself together. He leaned against the wall for a moment, fighting the nausea, then he walked into the bedroom and flipped on the light. The bed was unmade, the way he and Virginia had left it. He touched the side of his head and winced. He felt blood with his fingertips. The edge of the front door had lacerated the top of his head badly. He glanced around the bedroom. He'd seen the blonde through the window, he was sure. The girl must have walked from the next apartment into Martin's bedroom, but it seemed impossible now, looking around the room. He went to the closet door and opened it. Martin's clothes were still hung neatly, untouched. He flipped on the light and walked into the closet.

He pushed the clothes aside, looking for some kind of passage. The front door buzzer sounded twice. Standing deep in the back of the closet, looking for signs of a passageway or door and seeing nothing, he turned, tripping over one of Martin's shoes. He walked back down the hallway to the front door.

The buzzer rang again. His heart was racing. He approached the peephole and looked out. It was the doorman. Kline could see his big brown acne-damaged face close to the peephole. He saw a cold shark-like eye come towards the peephole and, for a moment, they both had their faces on the door. The buzzer sounded again. Kline didn't answer. He watched the doorman back away and go toward the elevator and then stop, looking back over his shoulder.

Kline turned from the door and started back toward the living room. Suddenly, there was a quick motion from the kitchen on his right and something smashed him in the face. He heard a tremendous crashing sound as he landed in the middle of a glass coffee table in the living room. He'd felt the glass break apart under him. The sound of the smashing tabletop seemed to go on long after he landed.

Lying in the glass shards of the destroyed table, he tried to pick himself up with one hand using the table's framework, but it was no good, his right leg was impaled on a triangle of glass. The sharp end stuck through his pant leg. He lifted his leg off the glass wedge. His leg flopped on the floor. Under pressure, blood began to pump out of the wound immediately like a hose that had been gashed. He turned around and saw the blonde girl running down the hallway into Martin's bedroom. He tried to stay conscious, gripping the metal sides of the table frame violently. The blonde slammed Martin's bedroom door closed behind her. The doorman came through the front door and rushed towards him. Kline remembered his bleeding leg and tried to reach for it to try and stop the bleeding as he passed out.

TWENTY-TWO

He couldn't remember where now, in the operating room perhaps, or afterwards lying in his hospital room alone, but he'd had one of those dreams that stay with you for weeks afterwards, truly memorable and disturbing. In the dream he'd been the character in Hemingway's *Snows of Kilimanjaro*. Like the character, he was dying. He and his parents were riding in an old DC-7. He could see the famous snow-capped African mountain out the window, and below that, the great African veldt. Sitting in the plane, he was bleeding from his leg and reading calmly the same Hemingway story that he himself was dreaming. Luis Borges came out from the cockpit wearing an airline captain's uniform and sat next to him and asked him how he liked his dream. Did he think it useful? He'd asked Borges if it was true that the man in the story died in the end.

The police came to the hospital and interviewed him but didn't believe his story about the blonde coming from the next apartment. A Lt. Cross told him it was impossible and that he didn't believe a word of it. They suspected, Kline surmised, that he and Cindy had quarreled and now Kline was lying about the fight to protect her.

Under the influence of painkillers, he casually mentioned that he was depressed to one of his nurses and, the next thing he knew, a pretty blonde psychiatrist wandered in and very casually asked him if he wanted to talk. The young doctor had dark freckles and a beautiful smile and she wore a heavy black sweater under her white doctor's coat. Her blue eyes took him in. She seemed very kind. Lonely and depressed, he sat up in bed, his body and mind narcotized for the first time in his life, and opened up to a complete stranger. He blurted out all kinds of things to her. He confessed that he was in love with a girl who didn't love him. He told her things about his parents, too; about his childhood and his mother's emotional distance from him.

He asked the young doctor why his father had never removed the hideous concentration camp tattoo from his wrist. It had always bothered him that he had refused to have it removed. Why? Why had he kept it? His mother had gotten rid of hers, but his father hadn't. Kline hated the thing–the fountain pen blue, the uneven numbers, the way people would look at it in stores when his father reached out to pay. It made his father seem like a branded animal. He and the psychiatrist talked for a good while in that special time zone hospitals seem to have, that colorless, dimensionless time zone where people come and go from your room as if you don't exist, that strange superreal environment where people die and are born on the next floor or down the hall without solemnity or joy, just efficiency, and an insipid "call out" from the PA system.

He even confessed to the doctor that he had the killer instinct and that it wasn't something the Marine Corps had taught him either. He said he'd been born with it. He was afraid that it would get out of control, especially now that he was depressed. But he doubted she could understand the killer instinct, the idea of it. He could tell it didn't really register with her, the savageness of it, or why it scared him that it was lying dormant on the dark side of his psyche to be called up like that tiger in Wordsworth's poem: ". . . burning bright in the forests of the night. . . ."

He and the doctor became friends after several of those timeless afternoons. Ironically, it didn't cost him anything. The hospital provided the service for its Victims of Violence Program.

And now, back in Martin's apartment, three weeks after the attack, he hated the fact that he'd told her anything at all, thinking back on it. He hated himself for spilling his guts to a stranger, and then two minutes later he wished to christ they could speak again because he did fear that he was losing control of that violent part of him, the part that could express himself *that* way, in the way that the military sanctioned and even gave you medals for. He stepped away from the window and turned toward Martin's living room. No. There could be no more painkillers. They were too liberating. Since he'd been released from the hospital, he'd been trying to forget everything that the sessions with the psychiatrist had dug up. But he couldn't; he would run into them like those speed bumps that catch you unawares.

His face was still discolored and swollen from the blow and he looked slightly monstrous, even with his sunglasses on. He limped when he walked. His right leg had been feeble since the attack and seemed to be sixty percent useless as far as he could tell. They had given him a cane at the hospital, but he'd left it at his office and refused to use it. He couldn't stand the idea.

He shifted more of his weight onto his injured leg, testing its capacity to hold him, as he stood looking at Martin's living room. The shattered table had been taken away. The kitchen had been put back together. He allowed the pain to build to a frenzy and then backed his weight off. Levine had just told

179

him on the phone—strictly off the record—that the story Kline had gotten from Count Moro was about right, and then Levine told him to not call him anymore if it had to do with the Anderson case.

The sound of the children playing far below in a schoolyard made its way up the hill and into the apartment. Kline limped back across the room, angry that someone had tried to kill him and angry with Virginia for not loving him. He lifted his cell phone to call her but stopped himself. He wanted just to hear her voice again. He and Virginia had had a falling out while he'd been in the hospital. She'd come twice to visit him after the operation to close up his leg and scalp, but each time he'd ruined it by asking if she was still seeing Boon. He'd been unable to stop himself. The last time she came to see him, she asked him to give up on Martin's case, telling him she was afraid now that *he* would be killed, too. Angry that someone had tried to kill him, he'd refused. So he'd made a pig's breakfast of it all, driving her away when he needed her most.

He wanted to explain to her that he'd been a fool and that she'd been right all along that Martin probably had been murdered and someone was trying to cover it up. He put his cell phone down halfway through dialing her number and limped into the kitchen instead.

On Martin's writing table, from left to right, he'd compiled the history of Martin's last days—the case file he'd been given at the very beginning from the law firm, the newspaper stories about Martin's suicide at Coit Tower and the attack on Fisher for which Martin had been accused. Cindy had taken Martin's laptop. He doubted she could prove anything with that.

Kline picked up Martin's cell phone and scrolled through its speed dial numbers, not sure what he was looking for. He stopped suddenly when he saw an entry for Dr. Susan Elders.

Elders had given him her card when he'd left the hospital. He'd carried it with him since, debating whether or not to go see her again. He took the card out of his pocket and compared the two numbers, making sure they were the same person. He called her number but only got her service. Someone asked if it was an emergency and he answered no, but he'd like to make an appointment.

He left the kitchen and walked back into the living room. The stitches in his leg were tugging. His leg looked as if someone had sown up a side of beef. It had taken thirty-six stitches to close his wound and, according to the surgeon, his right calf muscle was pretty much destroyed. The physical therapist who had brought him the cane to use told him he would walk with a limp for the rest of his life. Kline had told her that she was wrong and to keep the damn cane. *Screw that,* he thought, hobbling down the hall toward Martin's bedroom. He'd seen men come back from a hell of a lot worse. He'd get his leg working again at the gym or he'd die trying.

He walked slowly down the hall into Martin's bedroom and flipped on the light. Either he was crazy, or he'd seen the blonde cross from the next apartment into this bedroom. He was sure of it. Broken glass from the table had been tracked all the way into the bedroom when the police had come. He hobbled to the huge walk-in closet and opened the door. The closet was empty now. Someone had taken Martin's clothes away while he'd been in the hospital.

Kline had gone to City Hall the day he was released from the hospital and looked up all the names of the owners of apartments in Martin's building. He was surprised to see that Martin was listed as owning the entire sixth floor of the building. He stood in the huge closet and looked around him. The full-length mirror on the closet's back wall gave back his reflection. He looked at himself. He looked terrible; his face was black and blue. He couldn't look at himself any longer. He turned away, glancing about him, but he could see no obvious door or connection between the two apartments. Frustrated, he walked back into the bedroom and dialed Boon's number on his cell phone. Boon's secretary put him through.

"Hello Michael. It's Paul Kline. Look, I'm at Martin's apartment."

"Paul. Are you all right? I heard what happened. Jesus. Virginia told me you were in the hospital. I would have come by but I've been out of town on a case."

"Yeah, thanks for the flowers. I'm O.K. Listen, the record at the assessor's office shows that Martin bought the apartment next to his. Did you know about it?"

"Of course. I handled the deal for him, actually."

"You bought it?"

"Yes, as his lawyer. I had to. Martin didn't want neighbors after the incident with the dog. He had me make an offer on the place and it was accepted. Martin wanted to have the apartment completely remodeled and have the two places connected. They're still working on the place. Why?"

"Is there a key for the other place?" Kline asked.

"No. You don't need another key. We had the two front doors keyed the same. Paul, what is this about? Virginia said you were giving up the case. I hope you don't. Not now. Now that we know the blonde really *does* exist for god's sake." Kline walked past the bloodstained spot on the floor.

"Did you ever see the movie *Gaslight?*" Kline said, walking slowly toward the front door.

"What are you talking about?" Boon said.

"The movie . . . *Gaslight,*" Kline said. "With Ingrid Bergman?"

"Yes, of course. What's that got to do with anything?" Kline had moved out of Martin's apartment and was walking down the hall toward the next apartment. "I don't know yet. Hold on and I'll tell you." He tried Martin's door key on the adjoining apartment door. The key turned easily in the lock and Kline swung the door open.

"Paul, are you implying that someone was using the apartment next door to–" Kline took the phone down from his ear. He looked quickly around the living room, frightened suddenly. The feeling of how close he'd come to bleeding to death came back. His heart began to race as he stepped into the living room. A cold sunshine streamed through the dirty windows along one wall of the room, which was filled with carpenter's tools. He told Boon he would call him back. Kline closed his phone and wandered through the apartment. The hallway to the bedrooms was filled with ladders and tarp-covered tables. He walked into one of the back bedrooms where he was sure he'd seen the blonde. He went into the closet looking for some kind of connection to Martin's apartment but found only a mirror and blank walls.

TWENTY-THREE

A fixture from Kline's childhood, The Norton Psychiatric Hospital's rose-colored buildings sat on the hill in front of him. He had grown up nearby. The public hospital was huge, covering several acres on Twin Peaks. Kline drove through the hospital's ornate Victorian portals and up the narrow roadway. Once inside the grounds, he immediately felt the heavy atmosphere of the institution, the hugeness of it, as if the hospital buildings were an affirmation that sanity was, in part, a physical monolith, an imposing architecture of hallways and stairs on a sensible grid, and insanity was its chaotic antipode, a dark warren of senseless twisting alleys. He wondered if he'd been entirely sane himself since he'd laid eyes on Virginia. He imagined he wasn't, not really. Sexual desire—with or without love—makes you insane; it was a fact. He wasn't thinking straight, and he knew it, and he didn't really care.

Standing in the lobby waiting for the dirty aluminum elevator doors to open, he wondered why Martin Anderson had the doctor on his cell phone's speed dial. She could have been an old girlfriend, he realized, or had she been his doctor? The elevator door opened and he hobbled in and hit the black tarnished button, the number almost erased from years of use. He closed his eyes and rode the elevator as he leaned, exhausted, against the metal side. He felt utterly alone. The feeling had gotten stronger and stronger lately, even when he visited his mother's house. Only when he'd been with Virginia did he feel any real connection to the world. The elevator door slid open and he hobbled out slowly. The pain in his leg was intense. The wide hallways were busy with doctors and nurses coming on duty at this hour of the morning. No one paid any attention to him.

"Mr. Kline?" Susan Elders had just gotten off a call. She'd pulled an earring off and was putting it back on. Wearing a siena-colored suit with a black felt collar, she looked like a fashion model, not a psychiatrist. "I got your message. I thought I was going to see you at my office downtown?" she said. She was striking, in a *Sport's Illustrated*-swimsuit-edition way.

"Sorry. I had to see you sooner," he said. "Can I come in?" She nodded and he stepped into the small office. Elders went to the door and closed it. Like all old buildings—the hospital was a hundred years old—there were the marks of physical decay everywhere. The sense that the doctors were trying to hold back a rising tide of mental illness single-handedly permeated the cramped room with its stacks of files. He looked at the one free chair behind her desk. "Is it all right if I sit? The leg still hurts." He tried to smile.

"Of course." She offered him the metal chair from her desk, pulling it out for him. He sat down. He tried to do it gracefully, without making a face because of the pain. He waited a moment for the aching to pass before he spoke.

He noticed that there were papers and books stacked everywhere. There was a stack of files on one of the other chairs. She picked them up and unceremoniously took them to an even greater pile on the floor in the corner and set them down. She was working here, sharing an office, as well as at San Francisco General where they'd met. She explained that she was in the process of building a practice and she was forced to work several jobs. He let the chit chat go on while the pain in his leg eased.

"This won't take long. I'm here about Martin Anderson," Kline said finally. He looked at Elder's face. A flash of recognition quickly passed across it. It was barely perceptible, but the voltage in her blue eyes went up a notch. She'd cleared the other chair but didn't sit down.

"Martin Anderson," she said. "Did you know him?"

"Yes. I'm investigating the case. Someone's hired me to look into his death," Kline said.

"I see."

"I found your number on his cell phone. It was important enough for him to put on speed dial, so I thought I should ask. Were you seeing him? Was he a patient, or something else?" Kline asked.

She smiled. "Yes. He was a patient. My fiancé, Michael, suggested I see him. He and Martin were good friends."

"You know Michael Boon?"

"Yes. Very well," she said. He could tell by the way she said it that she was in love with him. He wanted to tell her that Boon was cheating on her, but couldn't, of course.

"Can you tell me about Martin?" he said instead.

"I'm not supposed to tell you any of this, so I didn't," she said, "but he's gone now. So. . . . Yes. He was seeing me in my private practice."

"I understand. Nothing you tell me will leave this room, I promise you. I need to know, was there anything about his behavior that would suggest he was . . . what's the word I should use?" Kline looked at her.

"Homicidal?"

"Okay," Kline said.

"No. But that's not surprising."

"Did he tell you he was adopted?"

"No," she said. She seemed genuinely surprised by the news.

"When he was about six years old," Kline said. She leaned against the edge of her desk. The phone rang behind her and she answered and told whomever it was that she would be right there.

"He never said anything to me. I wish he had," she said, putting the phone back down. "That would have been a very serious issue. He should have told me."

"Did you think his condition got worse towards the end?"

"I first saw him because he said he was having interludes, losing track of time. That's a very serious situation. Yes, it did get worse," she said "I have his session notes at my office downtown. He had hallucinations, and those seem to have gotten worse, too. There was a barking dog once in the next apartment that he thought he'd killed, but it turned out to be a hallucination. The police were called. He'd imagined the whole thing. I went to his apartment and gave him the MMPI test afterwards, and it indicated psychosis."

"I'm sorry; could you translate that into English, MMPI?" Kline said. He noticed that Elders was wearing her hair pulled back, probably in keeping with some dress code for doctors at the hospital. With her hair tucked up she was just as beautiful, he thought.

"It's a boilerplate test we use to ascertain a patient's mental fitness in emergency rooms and for psychiatric admissions. For example: Question–Do you hear strange voices all the time? Patient's answer–yes. Question–I never tell a lie. Answer–What do you mean by lie? He said he was a professional liar. I remember that answer. That's the first time I'd heard *that* one. You're smiling, Mr. Kline–"

187

"He was right in a way. I mean I understand his answer," Kline said.

"You do? Why don't you come work here, then? What's it mean, doctor?"

"It just means he's a writer. They're a kind of liar, aren't they?"

"Well, he was also a borderline schizophrenic with paranoid tendencies," she said.

"And the treatment?"

"Honestly, his prognosis was lousy. So many like him, his age especially, don't ever get better. We just stabilize them with psychotropics that address the worst symptoms. I tried a lot of different combinations with Martin, but the drugs were only partially successful. And he wouldn't take them regularly. That can actually make the interludes worse. Towards the end, he'd stopped taking his meds all together." He looked at her pretty face and realized how startled he was by the combination of beauty, practiced clinical detachment and intellect. She slipped on a doctor's lab coat, which was hanging near her desk.

"Doctor, what happened to him, in your opinion?"

"Ask half the psychiatrists in the country and they'll tell you it's genetic; he was programmed to fail. For some reason, serotonin levels plummet and never get back to normal. You can *measure* that. Ask the other half, and they'll tell you it was all his mother's fault. No one knows for sure what comes first, biochemical problems or just a bad history. How's it going with *you?*" she asked. He looked at her starched white clinician's coat, not wanting to look her in the eye. "Something told me you weren't ever going to show to that appointment you made."

"Schizophrenia, how does it start? What are the symptoms, I mean," Kline said, ignoring her question.

188

"Why, are you feeling a little lightheaded?" They laughed. It was the first time he'd laughed since he'd left the hospital.

"Very funny. I mean, what would you feel to start with?"

"Depends." She sat down in the other chair. "Might not feel anything. Might, or might not, hear voices. Might start to dissociate. Lose track of time, in other words. Lose interest in sex and life in general. Martin's illness probably started with a constellation of symptoms. By the time I saw him, he was seriously ill. He was losing whole pieces of every day. I put him on anit-psychotics immediately, the first day I saw him."

"Could you start killing people out of the blue? If you had his problems?"

"You might, but it would be a rare behavior pattern. Psychotics, even paranoids, in general, aren't violent. The police claim he tried to kill that director. That surprised me. Paranoids can act violently of course, but most aren't actually violent."

"What about seeing the dog in the closet that day?" Kline said. "Would it take an episode like that to convince you he was a schizophrenic?"

Her phone rang again and she put the call on the speakerphone. He tried not to listen to the conversation, but found himself attracted to it. An AIDS patient was suffering from depression. She adjusted the man's Zoloft prescription over the phone and hung up. He noticed that she had on pearl earrings. The feminine touch seemed a strain, here.

She moved away from the desk again and stood near him. "What are you trying to suggest?" Elders said. She forced him to look her in the eye. It was a professional look, examining him now like a patient for the first time since he'd walked in.

"Are there *key* events that convinced you that Martin might be a schizophrenic?" he asked.

"Yes. I have to go on behavior. That's all we *have* to go on. I can't see into a patient's soul. Behavior dictates treatment. That's the first thing you learn in medical school."

"What if I told you I think someone was trying to make it *look* like Martin were mentally ill, crazy even."

"Then I'd say they did a damn good job of it," she said, her blue eyes intense.

"Am I talking to a friend, or a doctor who could have me put away?" Kline said. "That's a joke."

Elders moved back and leaned on the edge of her desk. Her expression became warmer. "You know, I've worked here for only a few months, but it changes you. It has something to do with the vastness of the place and the fact that insanity is so commonplace. You stop seeing *people;* you only see their symptoms. Do you know what I mean? Being so clinical takes something away from your humanity, but you *have* to be or you aren't doing your job. Do you think that I was wrong about Martin? That I saw the symptoms and not the patient?"

"I think Martin was set up. I don't think he attacked the director. Sounds crazy, doesn't it? He may have been ill, I don't know, but I don't think he tried to kill anyone. I'm sure of it. Give me the test. The crazy test. The one you gave him," he said. She looked at him a moment.

"All right. Answer true or false to the following: I believe in God."

"No," Kline said without thinking.

"I would rather win than lose a game."

"Win."

"I am worried about sex matters."

"No."

"I believe I am being plotted against."

"No."

"I believe in obeying the law."

"Yes."

"Everything smells the same."

"No."

"Congratulations, you passed," she said. "But I think you're probably wrong about Martin. He was very ill at the end. I saw him for more than six months, and he was definitely getting worse. It's virtually impossible for someone to exhibit a whole constellation of symptoms like that and not be."

"What if I had answered differently to the questions?" Kline asked.

"Okay. What if?" she said. "We grade on a curve."

"Okay. You don't believe me. What do you think happened to him, then? What made him turn into a vicious man overnight, doctor? He'd never been violent in the past. No history of it." His kidding tone changed.

"When I read the account in the newspaper that he was using speed, I guessed that was the deciding factor. I mean, drugs can get anyone to do something stupid, mentally ill or not. He'd been taking amphetamines, so he and that director could finish their project. Illicit drug use–especially *speed*–is *extremely* dangerous. I warned him against it. Amphetamines are known to produce violence in otherwise normally non-violent people, never mind the mentally ill. My best guess is he probably wouldn't have attacked the director and he wouldn't have killed himself if it weren't for the drug use. That's my professional opinion." Kline looked at her. "I'm sorry, but your theory, Mr. Kline, is flatfooted."

"What about the fact that he'd just found out he'd been adopted? Could that have done something to him psychologically? I'm the one who gave him the news, and I saw how much it affected him."

"I see. You seemed . . . very involved," she said.

"Could the fact that he'd gotten that kind of dramatic news have made him *sicker?* Pushed him over the edge?"

"It's impossible to say, now. We'll never know. You can't rule it out as a catalyst."

"I think someone was trying to make him *look* crazy. And I think they just had to exploit his problems, his chaotic state of mind to do it," Kline said.

"Your issues with you parents. Those are very serious," she said, suddenly changing the subject.

"Yes," Kline said. He looked away immediately.

"I can help you with them," she said. "Don't ignore them, Mr. Kline. Your fear about becoming violent in civilian life is a serious symptom of your repressed guilt feelings. I don't want you to suffer. . . ."

"I'll think about it," he said, getting up suddenly. She saw him wince.

"Do you want something for the pain?"

"They gave me some Vicodan," he said. "But I don't like it. I don't like feeling muddled."

"What happened to your parents is not your fault," she said. He was getting up from the chair and trying to conceal the pain. He turned around, stunned by what she said.

"What makes you think I think *that?*"

"Isn't that why you joined the Marines?" she said. He didn't answer. But later, in the car, on the way down the hill, he knew she was right. He had always blamed himself for what had happened to them, crazy as that seemed. He'd never been able to explain it. It was irrational. He remembered Borges in the dream asking him questions. Maybe Borges could have explained why he should feel so guilty about something that happened before he was even born. Maybe Freud was really more of an historian than a medical doctor, he thought. And now Zoloft and Prozac made history totally irrelevant. He decided, by the time he got to his mother's house, he would suggest that she see Elders and discuss taking Prozac. Why not? It wasn't too late for her to be free of history, too.

TWENTY-FOUR

Limping badly now, Kline closed the gate to his mother's house. Since he was in the neighborhood, he'd decided to stop in and see her. The street was lined with white two-storey houses built in the fifties. The well-kept places spoke of hard-won savings, family meetings at kitchen tables and children anxious to kick in their two-cents' worth. Each house represented a thousand economies. It was a neighborhood where men (mostly Jewish) loaded their salesmen's cars (Cadillacs and Buicks) every morning with merchandise samples, sales books, red rubber bands, and the like, along with the *Examiner's* business section, thinking of tips and losses and nickel stocks.

Kline walked up the path past the camellias his mother had planted when he was a boy, their blood-red color vivid in the cold and gray foggy afternoon. When he got to the top of the stairs, he peered into the alley between the houses and noticed that several cars were parked nose to bumper. Seeing so many Buicks and Cadillacs in the driveway, he instinctively knew something was wrong. The front door opened and he froze for a moment, frightened, because he knew that the woman who was standing in the doorway, Carmen Rodriguez, only came when his mother was in some kind of crisis or when one of their circle of friends from the camp had died.

"Paul, what's with the face? You look awful," Carmen said. There were two other elderly women behind her, all in their seventies. There was a smell of cabbage cooking coming from the kitchen. Carmen was wearing an expensive-looking coat; obviously she'd just arrived, too. She threw her arms around Kline, speaking to him as if he were still a boy. Nothing had changed with her.

His father had always sent for Carmen, his mother's campmate, each time one of his mother's depressions had gone off the charts, when she would lock herself in her bedroom for days at a time, refusing to see anyone. Each time Carmen would fly in from Buenos Aires, and the frightened Kline, who thought his mother was going crazy, felt as if some kind of angel had arrived. Carmen would take command with her heavy accent, heavy perfume and zaftig figure, speaking in a peculiar combination of German and Spanish, and brighten up their home. Wealthy, she always brought gifts for him. Carmen's husband, an important Argentine banker, would come too, on occasion, and fascinated Kline with his worldliness, his intelligence, and Latin charm. The couple, with their open displays of affection, was so different than his parents. Carmen didn't look like a survivor from Dachau, but she was. She had been, like his mother, only sixteen when she'd walked through the gates of the death camp. After the liberation, she'd left Europe and gone, as many Jews had after the war, to Argentina, where she had distant relatives. She married the Argentine banker and dropped her German past altogether. She became Carmen Rodriguez.

She kissed him on the mouth with lip-sticked lips and then held his still bruised face in her hands, looking at it carefully.

"You in fights now?" she asked.

"A little problem at the office," Kline joked. Carmen could always get him to joke; to laugh in ways that were pain-erasing. It was a wonderful leftover of their past together, when she was the angel who had always kept things light, while upstairs in his mother's bedroom only God knew what was going on. He hugged her sausage-tight body, kissed her on the cheek and felt immediately better. They embraced for a moment more.

"I love you, angel," she told him. "I told you to be a violinist–then you wouldn't have these problems. Why don't you pack up and come back with me to Buenos Aires? Forget all this detective business," she said, still holding him. There was something in her face that scared him, something behind her tough smile that he'd never noticed before, a great sadness like his mother's. "I just got here, honey. I took the first plane I could get. I was in New York when she called."

"Mom called you?" Kline asked. Carmen nodded. She squeezed his hand and wiped something from her eye. One tear slid down her old face. He saw now that she'd aged, that the make-up was thicker than he'd ever seen it, that her platinum blond hair was thinner and that the lipstick wasn't on quite straight. But it was the tear that hit her cheek that marked some kind of awful change. He'd never seen her outwardly sad before. It was like seeing a bridge you need to cross everyday collapse right in front of you. If his Aunt Carmen was crying, then there was something *very, very* wrong.

"Where's Mom?" he said, peering behind her. He closed the front door and saw two young men in suits interviewing his mother in the living room. He looked at his Aunt Carmen. Rosenthal came out from the kitchen. He was talking on his cell phone. The two looked at each other. Rosenthal closed up his phone. He looked pale and very serious. Kline turned and headed toward the living room. Rosenthal tried to grab him by the shoulder, but Kline shook his hand off roughly.

"I wouldn't go in there right now, Paul," Rosenthal said behind him.

"She might need me," Kline said. Sitting in the living room, his mother was dressed very nicely, her white hair pulled back. She was wearing a simple blue suit. She turned to look at him; tears glistened on her face. "Mom?" he said, but his mother didn't answer; she turned back towards the young men. One of the young men gave Kline a strange, piercing look meant to shut him up. "I told you not to upset her," Kline said, turning back to Rosenthal.

"This isn't unusual," the other young man said, barely looking at him. "It's common, Mr. Kline. These matters are never easy to discuss." His aunt took him by the hand. She led him back to the kitchen and told him that everything was going to be fine. Somehow he didn't believe her. It had never been fine, had it? He told his Aunt Carmen in a petulant tone that he didn't like the men in the living room. He hoped they had heard him. He said he wanted to punch the one who had looked at him so arrogantly. They looked at each other for a moment. She told him she didn't think that would help anything. When Rosenthal came into the room, Kline and he started to argue. At one point Kline pushed him up against the wall. Rosenthal, shocked, shut up. On the verge of losing control, Kline backed away when his aunt pushed herself in between the two of them. Before he left the house, he tried to speak to his mother to get her to stop the interview but she refused to listen to him.

They'd never been close, but the rejection in front of complete strangers had been especially cruel, brutal in fact. As he stormed out of the house, his Aunt Carmen followed him to the sidewalk and tried to stop him from leaving, but he wouldn't listen to her pleas to come back into the house. It was the first time he'd ever been rude to her. He drove away angry with his mother for freezing him out and angry with them all for being victims and for being Jews.

• • •

It was after midnight when he drove out to Virginia's place in the Mission. Despite having Martin's apartment, she still lived at her old place on Treat Street. She'd left a message on his machine telling him he'd been invited to the group session out at Bolinas on Saturday and that everyone welcomed him back.

Kline parked and sat in his car in the darkness, watching the object of his desire like a shunned lover through the front windows of her ground floor apartment. There was a bar on the corner blaring tinny saccharine Latin music that spilled out into the night. The air smelled of car oil. Virginia was sitting at her computer working, her back to him.

After a long while, he got out and crossed the narrow street, limping up the worn-out wooden steps. The short staircase was loose and shifting, not unlike the shamoblic feelings he'd had since she'd called and left the message. He wanted to see her, yet he was afraid to see her. She wasn't expecting him, and when he knocked on her door, he wasn't sure how he would be received. They hadn't seen one another since their argument at the hospital. But after her call, he'd come directly here, like a carrier pigeon homing in, without really understanding why, exactly.

He watched Virginia walk toward the front door through a white lace curtain hung across the door's window. Kline immediately felt the world begin to spin faster when she smiled at him through the window. *What if Boone is in there with her? Then what?* His thoughts were no longer orderly and calm since the blonde had smashed a crystal bowl into his face. There was something profoundly wrong with him, he realized. He was in love with this girl and it was getting *to* him.

198

In a robe and barefoot, Virginia opened the door. Michelle Shocked's *Anchored in Anchorage* was playing. She kissed him immediately, before he could even say hello, surprising him. He felt the satin material of her black robe as he held her, the smell of cigarettes in her hair. They didn't talk for a moment.

"I'm so sorry for what happened to you. I feel somehow responsible for it," she said finally. "And I'm sorry I was such a *bitch* to you at the hospital," she said, holding him. "But you wouldn't *listen* to me." He looked over her shoulder, afraid he'd see Michael, but saw only the outlines of an empty kitchen table down the hall.

"Can I come in?" She took him into her small studio. Her computer sat on a metal desk under an architect's lamp. An old Janis Joplin poster hung above it. "But don't you see that you and Cindy were right about Martin?" he said, following her into the room. "I think now that someone was playing him, 'Gaslighting' him, and I want to know why. It was serious enough for that blonde to try and kill me. I want to take a look at the manuscript and the confession that were foisted on him. They're the key." He sat down on her worn out sofa. "Where's Cindy? I've called her several times but there's no answer. She's got Martin's laptop," he said. Virginia looked at him, a little spooked, he thought.

"She'll be at the group meeting tomorrow at the beach. She knows you've been looking for her. . . ." she said tentatively.

"If Martin isn't the author of the manuscript and the confession, then who is?" he asked. "Is it you? Did you write it?"

"Me? No. Of course not!" she said with indignation, but she looked away from him toward her computer screen.

"Tonight, while I was watching you write through the window, I remembered that Martin'd said that you could write anything, in any style. He said he'd always envied you that talent. He said you could do Amy Tan, Faulkner, even Henry James, if you wanted to." She picked up her cigarettes and took one out. She pulled the lamp down close to the table to keep the glare from her face. "You've got to tell me the truth," he said. "I won't tell anyone, if that's what you're afraid of. *You know* who wrote that manuscript, don't you?" She sat down on the wooden desk chair. The chair creaked loudly, flexing as she sat. She lit the cigarette, drew on it, and as she exhaled, he saw the smoke make a blue veil across her face.

"All right. I didn't, and I don't know who did, but I think I started it all somehow. I wanted to prove something," she said finally, looking at the floor.

"I don't understand."

"I wrote the first chapter of the manuscript and loaded it onto Martin's computer one night. I wrote it in the first person crime style as a joke because he'd said I couldn't do the Jim Thompson thing. Don't you remember, he even said that to you the day I first met you. I wanted to show him I *could* do it. But that's all that I wrote, just one chapter. And I didn't place the manuscript in Cindy's bag, either. The strange thing is, that Martin never mentioned it to me. The joke was a flop because he never read it. I thought he'd been too busy with the book tour and the screenplay to notice the new file in his computer. I kept mum about it because I figured he'd stumble onto it eventually and we'd have a giggle."

"Did you tell anyone else what you'd done?"

"Yes. I told Michael because I had to crow about it. I had to tell *some*one. Michael thought it was funny, too." She leaned over a little, holding the cigarette with the fingers of both hands. "Later, Cindy got the manuscript somehow and thought the story was about her. She *wanted* to believe it was about her. She was very flattered by it, warped woman that she is. But when she confronted Martin with it, he denied writing it completely. Now she believes him, and of course I do too, since I wrote the first chapter. We don't know who carried on with it and left it in her bag, but we figure that that person may have written the confession as well. I'm ashamed to have had a hand in it. I only meant it as a joke," she said, looking at him now.

"Could Michael have worked on the manuscript that you started?"

"No," she said.

"How can you be so sure?"

She hesitated a moment. "You've heard him read, haven't you?"

"Yes."

"Well, then you know why. Michael's got *one* style. It's kind of a college-clever style he's never been able to improve upon. It's very strange. He can't get any better," she said.

"Do you know that Michael is engaged to Martin's psychiatrist?" Kline said. He hated Boon, not because of Martin he realized now, but because Boon was his rival.

"I know all about her. He's going to let her down slowly."

"Are you in love with him?" he asked.

"Don't ask me about Michael anymore," she said. "It's starting to get boring."

"Did you tell Kevin about the chapter you wrote?" he asked.

"No."

"Could he have written the rest of that manuscript? Is he a good enough writer to have pulled that off?" She looked at him for a moment. "Yes. He's good enough. But why would he?"

"I don't know yet, but if you didn't do it, and Cindy didn't, and you claim Michael couldn't, then it had to be him or Betsy, and Betsy doesn't strike me as the devious type," he said. He could tell from the look on her face that she thought it might be Kevin, too. "Where does he live?" Kline said. "I want to talk to him."

"He's leaving for Los Angeles this morning on the first flight out. He called me today to say good-bye. He got an offer to write for one of those doctor shows on T.V. ER, I think. Anyway, Michael's taking him to the airport. He's arranged a first-class ticket for him with his United Miles so he can get off to a good start."

"Do you really love Michael?" he asked again.

"Yes, in my way. I need someone who understands me."

You mean someone your age, he thought to himself.

TWENTY-FIVE

For as long as Kline could remember, the San Francisco International Airport had been undergoing some stage of construction. To travel by air from San Francisco, one had to first maneuver through a gauntlet of raw concrete and steel, heavy machinery noise and confusing detours. He walked by one of the brand new cavernous buildings that was as yet unmanned. A jet passed low overhead with a great rushing sound, adding to the overwrought atmosphere. He saw his reflection in the new green-tinted glass of the windows along the concourse and saw that his pant leg was stained with blood from his bandaged leg.

Inside the United terminal, Kline came to an abrupt stop in front of a metal detector. He turned and studied the bank of TV screens showing departures and arrivals. The flight to Los Angeles was on time and scheduled to leave in a less than an hour. He passed through the metal detector, then down the long breezeway to the gate holding passengers for the flight to Los Angeles. Kline stood in the busy terminal and spotted Fitzgerald and Michael standing near the gate. The young doctor was wearing a white shirt and khakis and seemed uncharacteristically relaxed. He looked like any of the other young business types waiting for his flight, except he wasn't wearing a jacket. Michael, in sharp contrast, was wearing a perfectly tailored Brioni suit and was talking to Kevin quite seriously. They were saying their goodbyes when suddenly Boon kissed Kevin on the mouth and they embraced each other.

Kline couldn't believe his eyes. Stunned, he turned towards the wall, a little sick from the sight of the two men kissing, and tried to absorb what he had just witnessed. When he turned back around, Michael had gone.

Fitzgerald was reading a book, his carry-on luggage at his feet, and seemed to not have a care in the world, Kline thought as he walked toward him.

"Kevin." Fitzgerald looked up, his blue eyes intense.

"Kline? What are *you* doing here?"

"Why are *you* leaving town?" Kline said.

"New job. That's what people do when they finish their residency," Kevin said coolly.

"You're going to have to tell the police what you know about Martin's death," Kline said.

"Excuse me?" Kevin said, lowering the book to his lap.

"I think you wrote that manuscript and put it on Martin's computer. I don't know why yet. Why don't you tell me? I think you and Michael were trying to set Martin up somehow. Maybe it was you who went down to the hotel and attacked Fisher. Or was it Michael?" Kline said. Kevin looked at him blankly. He calmly closed his book. His plane ticket was in his shirt pocket. He took it out and held it against the large paperback he was reading, *Script Writing for Dummies*. "You planted that manuscript on Cindy, didn't you?"

"Yes, I did as a matter of fact. I wanted to prove to Martin that I could write that silly stuff like he'd sold. He just got lucky. It could have been me. It could have been *my* work. It *was* in so many ways. He stole all my best ideas," he said.

"So you were jealous of him. Is that why you tried to drive him crazy?"

"Don't be ridiculous!"

"You hated Martin. Everyone knows that. You found out that he was having emotional problems and maybe decided to take advantage and drive him over the edge. Is that it? A smart guy like you gets him to doubt himself so much that he takes a flier. Did you hate him that much?" Kline said.

"Yes. I did hate him. Are you satisfied? It was, after all, *in a way, my* book they bought, and it should have been *my* movie. Looks like you're leaking. You should see a doctor," Kevin nodded to Kline's leg. Kline looked down. There was a line of blood moving over his brown leather shoe, staining the dirty blue carpet.

"You'll have to come with me," Kline said. "You can tell the police all about what you did."

"Tell them *what,* exactly? That I wrote some fiction and put it on Martin's computer when he was out of the room? Don't be ridiculous. Do you think they'd care?" Fitzgerald said. "Go fuck yourself, Mr. Kline." Kevin picked up his carry-on bag and moved toward the queue of boarding passengers. Kline realized there was nothing he could do. Kevin was right. Why would the police care what he'd written, and there was no way to prove it anyway.

"Oh, by the way, Michael is two-timing you. Did you know that? And with your pal Virginia, no less." Kline said, hoping to sting him. Kevin gave him a quizzical look and suddenly looked a little worried, Kline thought.

• • •

It was the hidden world of the superrich, the kind of house that Kline had never been in before, truly palatial. Two huge Monets hung in the foyer. After exchanging very few words, Kline followed the old butler, dressed in a blue linen suit, through the house. They passed a cavernous dining room, its silence cryptic and full of melancholy. The old manservant led Kline through the gloom toward the garden. As soon as they stepped out into the garden, the ponderous atmosphere lifted and the sound of children playing came streaming over the lawn.

Kline, psychologically intimidated by the fabulous house and limping slightly, spotted someone he was sure was Kitty sitting under an umbrella near the pool, wearing a white sun hat. The silver-haired butler led him across a sea of lawn that made Kline's leg begin to throb.

A swarm of beautiful excited children—all white—surrounded the diving board, their bodies glistening in the sun. The boys were all prepubescent and physically awkward-looking. The girls were already budding sexual hips and breasts. The water in the pool was heaving from side to side and splashing over the coping, one chubby boy's cannon ball creating the watery panic. The poolside cacophony and the timeless look of the children gave the scene a movie quality. It could as well have been 1950 as 2000. The diving board sprang, the sound reverberating suddenly again, as Kline tried to keep up with the butler who led him past an empty table. He saw plates and colored glasses crowded on several abandoned tables. The perfume from the summer garden mixed with the aromas of barbeque leftovers, the aftermath of a birthday meal. Kline's shoes were sinking slightly in the lawn as he followed. Finally, he felt the *terra firma* of the patio under his feet. The old butler spoke to Mrs. Kolsrud over the din of the children.

The vending machine dowager sat under the heavy shade of an over-sized green captain's umbrella. Wrapped in muslin like an Indian princess to protect her from the sun, she was shrunken-looking, attentive, and intelligent, Kline guessed from her animated expression as he approached. She noticed

Kline's limp and bruised face immediately and asked him if he'd been in an accident. He assured her that he was all right and thanked her for her concern.

"I've come to ask you some questions about your grandson," Kline said. He took her proffered hand. It was a small hand that gripped slowly, as if thinking through the act and remembering how it was done. He'd expected to be turned away at the door but he supposed old people, even rich ones, are always accessible, unlike the young.

"Oh, he'll be here at six. That's my son's boy over there," Kitty said, turning her head slowly, the great wrinkles moving on her face and neck. Kline could tell she'd been a handsome woman once. She looked for a boy in the pool amongst the other children, who in one more year would be developing sexually and entirely different. "It's his thirteenth birthday," Kitty said. Kline tried to spot the boy but he could have been any one of the wet excited faces in the pool.

"No ma'am, I mean Martin. Your daughter Marguerite's boy." The old woman turned and looked at him differently, her wrinkles made more obvious by peach-colored makeup. The dark eyes, which were still pretty but rheumy, registered the warm sadness of the very old, as if they had one eye on the one clock that matters most now.

"I'm afraid there's been a tragedy," she said, her head shaking slightly all of a sudden. She tried to fold her hands on her lap calmly.

"I know. I'm sorry," Kline said. It sounded rather artificial and patronizing.

"Would you care for something to drink, Mr. Kline?"

"Yes. Thank you," Kline said. She picked up a small brass bell on the table and rang it.

"I wanted so much to *meet* Martin. I'd known him, of course, but as a little boy, not as a man. I had pictures taken by the lawyers," she said. "He turned out to be very handsome, and, just like his mother, so blond. Marguerite was *so* fair. She couldn't even sit in the sun, Mr. Kline," Kitty looked around her as if her daughter were suddenly there. A black maid came out of the house and crossed the bright lawn, like a little black bird, wearing a traditional black and white uniform.

"What would you like, Mr. Kline?"

"Coke is fine," Kline said.

"We need a Coke for Mr. Kline, Claire, and I think perhaps some fresh napkins too." The maid retreated without saying a word. Kline got the impression that throughout all of Kitty's long life people came out of one house or another and brought her the world in one form or another while she looked on passively. Kline watched the maid go into the pool house nearby.

"Thank you. Did you leave Martin some money as part of your estate?" Kitty looked at him a moment; there was a small patch of sun no larger than a playing card that lit the old woman's shoulder. He could see the quarter-sized age spots on her arm.

"Mr. Kline, why did I get a call from my lawyers telling me that you might be contacting me? What is your *interest* in all this?"

"Someone has hired me to find out what happened to your grandson, Martin," Kline said. "They think he was murdered." The word murdered made her shut her eyes. The maid returned and put a heavy-looking pewter bucket down next to Kline with several types of soft drinks in it. She handed him a fresh linen napkin and fixed him a glass with ice and lime. A young boy came lurching across the verge of the pool as Kline poured himself a drink. He was wet, slender and handsome and wearing a white baggy hip-hop style swimsuit. He came up and kissed Kitty, the water pouring

208

off his perfect skin. She became suddenly animated and hugged the boy around the middle, seeming to lose forty years in the act. The boy, enjoying his grandmother's affection, stared at Kline while she held him. After several more kisses, she sent him away.

"I'm afraid you don't understand," she said. "Martin saw his mother commit suicide. I can't imagine what that must have done to him. He was only six years old at the time. I fought to keep the boy, Mr. Kline. I fought with everything I had, but Jay, my husband, convinced me that he would never fit in with our family, that he would somehow hurt the rest of the children. I was much younger then. I listened to my husband in those days. It wasn't like it is today, you know. He convinced me that we should put Martin up for adoption, and we did. I made a mistake. . . . I know that. . . . It cost me my marriage. I resented my husband bitterly after that." She looked at Kline. Was she looking for sympathy, he wondered? "I'd been told he was a writer. I was afraid to see him; I thought he might resent me. I was afraid of what he would say to me for abandoning him." There was a silence. "Frankly, I didn't know how to tell the boy the truth about why we hadn't taken him in. I'm still ashamed of it."

"Why *didn't* you take him in, Mrs. Kolsrud?" She looked at him a moment, her dress still wet from the young boy's embrace.

"My husband hated blacks, Mr. Kline. He hated Jews and he hated Italians, of all things. Can you imagine? Italians, *really*. It seems all very silly *now*. Of course it wasn't silly *then*. He hated the thought that his daughter had fallen in love with this young man who happened to have dark skin. Actually, I thought they made a beautiful couple. I told him that when I met him. His name was Roberto. He was quite handsome. But, my husband became impossible. He threw

Marguerite out of the house. He wouldn't even let her visit. She called and called, but he wouldn't talk to her. He broke her heart. It was very sad because I know how much Jay loved her and how much she loved her father. He did, you see, *really* love her, but he couldn't stand the idea that she loved this Puerto Rican boy. It changed him. Really, it was like he'd been poisoned. Is your leg still bothering you, Mr. Kline? Would you care for another drink, perhaps something stronger?"

The past and the present seemed to be all one thing with her now. "Who set up the trust fund for Martin?" He put his glass down on the table and it made a sound. "Was it you, Mrs. Kolsrud?" A sliver of ice slipped out from the top of the ice bucket. He watched it hit the bricks at his feet and turn to water almost instantly, as if by magic, and then even the stain disappeared.

"No, it was my husband. I made him promise me that he would, or I wouldn't have agreed to the adoption. Martin wasn't to get the bulk of the money until he turned thirty-five, and I made sure his family got money every month. I did that on my own. That was my idea. I thought it was best. It was my way of being there."

"Is Mr. Boon your lawyer at the firm?"

"No, it's been Mr. Rosenthal for years now, since my divorce. I have spoken to a Mr. Boon. He's one of his assistants, I believe. Mr. Kline, it's really been quite terrible since Marguerite did what she did. I think she took us all with her in a way–the boy, her father and me." Kline looked at the woman and realized there was a strange connection he hadn't expected. Like him, history had its hold on her, despite her privilege and money, the way it had him, and they'd lived half-lives in the shadows as a result. He got up. Kline shook Kitty's hand. She held it for a moment in both of hers.

He hadn't expected to feel any sympathy for her but he did now.

"Do you know the strange thing, Mr. Kline? My husband had a black mistress during that time. He kept her in San Francisco. She was black as the night, my friends told me later. What do you make of that, Mr. Kline? You seem to be very perceptive."

"I don't know," he said. She closed her eyes for a moment, holding her hand over her face to block the sun.

"Mr. Kline, do you know why my daughter would want to kill herself?"

"No. I wish I did. I'm sorry," he said. He meant it. He reached over the table for her hand again and held it. He was about to tell her that, even though Martin may have had emotional difficulties, he thought someone had murdered her grandson, but he didn't.

"No one has ever been able to answer that question for me, Mr. Kline."

The breeze blew the old woman's sun hat off. It rolled across the concrete verge toward the pool. One of the kids, a long-limbed and freckled blonde girl, the spitting image of what he thought Marguerite must have looked like at her age, tried to catch it but missed. *It seems all very silly now. Of course it wasn't silly then.* Kline heard the old woman's words again as he crossed the beautifully manicured lawn on his way out.

TWENTY-SIX

The Cadillac, a hulking rotten-metal testament to a bygone America, had been the only thing his father had left him that he cared about. Kline drove the car for all it was worth that afternoon, making it squeal in the turns on Highway One, the Pacific Ocean far below him. The seventies antique swayed angrily up the beautiful country road, spitting a blue acrid smoke, left behind for others. The interior was living-room-worn and contained the distilled orgone of two generations of Kline males; the black steering wheel had been rubbed pearl smooth by his father's anxious hands. There was angst in the screeching new tires now, and angst in the people's faces who happened to see the white tank's thrusting aristocratic grill flash by with Kline's face coming at them, his hands placed squarely at ten and two on the wheel, something unforgiving and atavistic in his expression.

On the cliffs above Stinson Beach, there were moments where Kline could see the stark two-fisted beauty of the surf sliding over the rough black lattice of crenellated rocks hundreds of feet below. Some water-bashed rocks held groups of torpedo-shaped seals. The Marin coastline all the way to Bolinas and beyond was clear and clean of fog. He passed when he shouldn't have. He glanced in the mirror behind him and could see just the tops of buildings in San Francisco showing above a wall of fog.

He looked down to his left again and saw one of the tide pools, a kind of sorrow of water and darkness and boiling foam, like hope's birthplace. But there was only hope for the seagulls that floated below, skimming the sun-shattered water—stark, free creatures. "Glide, baby, glide," he said out loud. Loving Virginia was like trying to hold the ocean. *It just slips by your ankles and then pulls away.* Somehow he knew that about her.

Boon's beach house, very grand, was on a cul-de-sac right off the beach, the Bolinas Lagoon behind it, the ocean in front. Kline parked the Cadillac and walked down the sandy driveway. He stood outside the door for a moment and listened to the surf bang against the beach. He thought twice about turning around and leaving, not wanting to see Virginia and Boon together in the same place, but he was afraid someone had already seen him park. He looked for a doorbell but didn't see one. He finally gave up and knocked on the door. He looked down at his feet stupidly as he waited for it to be opened. When it was, he was surprised to see Susan Elders looking at him with a keen smile, dressed in green capri pants and a man's white shirt.

"Paul!"

"Hi."

"You didn't say you were a member of Michael's writing group. You should have said something," Elders said, genuinely surprised.

He followed her down the bright beach house hallway. Kline could make out a huge living room ahead that looked out onto the ocean, framed by several huge windows. Outside, the beach seemed to be decorated with beautiful people, all of them in their late twenties, the weekend glitterati from San Francisco's elite families. This was *their* beach and they knew it. He caught the reflection of the fireplace on the glass covering a photograph of a naked woman standing on the beach in the rain, her nipples dark, her hair wet.

"Michael and Virginia are taking a walk on the beach. They left me a note. I just got here myself. I didn't know you were a member, too," she said again, smiling. She offered him a glass of wine and he took it. They sat down on the oversized down cushions of the couch to wait for the others.

The sun was setting. It looked like some tagger had spray-painted the horizon orange. "When I joined the Marine Corps it was very hurtful to my parents," he said. Elders looked at him. The couches looked out to the rolling Pacific and the seagulls that were riding the airwaves.

"How was it hurtful?" she asked. He'd slipped into a conversation with her without thinking about it. The glass of wine made him want to talk. She had guided him gently toward the subject of his parents, and he'd let her.

"The uniform for one. It scared them. And I knew it would, of course, but I joined anyway." He had another sip of wine.

"Certainly they tried to understand," she said.

"No. They never talked about it. It was as if I were doing something else. It was very strange. We never once talked about my years in the military. I stopped going home in fact. My father died while I was overseas," Kline said. He looked around the living room. The house was worth at least a million dollars, he thought, probably more.

"Why does it matter what your parents thought about your career as a soldier?" she said. "I mean, as long as it made *you* happy?"

"Is this session for free?" The wine made him a little light-headed. He tried to smile at his own joke but couldn't.

"It's on the house," she said.

"Okay. Of course it matters." That seemed an odd question, Kline thought.

"But why?" she asked.

"Because I owed them so much, and I never paid them back."

"Why did you owe them so much?" she asked.

"You don't understand." He moved on the couch uncomfortably.

"I'm trying to," she said looking at him. She was a remarkably beautiful woman. It seemed sitting here in his house that Boon had it all. Kline finished his drink. He had *his* girl *and* this one. He had *too* much, Kline decided, and so do the dot.com assholes out on the beach, he thought, finishing the drink.

"They went through hell to have me. My mother. . . . My mother. . . ." The words felt like ashes in his mouth. "In the camp, my mother–had to do things to survive. Sexual things." He turned his face away, embarrassed and ashamed.

"What does that have to do with what you owe your parents?" she said.

"I owe them my life. Do I have to spell it out for you? Jesus!" He didn't want a stupid psychiatrist, he thought, wiping his mouth with the back of his hand.

"Are you saying she had some kind of sexual dysfunction, Paul?"

"She hated sex. That's what my father said. She hated it, but they had me anyway. She wanted to have children despite what had happened to her. I owe my existence to an act of her will." He felt cold inside. He'd never articulated all the loose bits that he'd felt for years. His father had told him this, out of the blue, while they were eating breakfast, one summer when he was home on vacation from Stanford. He'd said it almost as if he were speaking to himself about something he'd read in the paper. It had been shockingly clinical. "My father told me I had to succeed, that it had cost her too much to have me for me to fail."

"Where is she now? You said your father had passed away."

"She lives here in town, in San Francisco. She does volunteer work. She spends part of every year in Israel. She has a sister there. I don't let her stay all year in Israel because of the violence. I don't want anything more to happen to her. Look, I want to be able to write about these issues, but most of the time when I try to write, nothing comes. I can't. Something stops me. It's almost physical. Do they have drugs for that, something that would force me to relax? Martin seemed to be able to write, even about painful things."

"There's no drug for that," she said, her face passive and nonjudgmental.

"I'm a little jealous of him. He was everything I wanted to be but never could be. He was free—unaware of his own unhappy history, at least until *I* showed up. He wrote about his mother's suicide. I found something in his papers the other day. That must have been very difficult."

"I think you should put Martin behind you," she said, and stood up. "It's better when we don't obsess about someone else. I would drop his case. I don't think it's doing you any good."

"Right now I'm trying to find out who killed him, so I can't."

"I see. You think he was *murdered?*" She looked at him, clearly shocked.

"I'm not sure. I didn't think so until someone tried to kill *me,*" Kline said. "But I'm going to find out."

In the strange almost florescent beach light, they caught sight of Boon and Virginia as they crested the dune. Elders began waving to Boon, who was holding Virginia by the elbow, helping her navigate the dune. Seagulls scattered as they approached the house. The doorbell rang suddenly and Kline went down the hall to answer the door. Several new members of the writing group had all come out to the beach together. He didn't know any of them.

TWENTY-SEVEN

The new group was large, about fifteen people, too large for a writing group, but Virginia told him that she expected most of them to quit soon enough. Some of the new people had to sit on the red Oriental rugs near the fireplace. A pretty woman in her forties, Klein's age, in well-pressed Gap garb and obviously a homemaker, took the seat next to him on the couch. She gave him an eager smile. Kline introduced himself. She seemed nervous, he thought, and he tried to put her at ease. Virginia took the floor and hushed everyone, asking for quiet. She introduced Betsy Austin, who was back from her latest sojourn in Europe, to the new members and told everyone that Betsy was armed with a brand new novel.

Betsy read from her first chapter. The novel was a comedy of manners set in New York. Over Betsy's words, Kline heard the crackle and pop of the fire. Her novel was about the East Side patriciate, types Kline didn't really know about. Austin assumed everyone knew what an "East-Side-of-the-Park bitch" was. Kline had no idea exactly, but he could imagine and responded to the novel's dark humor and clever insights. Like Bingham's *Lightning on the Sun,* everyone was too miserable, too talented and too rich. Someone had just drowned in a pool. Whatever Betsy had gotten up to in Europe, it had made her a better writer, he thought.

At the break, Michael made his way across the vast art-plastered living room. "How's the detective?" Michael asked

218

him. He was dressed like one of the characters in Betsy's sybaritic world—baggy green corduroy pants, worn Sperry's with no socks, a black turtleneck. All the women in the room, married or not, kept eyeing him.

"I know who they are," Kline said. Michael looked at him a moment and then smiled. Kline tried to keep his voice down. "I saw his grandmother yesterday."

"I asked you not to do that, Paul," Michael said.

"It was a free country last time I checked," Kline said, trying to keep the hostility out of his voice and not doing a very good job of it.

"Is it? I'll have to tell Mr. Rosenthal what you've done. He won't like it," Boon said under his breath.

"I don't give a shit who you tell. Someone tried to kill me. I want to know *why*," Kline said. Elders was standing nearby and telling Betsy how much she'd enjoyed her work. She had been very friendly towards Virginia earlier in the evening. Elders obviously didn't have a clue about Michael's two-timing her, Kline thought, looking at her.

Virginia walked toward them from the kitchen. She was wearing white jeans and an orange top. Her hair was clipped up, coquettishly, on her head. Both men turned to look at her. "What's with the serious faces? It's important to me that you're both friends, you know," Virginia said, looking first at Michael, then Kline.

"Of course we're friends," Michael said quickly. "Why wouldn't we be? Where's old Cindy?" he said, changing the subject. "I thought we were going to see her, finally. It's been ages. Has she run off and joined the damned circus or something?"

"She said she'd be here, but you know Cindy," Virginia answered. Michael scooped up a few peanuts from the dish on the side table.

"I think I'll get a beer," Michael said curtly. Elders, obviously sensing the tension between the two men, followed Michael like a puppy dog as he started to walk away.

"Why do you bother coming, Michael?" Virginia asked suddenly, her question stopping him. "You haven't read anything in weeks." Michael turned and looked at her.

"I thought we dropped the brutal rule," Michael said, a little taken aback.

"I'm bringing it back," she said. "What do you think, Paul?"

"I don't know," Kline said.

"Then why did *you* come?" She turned on him now.

"The friendly people?" Kline said.

"Go ahead. Bring it back. I always thought it was our best friend," Boon said, rolling the peanuts around in his palm. Taking Elders by the hand, he turned and walked away.

Virginia took the floor again after the break. Icy and petulant just a moment ago, she was gracious and affable now as she led the group, which was radically different than what it had been. Scattered in with the typical young Iowa-Writer's-Project types were people of color and older women. The group was no longer just the hip and the young as it had been when Martin was alive.

Virginia introduced the brutal rule to the group and suggested to everyone that it be implemented. "It was a very simple rule," she said, looking at Michael, who'd appeared at the kitchen doorway.

"I second that. I mean I'm one of the old guard. It was a good rule. Made you *really* work," Michael said

"Everyone in favor raise their hand," Virginia said. The soccer mom next to Kline shot her hand up eagerly like one of her kids at school. It was settled.

"Paul is going to read for us now. He's been away from the group for awhile," Virginia said. Kline felt his face turn red. He had a terrible deep blush whenever he was embarrassed; he felt it run across his face now. His heart seemed as if it had suddenly stopped beating. He hadn't expected to be called on to read. He had no work of his own to read, only those pages of Martin's that he'd mentioned to Elders and had brought with him, intending to give them to Virginia. He heard the fire crackling and looked up. Michael had gone to the fireplace and tossed a log on the fire from a neat stack on the hearth. Virginia sat down on the arm of the couch near him, tapping his sweatered shoulder as she did. Embarrassed, Kline stood up and removed Martin's pages from his back pocket. Like some psychic infection that his system had fought off and finally killed, his jealousy of Martin Anderson left him as suddenly as it had come.

"This isn't my work. It belonged to a friend of mine, but I want to read it tonight. I was envious of him for a while. You see, all my life I've wanted to write, but I can't. I'm not an artist. I'm not a writer," Kline said. "I understand that now." He looked around the room. Some of the faces looked surprised. He looked at Susan Elders. She was sitting alone in a big white chair, her blonde hair spilling over her shoulders. The yellow light from the fireplace painted her beautiful face. Betsy Austin looked at him quizzically, drink in hand, the perpetual college girl.

"Is it really Martin's?" Austin asked from across the huge room.

"Yes," Kline said. "It's Martin's. It was one of the last things he wrote, I think," he said and then started to read aloud.

"He was born in this city, and although only a boy, he could feel that it would be his home forever. He was wearing polished Buster Brown shoes, and a jingle about "Red's Tamale Day" was playing on the car radio. The cars in those days were big. This one was white, with a roomy upholstered interior and a big steering wheel and a chromed horn bar. He could feel the heft of the car as they drove down Lombard Street. He was happy that afternoon as he heard a woman's voice, very splendid, very young, say, "Martin, this is the crookedest street in the world. I bet you didn't know that, did you, darling?" And he remembered standing up on the seat and looking at the houses and the yellow and white flowerbeds and repeating "crookedest street in the world!" with a little boy's quickness. He was a bright boy, like the sun. "Look, a blue sky," the woman said. "Blue sky, darling, blue sky."

"It wasn't until they approached Coit Tower that he felt something else. Something that a child feels when they suspect an adult is not behaving quite right, when their shadow falls over you, and the joy and the love turns into a kind of apprehension and fear of the next word. He knew something was wrong with her. It came to him quicker than a thought, so quickly, as the car drove past the small wind-bent cypress trees along the serpentine strip of road to Coit Tower.

"The young woman, who was driving, looked up at the tower ahead of her, not out to the bay that was crystal blue that afternoon. They came to a stop. It was as if the world stopped. The little boy was still. She was looking up at the tower, and then she turned up the radio. The little boy pressed against her, afraid that the shadows were winning and coming between them. He could smell the liquor on her breath, and he could feel the lack of response from her, a kind of deadness where love was lost. The black hole of his need for her love opened as he tried to get her to look at him. *Was it a kiss he'd wanted?* And, then, she looked at him, but her face was blocked by the sun that was streaming through the driver's side window. Sharp and bright, the sun shone around her, like the halos that surround Catholic saints, obscuring her features. She was the faceless icon of a lost world where there had once been happiness.

"'Do you know what day it is?' she asked him. He shook his head no.

"'It's my birthday. I'm twenty-seven years old today,' she said. Her tone had changed and she was talking to him in the way that scared him, in the way that had to do with the vodka bottle. She kept one in the glove compartment and one in her closet. Once, she'd slapped him when he'd found it, and he'd cried and never been the same afterwards, a little piece of his security slapped away forever. Then she kissed him on the cheek where she'd slapped him once and held him for a moment. He thought he might cry because the shadows were stronger than he'd ever felt them.

"She turned down the radio and let him out of the car. She told him to stay and wait for her. Then she simply walked through the crowd and up the white steps alone. She was wearing a long dress with big polka dots and a straw summer hat, and she must have been tall, he realized. He was left alone with the throngs of tourists and the sound of gay holiday voices, and the smell of the bay in July, which is really the smell of grass from Angel Island. The sun rotted gold, like some Roman coin. Girls in hippie dresses stood nearby.

"And then he heard the terrible ululation from a woman standing near him. The sun screamed as he ran toward the steps where he saw her land, all broken—different now. And while he ran, he started to cry for help. But no help came.

"She was on the steps, and the shadows had won and the love was gone, defeated and dead; he knew that instinctively. It was like the wind in the city at the corner of Sutter Street, full of noise and loneliness."

Kline stopped reading. He put the pages down on the coffee table. Teary-eyed, the soccer mom clapped slowly. Shocked, Kline noticed that Susan Elders was sobbing uncontrollably. Michael crossed the living room toward her. She cried out again, hysterically, and this time she didn't stop. They all watched as Michael and the soccer mom, who said she was a nurse, took her out of the room. It was so quiet in the room afterwards that you could hear the surf outside hitting the beach, like gods stepping out of the water.

• • •

Bolinas's tiny main street was a nestled hodgepodge of cottages and restaurants. Unnerved by Susan Elders' reaction to Martin's story, Kline had gone to Smiley's Bar in Bolinas to have a drink. Outside the bar, it had rained hard. After that, he checked into a dank room at one of the funky motels in Stinson Beach.

The next morning, he woke up very early, not feeling quite himself. The windows to the motel cabin were streaked and steamy. Through the curtains, he saw the sky was pinkish gray and overlaid with scud. His neck was stiff from the Vicodan. He'd had to get up in the middle of the night because of the pain in his leg; he'd taken two of the painkillers so he could sleep. It was pouring outside and the room was ice cold. He walked over and clicked on the TV and then the wall heater. He went into the bathroom and made coffee in the tiny sink.

When he walked back into the room, Cindy was sitting in a chintz-covered chair in a dark corner by the TV set. He hadn't heard her come in. Startled, he just stared at her. She was wet and was clutching a laptop, her long hair shiny from the rain. Her face was pale and she'd lost weight since the last time he'd seen her.

"Virginia said you'd be here. The desk clerk gave me a key. I told him I was you're girlfriend." She was shivering from the cold.

"Where the hell have you been?" he said.

"County Jail." She reached over and turned the volume down on the TV. She was wearing black bib-overalls. "Possession of heroin. They gave me probation. Any more trouble with the police, and I'll have to do some serious time." He looked at her a moment and then pulled the covers back to lie in bed where it was warmer. He watched the overly coifed TV anchor laughing on screen about something terribly funny that was going on out in the world that morning. "Virginia bailed me out. She promised to keep it a secret. I called Michael, but he wouldn't help me with the bail. He's mad at me. I don't know why," she said. She started to shiver again. He got up and turned up the wall heater as far as it would go.

"Michael is afraid you're going to screw up Virginia's inheritance," Kline said.

"Is there any more of that coffee? I'm freezing," she said.

"It passes for coffee, I guess." He got her a cup of coffee from the bathroom and handed her a towel and got back in bed. He turned around and looked at the clock radio on the nightstand. It was only nine o'clock, too early to call Michael's place and see how Susan Elders was doing. The rain drummed intensely on the roof of the cabin suddenly.

"I went to Michael's last night but you'd already left. I was pretty drunk. Michael wouldn't even let me in the house. Virginia said you were here. She said I shouldn't come until I sobered up. I passed out in my car."

"You've been here all night?"

"Since about two A.M., in the parking lot. Us dope fiends don't keep regular hours. I took a walk on the beach this morning in the rain to sober up."

"Why are you trying to kill yourself?"

"I don't know, really. I think I wanted to be different. I didn't want to be the passive Chinese girl who always got A's. I wanted to be Virginia Wolf or Amy Tan or, shit, *anybody* other than who I was. I was so fucking *obedient.* You wouldn't have believed it. I traded one jones for another, I guess."

"That's why I joined the Marine Corps," he said. "But I think you should stop hurting yourself," he said. The coffee was finally doing him some good.

"Thanks. I'll keep that in mind." He could see that she was keyed up, either from withdrawal or something else.

"Virginia told me you might be able to prove Martin didn't write that confession about Fisher."

"I can and I did. And I don't think he wrote that manuscript, either," she said.

"I *know* he didn't write that."

"You *know?*" She looked surprised.

"Virginia wrote it, the first chapter anyway. Kevin wrote the rest. He told me he did," he said.

"Why would she do something like that? That wasn't right," Cindy said.

"It was a joke that went sour," he said. "But we have to find out who wrote the confession in order to prove that Martin was murdered, that he didn't kill himself."

"That's why I went up there that day to the apartment to meet you. I wanted to get my hands on his laptop so I could prove it. The confession was found on it, but he didn't write it."

"How do you know that?"

"Because I have a Ph D in Computer Science from Harvard. Personally, I wished I'd never got the fucking degree. Anyway, I took the document file and took it apart. You'll have to trust me when I tell you that I *know* what I'm talking about."

"All right. I believe you, doctor."

"The confession was originated on a computer owned by Sir Speedy's on 24th Street, *days* before the crime even took place. But their records can't tell me *who* wrote it. You don't have to show any identification when you use one of their computers. It was a cash transaction," she said.

"Martin still could have written it," Kline said.

"Why would he go to 24th Street to write a fucking confession to a horrible crime? That doesn't make any sense," she said. "I'm betting it's the same for the manuscript I found at Betsy's, which you say Kevin admits to. I just haven't had time to tear into the manuscript's files, but I will. I was 'girl interrupted' for a while. But I'm back now. I think we'll find that Virginia wrote the first chapter of that manuscript on her computer and the rest was written at a Sir Speedy or some place like that. You know, that Sir Speedy on 24th Street isn't that far from the hospital where Kevin worked."

"It isn't that far from about a million other people either," he said. "You still haven't proven Martin *didn't* write the confession. Or that anyone else *did*."

"You're right, but it's a start," she said.

"So tell me, doctor, what's your theory? If he didn't commit suicide, what happened up there that day? I haven't been able to put that part together."

"Virginia says that you were hired by Michael's law firm to tell him he was adopted and that he'd inherited a lot of money. Well, maybe someone *wanted* that money, and maybe Martin needed to die for them to get it."

"I've been over it a thousand times. If someone pushed him, the police would have found them. The tower's elevator was closed down. The guard had locked the door to the stairs as soon as Martin took the elevator. The police came a few minutes later. They went up the stairs, as well as the elevator, and didn't see anyone. So whoever it was that pushed him was able to vanish into thin air. That doesn't make any sense, does it?"

"Or they waited in the stairwell until everyone left and then just walked out," Cindy said. "I played in that stairway when I was a kid. There are lots of places to hide."

"Hold on," he said. Kline became distracted suddenly and climbed over the bed to turn up the volume on the TV. They were showing his mother's house. His mother was standing at the front door and talking to a horde of TV news people and cameramen. "Is it true that your husband was a Nazi and that he lived here with you, pretending to be a survivor? Is that true?" A reporter shouted over the crowd of other reporters gathered around him. Kline watched his mother in disbelief. His Aunt Carmen tried to lead her away from the front door. His mother pulled away from her and turned back toward the gaggle of reporters. "My husband was a good man," she said.

"Yes, but the Weisenthal Center is claiming that your husband was a Nazi that worked in Dachau. Is that true? Did he lie about his past? They are claiming that your husband wasn't even Jewish," the reporter said. The camera zoomed in on his mother's face. He saw the network call letters on the microphone.

"I have to go," Kline said mechanically.

"Kline, what's wrong?" Cindy said. She tried to look at the TV, but he'd climbed to the edge of the bed and switched it off.

"Nothing."

"There's one thing I can't figure out . . . the blonde. The one who tried to kill me that day in the apartment. She was there for the computer *too,* I think," Cindy said.

"Maybe," Kline said quietly, not really paying attention now. He wanted to turn the TV back on, but he couldn't.

"Can I take a shower, Kline?"

"Okay," he said. He left while she was still in the bathroom.

He'd forgotten his raincoat in his hurry to leave. He trotted hurriedly down the gravel path. Windblown rain hit him in the face. He caught glimpses of the traffic on Highway One. The gravel lane wound past several motel cabins. He came around the corner of the last cabin and saw his Cadillac across the two-lane highway parked in the public beach parking lot, the lot mostly empty because of the bad weather. As he waited to cross the road, he spotted a big American car parked next to his Cadillac. He ran across the road and was going to ignore the man in that car who was face down on the steering wheel, a drunk, he thought. Then he looked again, peering through the car's rain-splattered windshield for a better look. He thought it looked like Rosenthal's profile through the driver's-side window. Kline knocked on the window. Sure it was Rosenthal now, he pulled the car door open. He saw the back right side of Rosenthal's skull was avulsed, fragments of it showing white shattered edges. Kline reached in and brought the chin up enough to see exactly who it was. Rosenthal's head lolled back grotesquely. He had been shot in the face, point blank, a bullet hole for a nose now. The eyes were lightless and clouded, expressionless. His rubbery face was specked with black from the close fire.

TWENTY-EIGHT

All his life he'd had nightmares about just such a room, a room at the end of a narrow quiet corridor. A room where the police—efficient and base—waited for you. A room where unspeakable things happened. The kind of room his parents had been taken to when they were first arrested in Berlin. "I'd like to get on with this," Kline said nervously. The interrogation room at the San Francisco Hall of Justice was claustrophobic and rank. The stink of cigarettes and fear seemed to have permanently soured the air. A sole metal table fixed with a tape recorder and two chairs sat in the florescent gloom. Above the table, high on the wall, were two filthy windows that punctuated the room's officious sterility. A large mercury-colored mirror hung on the wall to Kline's left.

"You seem upset," Lt. Cross said. The policeman had stood up when Kline was led in by the jailor. The lieutenant's pock-marked face squared off in a smile. "Can I get you anything? Cup of coffee? Did they feed you this morning?" Cross's tone was respectful; he'd been a Marine too, he told Kline. There was a genuine respect for Kline's war record amongst the jailors and the policemen, most of whom were ex-military themselves. Curiously, the story about his father's alleged past that filled the newspapers and TV didn't seem to matter to them.

The lieutenant opened up his notebook. The sound of the book's pages being flipped filled the poorly lit room for a moment. Kline, still standing, pulled back a metal chair and sat down without answering Cross at first; he'd gotten some tasteless breakfast—horribly greasy scrambled eggs—he said finally, his eyes still taking in the room.

He tried to get his emotional bearings as he looked at the policeman across the table from him. It hadn't helped when he saw himself in the mirror as the jailor brought him in. His face had appeared slightly distorted. He knew, since the moment he'd heard the news about his father, that he was no longer exactly sane. How *could* he be? And now, even the mirror was telling him he was a lead-colored monster in an orange jumpsuit with two day's growth of beard. Yet he wasn't *outwardly* insane.

Dirty and ashamed, he'd experienced moments of fear and self-loathing in his cell—moments when he just wanted to be alone and free of the filthy jail cell with its racist graffiti and swastikas etched into the walls. He wanted to be free to walk on the street or get in his car and drive. He wanted to be completely alone and piece it all out. Why had Rosenthal been murdered? Where had the gun the police found (identical to the one Kline had found at Martin's) come from?

Since he was a child, he'd been afraid of jail and everything it implied. He was not afraid of being harmed by the prisoners, he was afraid instead of the state's unseen apparatus getting ahold of him. He'd been taught to fear the police by his parents. They had filled his head with stories about the Gestapo and the way they, like ferrets, methodically and systematically stripped their victims of their property and their dignity before shipping them off to the camps. Whole bank accounts were signed over to the Gestapo, the families believing it was in payment for exit visas to Switzerland. (He remembered having read a news story about a rich French businessman with a huge art collection of stolen Jewish

232

paintings in which the man had said he didn't really believe there had been a Holocaust! He'd said that he'd paid good money for the paintings and he planned on keeping them.) His parent's stories had had a horrible impact on him as a child. The idea that the authorities could be madmen, who could keep you against your will, unfairly, was profoundly disturbing.

"I've never been in jail before," Kline said. He was sweating and he felt like he wanted to sprint to the door, but he had a plan now and he was committed to it. His feet tapped the floor uncontrollably in his jailhouse slippers as he looked at Cross. Unable to sleep, he'd slowly worked through the case and had come up with a plan. Still protean, his plan required him to convince the authorities that he was guilty of murdering Rosenthal, but in stages. He had to be convincing.

"Why did you do it?" Cross said.

"You tell me."

"You had a motive, didn't you?" Cross said.

"No. I didn't."

"Hadn't Rosenthal ruined your family by investigating your father?"

"Albert didn't do anything. My father did that to himself," Kline said very calmly. He tried to fold his hands and appear normal, but it was difficult somehow getting them to fold. It was as if they belonged to someone left to stand in for him, a guilty doppelganger sent to face the world with what his father had done. There was a pause then as Cross watched him fidget. *Guilty men fidget,* Kline thought.

"What's it like? I mean, all of a sudden, your father turns out to be some big-time Nazi."

"What do you mean?"

"Does it make you angry? People hate you now. The Press says you and your father were just alike. . . ."

"Ask me that again and I'll. . . . I'll kill you," Kline said. It came to him that he had to make the police hate him, too. He had to negate the respect they had for him and his medals. *Everyone* would have to hate him for his plan to work.

"You'll WHAT?"

"I said I'll kill you," Kline said, looking at him. He turned towards the machine recording his words.

"Do you know you're being recorded, Kline?" the policeman said incredulously. "The D.A. will hear this."

"Yes. I understand that. And I'm telling you. . . . I'll bash your fucking brains out if you ask me any more questions about my father," he said.

"Are you *crazy?*"

"Maybe. Ask me that question again and find out." Startled, Cross looked at him for at least a full minute, tapping his notebook with the eraser end of his pencil. *Yes, I'm a big motherfucker,* Kline's face seemed to say.

"Okay. I apologize. We won't talk about your parents," Cross said. "Did you shoot Albert Rosenthal?"

"No. I didn't. Someone did it to stop me from investigating Martin Anderson's murder." He decided to tell the truth because he knew that, perversely, it would sound lame to the police. The truth, ironically, would convince them he was guilty.

"Martin Anderson?" Cross said incredulously.

"Yes," Kline said.

"What murder, Kline? He jumped off fucking Coit Tower in front of witnesses!"

"The witnesses were all down on the parking lot, weren't they?" Kline reminded him. "I was one of them."

"He was alone when he jumped. I investigated that case myself," Cross said.

"You fucked up. Somebody was up there with him. They pushed him off, then got away on the stairs." He told Cross the truth again and smiled, knowing he wasn't going to believe a word of it.

"We're not here about Martin Anderson's suicide, Kline. Anderson is dead. That's got nothing to do with you shooting Rosenthal in the face."

"I realize that. But I'm just trying to answer your questions," Kline said, smirking. "Honest Injun."

"The gun found in Rosenthal's car was the murder weapon. It has your fingerprints *all over it*," Cross said. "How do you explain that?"

"I can't right now," Kline said. He looked up. He had been over that point a million times in his mind. He remembered the gun at Michael's office that day and putting it back in his coat pocket after Michael told him to keep it. He'd taken it home and he was sure it was still there, locked up with his other pistols, but he didn't say that. He just looked at Cross fatuously. He had no idea where the gun the police found could have come from. "The only thing I can say is that it isn't my gun," Kline said.

"You're right. But they're your fingerprints, Kline," Cross said. "There's no question that they're your fingerprints."

"I want to call an attorney," Kline said.

"All right." Cross said. "All right." A half-hour later Kline was standing in a hall in a queue of prisoners, most of them black and young, all of them waiting for the one pay phone. He finally got to the head of the line and called Virginia.

"I want you to ask Michael to defend me," Kline said. "I don't want anyone else. You have to get Michael for me. Do you hear me, Virginia?"

"Yes. Of course," she said. "Of course, Paul."

"I have to go," he said.

235

"Paul." He hung up before she could bring up his father. He didn't want to talk about it. He had a plan now. It was taking shape every second and he clung to it. As they were lined up and walked back toward their cells, he thought it felt a lot like boot camp, only no one was yelling at him. One of the younger men looked at him aggressively. Kline mouthed the words "FUCK YOU" carefully, just so there wouldn't be any misunderstanding about his attitude. He wasn't going to be anybody's punk. The kid, who had expected to scare the older man, looked at Kline like he was stone psycho.

TWENTY-NINE

Everyone in America expected Kline to be found guilty. His conviction was a given in the newspapers. After all, he was the son of a Nazi, as the press reminded everyone constantly now. As one Associated Press writer put it: *Nazi blood coursed through his German veins.* In fact, the reporter said, it was possible that Kline was responsible for war crimes himself. An A.P. investigation was ongoing into his war record in Panama, the Gulf and a host of other military actions.

Kline's trial had become the hot ticket and the most sensational murder trial of the year. Court TV was covering it. *USA Today* dedicated a quarter page to it *every day.* The coverage spanned all media from *Entertainment Tonight* (there was speculation about a movie and who would play Kline) to the *New York Times.* The case had even caused problems for the U.S. Government internationally. Kline's father had, according to reports, worked for the C.I.A. during the sixties in Chile during Operation Condor as an advisor to Chilean intelligence and then later in Brazil. Civil rights groups were demanding that his files and others, including those of the famous rocket scientist Von Braun and Klaus Barbie, be released to the public immediately. Outraged, the group demanded to know why former Nazi war criminals like Barbie and Kline had worked for U.S. intelligence during the Cold War.

The trial had become—like Clinton's sexual travails—the kind of thing people talked about at lunch, speculating whether

Kline's mother was a victim or a criminal herself. As one wag put it: Even war criminals have wives. (*USA Today* conducted a poll on the subject: *If your husband were a war criminal, could you go on?*) It had all reached a frantic pitch that morning in June in San Francisco as Michael Boon stood up and approached the bench in his thousand-dollar suit in a dreary courtroom on Bryant Street.

There was a heated sidebar meeting. Kline watched Michael and the prosecutor discussing with the judge the unusual tack the State was planning–to call Michael Boon to the stand to testify for the prosecution. Kline turned to the gallery looking for Virginia. The gallery was crowded with press and spectators; no seats were left empty. Kline had been fashioned into a pariah by the reporters covering the trail. None of them now would look him in the face as he searched for Virginia in the crowd of spectators. Michael came back to the defense table, obviously frustrated.

"The State calls Michael Boon, your honor," the prosecutor said. The courtroom turned into a mob scene. It was the moment the press had been speculating about for days. "For the record, your honor, I want to have this witnessed deemed hostile," the prosecutor said in a take-charge tone.

"Granted," the judge said, afraid of her. The judge, a physically small man, seemed to be hiding behind the bench, his robe too big for him and his toupee the subject of endless jokes on late night T.V. Like Judge Ito, he'd failed from the outset to get control of the courtroom, and now it was too late. The prosecution seemed to be running the show from the outset. The press–always on the side of the State–had only added to the prosecutorial snowball. They'd given the black female D.A. godlike qualities in their coverage.

Michael, looking like a young movie star, turned to Kline at the defense table. "I have it under control, Paul," he said over the hubbub as he stood up. Kline had barely heard him over the sound of the judge's pounding gavel. The courtroom seemed to inhale as Michael left his place at the defense table, where he'd been by Kline's side for weeks fighting the torrent of evidence that pointed to Kline's guilt. The camera from Court TV panned the courtroom and then moved in on the young lawyer as he crossed in front of the three lawyers at the prosecution's table. There had been a lot of comment in the press about how handsome and dashing Boon was, and he was living up to it today. There was speculation Boon might even run for Congress. All the press agreed that Kline was lucky to have him as his attorney. There were dozens of stories filed about how brave Boon was to represent such a hated defendant. A Holocaust survivor had actually spit on the young lawyer in a restaurant for defending Kline. The story spread around the world.

Kline turned to look for Virginia again, the way he had every time someone came to the stand to testify. Virginia and Cindy had been there every day without fail. He spotted them finally in the back. He tried to catch Virginia's eye, but she was speaking to Cindy. The judge gaveled the courtroom down. After repeated warnings that he would have the gallery cleared, the room finally came to order.

The prosecutor stood up, still glancing at her notes, seemingly unruffled by the hoopla. She hadn't even looked up as Boon walked by her and took the stand. The woman, in her forties, continued to study her notes for a moment as Michael settled into his chair. She finally came out from behind the prosecution table holding her glasses, esurient.

"Good morning, Counselor."

"Good morning," Michael said. He leaned forward and spoke into the microphone to his right as if to test it.

"How long have you known your client, Paul Kline?"

"About two years."

"You knew him socially?"

"Yes. He had joined my writing group."

"Can you say he was a close friend?"

"No. I can't say that. He had worked for my law firm, so I knew him professionally as well."

"Did you know the defendant's father was a war criminal? Strike that, your honor. Did you know that Mr. Kline's father was an S.S. officer who had joined the Nazi Party at a very young age and that Mr. Rosenthal had been suspicious of the defendant's father for years? And for the record, your honor, Mr. Kline's father's family name was actually Neizert."

"I object, your honor, to this characterization. It prejudices my client and is irrelevant," Kline's second attorney, a friend of Michael's who was brought in for just this phase of the trial, sprang to his feet immediately.

"Sustained," the judge said.

The prosecutor, cocksure, like one of those battlefield surgeons Kline had seen in action, had a sense of what was about to happen next and could move from point to point keeping the whole show in mind while she worked over the bloody details. She shot a glance at Kline. He thought she looked a little done-in this morning, as if the trial was beginning to wear her down. Her brown suit was rumpled and she didn't look quite right. Her lipstick seemed to be off center. Kline imagined she'd been up late preparing for perhaps the most anticipated and important witness of her career. "I'll rephrase the question, your honor. Mr. Boon, had you spoken with Mr. Rosenthal about his investigation of the defendant's father? The investigation he was conducting with the Simon Weisenthal Center in Los Angeles?"

"Not until the night he came to my house in Bolinas."

"But you saw the victim, Mr. Rosenthal, every day at the law firm where you are employed, didn't you?"

"I would see him occasionally, but there are forty or more attorneys at our firm. Mr. Rosenthal and I didn't speak normally, other than to say hello, that type of thing. He was much older and not involved in the day-to-day affairs of the firm."

"I understand." The prosecutor moved back to her table and picked up the automatic pistol the police said Kline had taken from Martin's apartment. "Did you ever see the defendant with this pistol? Please answer yes or no." She brought it first to the bench and then back to the stand so Boon could take a good look at it. The pistol's distinctive silver plating stood out. Boon leaned over and examined it carefully for a moment.

"Let the record show that the prosecution is bringing Exhibit A for the witness to examine," the judge said.

"Yes. I was the one that suggested he might want to keep it," Boon said.

"Your honor, would you please tell the witness to keep to yes or no answers unless otherwise instructed."

The judge cleared his throat for effect. "Mr. Boon, as an officer of the court, I don't think it's really necessary for me to explain your duties while on the witness stand," the judge told him.

"Yes, your honor," Michael said. He looked up at the judge like a little boy.

"Counselor, you told the police that Mr. Kline removed this gun at your request from Ms. Winston's apartment, that he brought it to your office but then took it away again. Is that correct?"

"Yes. Your honor, can I explain?" Michael looked toward the judge. The judge nodded. "Your honor, that pistol *was* delivered to me at my office as I requested."

"Then how did it get into the defendant's possession?" the D.A. asked.

"Objection, your honor. We have no direct evidence that the murder weapon was in Mr. Kline's possession at the time of the murder." Kline's second attorney had stood up again to object.

"Sus...tained," the judge said, dragging the word out.

"I'll rephrase," the prosecutor said. "You told investigators that Mr. Kline took the pistol with him when he left. Why *didn't* you ask for it back before he left? Wasn't your intention to take possession of the pistol to begin with?"

"I have a fear of guns and, to be honest, I was upset that day. I decided it would be best if Mr. Kline simply kept the gun."

"Why didn't you call Mr. Kline later and ask for the pistol back? It was estate property. You had a duty as trustee to include it in the estate property, didn't you?"

"I didn't want to ask him for it. I thought he'd earned it. He'd done me a favor by removing it from the apartment, and I thought that it was better off with him. I really didn't want it around the office. I had no idea what to do with it otherwise. I reimbursed the estate for it myself and left it at that."

"For the record, Mr. Boon, you never asked for the gun back? Yes or no?"

"No. I did not. I saw no reason to. In fact, I was relieved when Paul took it with him."

"So, as far as you know, Mr. Kline was in possession of the murder weapon? Is that your testimony?" This was the question she'd worked out and built for, the question that had caused her to stay up half the night plotting. She was sure it was the question that would put Kline in the gas chamber. "I'd like an answer, Mr. Boon. Yes or no?" The entire courtroom waited for the answer.

"Yes." There was an audible gasp from the gallery.

"Did Mr. Rosenthal come to your house in Bolinas a few hours before he was found dead at the Starlight Motel at Stinson beach?"

"Yes."

"Why had he come out to the beach? Why had he come to your house?"

"To speak to Mr. Kline."

"Why did he think Mr. Kline would be at your home?"

"Paul, Mr. Kline, mentioned to his mother that he was coming out to my place for the weekend. She must have told Mr. Rosenthal of his whereabouts."

"What did Mr. Rosenthal want with Mr. Kline?"

"He wanted to tell Paul what was being said about his father by the press. Mr. Rosenthal was quite upset by what he'd discovered about Paul's father. He'd known Paul since they were children. They were old friends."

"You mean he wanted to inform Mr. Kline of the fact that his father was a Nazi who'd escaped prosecution for war crimes and lived with his mother as a Jew and a survivor, deceiving everyone in the most horrible way."

"I object, your honor," Kline's second lawyer said. "Mr. Kline's father has no bearing on this case."

"Your honor, I'm trying to establish motive here," the prosecutor said.

"Objection overruled. Answer the question, Mr. Boon," the judge said.

"Yes," Michael said.

"What did you tell Mr. Rosenthal when he came to your home that evening in Bolinas?"

"I told him Paul had been there earlier, but was staying at the Starlight Motel in Stinson Beach."

"And what did Mr. Rosenthal say to you about Mr. Kline?"

"He said he knew that Paul was going to be upset, that the news about his father would be devastating to him. He wanted me to call the motel to see if Paul was all right, in case he'd heard something."

"And did you?"

"Yes. But there was no answer."

"Mr. Rosenthal expected Mr. Kline to be very angry. Isn't that what you told the police when they first questioned you about that conversation?" The prosecutor went back to her notes, putting on her glasses, and picked up what she needed from the table. "'He was afraid that Mr. Kline was going to be terribly angry with him,' you said."

"Yes. He was afraid that Paul was going to take the news about his father very hard and perhaps blame Mr. Rosenthal. Albert wanted to be the one to break the news to him before anyone else. He said he owed it to Paul to be the one, no matter what happened."

"So Mr. Rosenthal had left San Francisco that evening to find the defendant and try to console him because they were friends."

"Yes."

"And where did you understand Mr. Rosenthal was going when he left your house in Bolinas that evening?"

"To see Paul at the motel and to take him back to San Francisco to his mother's house."

"Why? Why did Mr. Rosenthal want to take Mr. Kline back to San Francisco?"

"He said his mother was desperate to speak to her son. Mr. Rosenthal had promised her to bring him back home."

"But he never got that chance, did he?"

"Objection, your honor," Kline's second lawyer said.

"Strike the question," the prosecutor said. "No further questions, your honor."

"You are excused, Mr. Boon," the judge said.

It was suddenly over. There was quiet in the courtroom. The prosecutor milked the pause. The gallery saw that Boon had done his best but it was no use. Like the rest of the testimony during the trial, the blocks of evidence had fallen into place against the defendant. Each one–when it fell–had made an almost audible sound in the jury box. Looking around him, Kline knew that he was finished. There was little question. Michael got up and left the stand and came back to the defense table, a little shaken, Kline thought. Kline turned and looked for Virginia again. She'd had to admit on the stand that they'd been lovers. She'd admitted on the stand that she didn't love him, but had used him as a kind of surrogate for a former boyfriend. He had turned away, recalling how much that hurt and how much he still loved her. Now he thought. Now. He'd been waiting for three weeks, and now was the time. Kline leaned over.

"I want to speak to the judge. I want to confess." Kline had leaned close enough to Michael to smell his aftershave.

"What?"

"You heard me. I want to confess. Get up there and tell the judge."

"Paul, you're not making any sense. There's still a chance the jury. . . ." Michael whispered.

"You heard me. Tell him." Boon turned to stare at him. Kline could see the clear cold blue of Boon's eyes. Michael stood up.

"Your honor, I'd like to approach the bench," Boon said.

There was an exhausted quiet in the courtroom when the prosecution finished its summation. Kline watched the jury—six women and four men—receive their instructions from the bench with stern faces. A middle-aged Latin woman turned to look at Kline a moment. It was a strange and frightening look, an articulated hatred for him after his confession to the cold-blooded shooting of Rosenthal. He'd been called to the stand as soon as they'd come out of the judge's chambers. He'd made up the details. He'd said Rosenthal had begged for his life and how he'd shot him in the face as he sat there, begging him not to. He'd said it and turned to look at the jury without any remorse on his face. There'd been a stunned silence. The prosecutor had looked at him slack-jawed. The prize—his head—was being handed to her and she couldn't believe what she was hearing. He'd said in the judge's chambers to all the assembled lawyers on both sides that he wanted to confess to the charge but that he wanted to do it on the stand in front of the jury. That was the deal, he'd told them, and that he be allowed to visit his mother while the jury was out. He was out on bail and, technically, they couldn't stop him from walking out of the courtroom before the jury delivered its verdict. The prosecutor had agreed to the terms, of course, because it meant she could ask for the death penalty. The judge had to agree to allow him to walk out of the courtroom or no deal. Michael had spoken up and said that he was opposed to his client's decision but if it was what his client wanted, he couldn't stop him. The judge took a call while they waited. When he put down the phone he stood up and nodded to Kline.

"All right, Mr. Kline, you have a deal. You'll be allowed to see your mother."

The judge explained from the bench that a verdict of guilty in the first degree would mean he would have no choice but to sentence Kline to the gas chamber. The law, he said, looking down at the jury, was very clear on that point. Even the jury looked startled after he'd said it. It was the first time during the three-week trial that the obvious had finally been spoken. They now had the power of life and death over him. The judge adjourned the trial for the day. The jury was allowed to go home. Deliberations would start in the morning. It was what Kline had asked for. It gave him twelve hours to be with his mother. Kline watched the men and women on the jury troop out. Michael leaned in and said something to him but Kline barely heard him over the mad dash of reporters rushing out to get their stories filed. The *Examiner* sold more papers that evening than it had in years.

The city was beautiful on the ride downtown, the streets foggy and quiet the way they are in summer, oddly passive. They walked alone into Boon's office on Maiden Lane. Michael put his briefcase down. Kline closed the door behind them. They'd taken a Town Car from the courthouse. Neither one of them had spoken a word in the car. "They'll have to find you guilty. You should get your things in order. Why did you do it, Paul?" Boon sat down. He looked exhausted. Kline felt happier now that he was free of it all. Everything was working now the way he'd planned.

"I killed him," Kline said.

"I don't believe you," Michael said. He sat down behind his desk and looked at him. "I'm sorry I called you that first day. I wish to God I hadn't now." Kline could see the café from where he stood through the office window. "I know you're lying. I suppose you have your reasons. Are you going to tell me? You must have a reason for lying."

"How do you know I'm lying?" Boon stood up and opened his briefcase.

"Let's say I want to believe it. You always want to believe your clients are innocent," Boon said. "And I've come to like you."

"Well, I'm guilty," Kline said. "I had good reason to kill him, didn't I?"

"I suppose you did," Michael said, hauling his files out of the briefcase.

"I have to see my mother," Kline said automatically. "Will I be arrested as soon as the verdict is in?"

"Yes. Right away. You'll be taken into custody on the spot. You'll be in San Quentin within the week," Michael told him.

There was the sound of a cable car bell in the distance. Kline nodded. "I'll see you tomorrow then. I want to thank you," Kline said quickly. "I want to thank you for everything you tried to do for me during the trial."

"We'll appeal if you like. It's automatic in a death penalty case. I can say that your confession was due to some kind of temporary insanity. God knows you've been under enormous stress," Michael said. Kline nodded and he left the office. He was leaving when he saw Virginia. She was coming down the hallway on the way to Boon's office. They hadn't really spoken since he'd been arrested except on the phone. He had been careful not to see her, afraid that it would weaken his resolve and destroy his plan.

"Paul?"

"I'm still in love with you. That hasn't changed," he said. "I want you to know that." The hallway was empty, just the two of them.

"Paul, I'm sorry," she said. "Whatever happened. . . . It doesn't change the way I feel about you." She was wearing the white suit she'd worn in the courtroom. He loved the way she looked in it. She hadn't missed a day of his trial. He had been told by Boon that she'd paid his bond. He looked at her a moment, and it dawned on him that this might be the last time he ever saw her. *The plan could go wrong,* he told himself. She was looking at him in a strange way, obviously frightened by what he'd confessed to on the stand. For the first time in his life, he wanted to beg. He wanted to get down on his knees and beg her to love him. But he couldn't allow himself to say a word or he wouldn't be able to go on.

"There you are." Boon had stepped out of his office. "You should tell Paul, Virginia. It's only right," he said.

"Tell me what?" Kline said, turning for a moment to look at Michael.

"Paul. You haven't heard? I thought Michael told you. Michael and I are going to get married," she said. She reached forward and kissed him once on the cheek and told him she would come to the courtroom tomorrow morning to be with him. He thanked them both and forced himself to turn away and leave.

THIRTY

Before he left for his mother's house, he sat alone in his office in a daze and watched Larry King interview the prosecutor from the trial. At one point, the prosecutor looked into the camera and told the audience that Kline was an evil man from an evil family. Before cutting to a commercial, they showed a photograph of them—his mother and father and him—taken sometime during the sixties at a party. He'd been just a boy, and his father, well into middle age, smiled happily at the camera, his arms holding onto his son's shoulders. He and his mother hadn't spoken since the trial. Angry about his father, he couldn't face her and what she'd done. He hadn't wanted her to come to the trial; he didn't want her to be humiliated any more than she had been already.

It was late, and the houses on his mother's street were dark, the asphalt street slightly luminescent. Close to the ocean, fog descended in the form of mist and surrounded the streetlights, enhancing their light and making eerie halos. He stood for a moment at the gate. The press, which had been camped out in front of her house since the trial started, were in their windowless riot-proof vans or gone until morning. He stared at the house he'd known so well. They had shown it on TV a thousand times during the trial as some kind of iconic flashcard of shame and perversity. So much about his strange childhood and the terrible shadow that had been silently present all those years had been revealed now. He walked through the gate and up the stairs. Opening the door, he pulled his key from the lock and reached for the light switch in the foyer but decided against turning it on. He climbed the stairs toward his mother's room in the dark. His Aunt Carmen came out of the shadows in the hallway. Had she known he was coming? He knew instinctively from the look on her face that she'd been enlisted somehow in his mother's conspiracy and in her final defense of the past. He walked up the stairs toward her. She moved backwards, shaking her head, stopping finally, her back against his mother's bedroom door.

"No," she said. "No, Paul." He blamed her, too, for some reason. She was part of the secret, the infection that had always been out there threatening them, part of the affliction that had awaited his mother and father, the affliction that he thought they hadn't deserved and now knew they did. He was sorry he'd ever set eyes on any of them. He hated them all now but he wanted to hear the truth from his mother's lips once and for all. He wanted to tell her that he wasn't her son.

"I want to speak to her, Carmen. Get out of my way. I don't have much time."

"She made me promise to keep you out. She doesn't want to talk about it."

"Why? Why can't she tell me the truth now?"

"It doesn't matter why," she said.

"*I'm her son for christ's sake!*" he yelled. He reached over and struck the door with his fist. "Momma! It's me, Paul. Please let me in, *Momma!* I have to know what happened, if it's true. *Please!* I have to know. I have to hear it from you," he said, speaking to the door the way he had as a child when she'd locked herself in.

"Why, Paul?" his aunt said. "It can't matter now."

"Shut up. If you don't get out of the way, I'll–I'll. . . ." He picked her up by the arms. His aunt fought him, slapping him hard, kicking at him. He pushed her against the door. She slid down on her haunches, stunned.

"She doesn't want to see you. She's suffered *enough*. Can't you love her enough to understand how *ashamed* she is?" Carmen said, looking at him from the dark.

"Mother! Please come out. Please, Momma, I love you," he said. He fell to his knees on the floor by his aunt and burst into tears. His aunt reached out and touched his face. He knew it was true; Elders had been right. All these years he'd been grieving for *himself,* not his parents. He'd wanted to be unselfconscious like all the other children, but his parents' unspoken lies and pain had made him see, made him feel, made him think too much too early. He'd developed a strange consciousness early on, one that he hadn't wanted, one that he'd hated and blamed them for. And now he felt guilty too, as if he'd been part of their dirty conspiracy.

The bedroom door opened suddenly; light bathed the hallway. His mother, in a robe, stood there looking at them, her old face terribly pale. Her expression was strange– resigned and frightened all at once.

"Carmen," she said softly.

"Yes, dear."

"It's time to tell him," his mother said. His mother motioned for him to come to the door. He saw she'd been crying; her bed hadn't been slept in. She reached out for him and kissed his face as he stood. How could he tell her he wasn't her son? They both cried, holding each other and, for the first time, he sensed a real closeness, a new bond between the two of them that had never existed before, as if he too had ridden the train that day to Dachau, as if he too had been in Berlin the day she was arrested by men who were acting with the sanction of law. The truth would be their new bond, a bond that had escaped them until that moment. The ghost that had stood between them had vanished now, finally and forever, he thought, holding her.

His Aunt Carmen made coffee without speaking. He sat numbly, watching her moving around in the shadows of the clean dining room. He was afraid of what he was going to hear. He had avoided the newspaper accounts outright, refusing to believe any of it until he heard it from his mother, but somehow knowing that it was all true.

His aunt put a tray with coffee pot, cups and cream on the table. She poured him a cup. The room was dark, only the light in the foyer was on, so the details of things were obscured. He could make out only the general impressions of the porcelain cups and his aunt's face as she sat across from him and started to speak. It was as if she were literally afraid of the light.

"I am a Gypsy, not a Jew," she said. "I met your mother on the train to Dachau. It was 1944. That's how long I've known her. I was fourteen, not sixteen; we both lied about our age later. I was a Gypsy living in Hungary. It was all very nice before the war. Then the Ustashi came to our town and murdered my parents, my brothers and sister. The Germans were paying a bounty for pretty girls then, and so I was sent to Dachau. Your mother and I were two girls alone. We clung to each other because we didn't have anyone else in the world. No one else. We didn't talk about what had happened to us. We knew instinctively we'd suffered the same thing. We became sisters on the train." Kline looked at her. She reached over the table and touched his hand.

"We were segregated into a women's dormitory, Dormitory 16, people called it. It was named after the age of most of the girls there. I was so glad that the S.S. had kept your mother and I together. The officer at the station didn't try to pull us apart the way we'd seen the people in front of us pulled apart, mothers from their children, husbands from their wives. We held onto each other when we got to the head of the line, like family. There was so much confusion and crying. An officer was standing on a luggage trolley. I remember that officer, his jackboots and black trousers, and I heard him speak, but I didn't understand any German then. I learned that later in the camp. But that particular day, I just remember holding onto your mother and finally hearing the officer say something to her and feeling so happy that we weren't torn apart like the others we saw. We went and stood with the other girls our age. They marched us through the town, Dachau, to the camp. I remember people on the street stopping to stare at us. I remember we walked by a school. I'll always remember seeing the children through the window of the school doing their schoolwork. They were so used to people being herded by the school they didn't even look up. And I remember the sound of the train as it left again, the whistle, the sound of the cars the way they banged against each other.

"At the camp, the older people and young children were taken off one way, and all the young women and men were led to the barracks. I thought at first when we came to the barracks that it was going to be all right because there were so many girls there my age that I thought somehow that meant it would be all right, because surely they wouldn't harm all these young girls." He saw his aunt was crying now, the tears rolling down her old face that was connected by time to that place. "It's strange, even when you know better, you still can't believe some things about people." Kline couldn't look at her. He had to turn away.

"I learned, of course, that it was a brothel for the Germans almost immediately. Your mother was a blonde and quite beautiful; she went with some guards almost immediately. I understood my fate then, when they were taking her away. We never talked about what they did to us. It was our way of keeping our innocence about it. We still don't speak of it." Carmen looked at him. "There was one S.S. officer, who was very young and handsome who used to come regularly from somewhere nearby. He always looked for your mother. She started having more food then, and more privileges. Little things in the camp were everything, the difference between life and death. They fell in love. You're father was that officer," she said. He stared at her in the dark. It was as if suddenly English were a foreign language. He'd held out the hope that somehow it would all be a lie, that his father was innocent, that it had all been a terrible mistake.

"I don't understand?" he said.

"They fell in love. He took us away in the last hours of the war to the American front because he said the Russians would kill him. Your mother made him take me too or she wouldn't go with him. We all ended up in a refugee camp run by the Red Cross. We stayed in the camp for months. Your father had come dressed as a regular German soldier. The American O.S.S. were recruiting *Schutzstafl* and Gestapo officers and taking them out of Germany with Vatican passports to work for them abroad. There was a Serbian priest who was going to the Red Cross camps and recruiting for the Americans. He worked with a high-ranking Gestapo officer who was posing as a Red Cross worker. He knew who was who in the camp. Your father said he wouldn't go unless we were given passports, too. The priest got us all Vatican passports. I left for Argentina. It was all arranged for me. Your father went to work for the American O.S.S., first in Italy, then Mexico City, and then in Argentina and Brazil. Finally, they came here to the U.S. Your mother and father were married in Mexico City. Your mother and I ran into each other in Buenos Aires on the street by accident in 1956. She made me swear that I would never turn your father in. I remember she was pregnant with you. They were very happy, but they were afraid that your father's secret would come out."

"Turn him in for what?"

"He'd been on the list of war criminals the Israelis were looking for. I kept my word because your father kept me alive. He was kind to me. I loved you father like a brother. I don't expect you to understand that. In the camp, if it wasn't for your father and mother, I would be dead. I wouldn't have had my children. I would never have met my husband. I would have been gassed."

"Kline. Where did that name come from?" Kline said.

"The Vatican people issued passports using Jewish names for obvious reasons. Jewish names were safe. The people were dead, there was no way for anyone to check to see if this Kline was dead or not."

"You're saying that it's all true about my father then?"

"Yes. That's what I'm saying. But he never actually worked in the camp," she said. "We never knew what he did." She put her cup down on its plate. "He loved your mother, if that makes any difference."

"How dare she," he said.

"They fell in love. Can't you understand that the camp wasn't a normal place?"

"No. I don't," he said. "I don't understand at all. He was a murderer. No, worse."

256

"Then I can't explain it to you," she said. "If you love your mother, you'll try to understand. She loves you very much. You don't know how much. One other thing, dear, my children think I'm Jewish. They think they're Jewish. No one wanted the Gypsies. They weren't included in the refugee quotas. I would have been sent back to Hungary and the Russians. Nobody wanted Gypsies in Argentina. So now you have my children's lives in your hands," she said. He watched her get up. She bent over and kissed his face. "I'm not a victim, Paul. I'm a human being. Love is the only thing that matters, dear. It is the only thing we can make happen, the rest just happens *to* us," she said.

"Was he a war criminal?" Kline asked before she left. She stopped and turned around, her old face looking at him. She'd stepped into the light now. He tried to imagine that girl on that train with his mother, the two of them facing everything they were to face alone.

"Every day at Dachau they would march children through the streets of the town to the camp to die. No one did *anything*. They all knew. Were *they* war criminals? You answer me that first," she said. "Unless they put every old man and woman in Germany in jail, it doesn't make any difference to me who you call a war criminal. What about the Americans and the Russians that used the S.S. after the war to fight each other? Are *they* war criminals, too? How do you think they got the atomic bomb? Do you think they cared that Von Braun was a Nazi? Were Eisenhower and Truman war criminals, too, or just sad human beings? Marry that girl, Paul, the one you told me about, the one that comes to the trial, and try to forget."

"Aunt Carmen," he called to her as she was crossing the foyer. "Thank you for telling me. I'm glad it was you." She smiled at him.

257

"I have always loved you, Paul. You're my son, too; I'm your godmother. Do you know how much I love you and your mother?" He nodded.

"Does she know that I didn't kill anyone? I confessed, but it's all a lie. You'll tell her that."

"Yes. I already did. We never believe what the police say anyway," she said. He went up later and sat with his mother and aunt. They didn't talk about the trial or the camp. They talked instead about his father and the little things about him they remembered. His mother said she missed him. He was content to finally talk to her in a way he never had before, like a son instead of a stranger.

THIRTY-ONE

"Your honor, we find the defendant, Paul Kline, guilty of murder in the first degree."

"So say you all?" the clerk asked.

"So say us all," the foreman answered.

The foreman's words kept playing in his head as he drove through San Francisco's crowded noontime streets that, ironically, never seemed more alive. A convicted murderer and the son of a war criminal now, he'd watched the foreman read the verdict on CNN. Boon had sat grim-faced at the defense table without him. The judge was very angry and grilled Boon as to his client's whereabouts. Boon told the judge he had no idea.

After the verdict was read, he'd left his mother's house, he realized, probably for the last time. The police would be looking for him, and he knew they would go there first, policemen in uniform demanding to come inside. It would be the scene he knew his parents must have always feared. He had stood outside his mother's bedroom wanting to warn her, tell her not to be frightened, but found her door was locked again. Did she know they were coming, too?

He drove to North Beach, hoping to use his office until he organized his plan, but the police were already surrounding the place. Kline sat at the intersection, waiting at a red light, and watched Cross walk into the building. The lieutenant was talking on his radio. The news reporter on Kline's car radio said that Paul Kline had been found guilty and had failed to appear in court. The police had gone to his mother's house looking for him, but he'd fled. The reporter said the police were surveilling the airports and freeways. They interviewed a police spokeswoman who assured everyone that Kline would be caught, and soon. He switched off the radio and turned right on Lombard and drove past a line of black and white police cars. He thought for a moment of simply pulling his car over and turning himself in because his plan might not work, but he kept driving, surprised that the Cadillac hadn't been stopped already. He wondered if his mother had felt this way as she and her family tried to get out of Berlin. He recalled his father once said that the day they were arrested everyone on the street seemed to be a policeman, everyone was looking at them. It seemed that way now as he drove up the street, stealing by people. He couldn't get his father's stories out of his head, even now, when he knew they had all been lies. In the story, told countless times, his parents had finally been caught on a trolley. The conductor, unbeknownst to the young couple, had flagged down a policeman because he suspected them of being Jews. They were in Dachau a week later, the story went.

He gunned the engine. The idea that the state was after him—a decorated Marine officer—seemed ironic. Without realizing it at first, he was heading towards Martin's apartment. He needed a place where he could sit down, use the phone and wait for dark in order to execute the plan that he clung to now. He had to kill Michael Boon, one way or the other, or Virginia would never be safe, he was sure of that much. He would kill Boon and then turn himself in.

THIRTY-TWO

The outdoor elevator moved slowly then stopped with a shudder at the top floor. Outside the elevator, the city was taking on a mother-of-pearl sheen at two P.M. Kline still had a key and thought that Martin's apartment might be the safest place to hide. Is that why he'd come? Or did he want to see it one last time, as he'd seen it and Virginia that morning that had changed his life forever. He'd never forgotten that moment when he'd first seen her. Whenever he thought of it, it made him smile.

Standing in the hallway, he looked at the apartment door a moment, then turned the key and stepped in. It smelled of paint. The floors had been refinished. They weren't bleached white anymore. Martin's furniture was gone. There were painter's ladders and drop cloths in the living room. He walked in and saw Cindy standing in front of the windows, alone in a black mini-dress and black sweater, the same thing she'd worn to the trial. She turned around and looked at him. Somehow, he wasn't surprised to see her there.

"Hi," he said.

"I guessed you might come here when I heard that you didn't show up. It's all over the news," she said. "I wanted to hear the verdict here," she said. "I don't know why. It seemed like the right place." He walked into the middle of the room glancing down the hallway.

"I didn't do it, Cindy. I swear to you. Someone killed Rosenthal out there when he pulled into that parking lot. I lied on the stand."

"I know that," she said. "You're really not a very good liar."

"I'm scared to death," he blurted out.

"You look it, " she said.

"Is she here?" he tried to forget his fear.

"Virginia? No. She's been letting me stay here," Cindy said.

"I can't go to jail. I can't do that," Kline said. "I'd rather die." He walked across the room and stood next to her looking out on the view.

"I don't think you'll have to," she said. "My uncle worked at Coit Tower in the sixties. I still have cousins that work there. He called me last night. He's been reading about your trial in the paper. He remembered Martin. He said that day the girl jumped, there were two children in the car, a boy and a little girl. He remembered the little girl's name finally, Susan. He's sure about the name. He was the one who found them in the car waiting for their mother. No one had noticed them in all the excitement. The girl was just a toddler. My uncle was the one who called the police and told them the kids were there." Kline looked at her.

"You're sure? *Susan?*"

"Positive. My uncle is old but he remembers everything."

"But there was no mention of a sister," Kline said. "Never. The grandmother never mentioned a granddaughter to me."

"Don't you think it's strange that Michael didn't know about a sister?"

"What do you mean?" Kline said.

"Wake up, Paul. Michael hasn't liked your looking into Martin's case, and he hates me for not letting go of it. What is he afraid of? Why didn't he tell Martin he had a sister? He must have known if he was working for the family."

262

"Maybe he didn't know," Kline said

"Why was he so afraid you would talk to Martin's family then?"

"He was trying to protect Virginia. I understand that now. He's in love with her. He was thinking about her." He lied. He couldn't tell Cindy that he planned on killing Michael. There was no point in making her an accomplice. He didn't tell her that his suspicions about Michael crystalized the moment he found Rosenthal's dead body in the parking lot and were ultimately confirmed during the trial with Michael's testimony about the murder weapon, which couldn't be the gun Kline had taken with him because he knew *that* gun was still locked away in his apartment.

"So why did he want to represent you? You were accused of murdering his boss after all. Virginia said he would never make partner now because he'd taken your case. The law firm has asked him to leave. Why would he give up so much for *you,* Paul? Someone he barely knew until last year? Answer me that?" she said. "You. The person who is hopelessly in love with the woman he's going to marry. His rival in every sense of the word."

"What are you getting at?" he said.

"I went to Michael during the trial and told him what I'd found on Martin's laptop, everything I'd told you. I told Michael I could prove the confession had been written two days before the attack on Fisher. I wanted him to bring it up at the trial. I told him I could prove that Martin hadn't written that confession, that Kevin probably had. I told him I thought the two cases were connected, yours and Martin's. I told him I thought you were being framed just like Martin had been framed. He told me to quit meddling, that I was a dope addict and should stay well out of it if I didn't want to screw up the little chance you had. He told me I was the last person in the world he would ever put on the stand. I think Michael had something to do with Martin's death and so do you, Kline. You're going to kill him, aren't you?" she said.

"Don't be ridiculous."

"I thought about it. Why you were playing along. At first I didn't understand, now I do. You wanted to smoke him out. You suspected him but you had no proof. So you figured you'd hire him as your lawyer and see how he "defended" you. You're pretty smart, Paul, but you got the death penalty."

"If I were going to kill Michael, I could have done it a lot sooner."

"I called him this morning about what my uncle told me. He was very upset. I told him I thought he knew all along that Martin had a sister. You see, he has to be stopped. So we'll get our chance now. He's on his way over," Cindy said.

They heard a voice coming from the hall. Kline looked at Cindy and she shrugged her shoulders. "I'm alone," she said. They watched as a black man in white painter's overalls walked down the hall from Martin's bedroom seemingly coming from nowhere.

"Hey, what do you want to do with the clothes in the other apartment?"

"What?" Kline said.

"There are some clothes in the other apartment," the painter said. "You want to keep them or not?"

"You'd better show us," Kline said. He and Cindy followed the man back down the hallway into Martin's bedroom. He opened the door to the walk-in closet and they followed. The huge closet was completely empty now. The painter pulled at the dressing mirror in the back and it swung away from the wall, obviously hinged. There was an old-fashioned pocket door behind it. Kline stopped to look at the mirror; it had hidden the pocket door perfectly. They walked through the passage, following the painter into the next door apartment.

The painter walked them down the hallway into one of the apartment's other bedrooms. He opened a closet that contained some women's clothes. Carpenters were busy working, sheet-rocking the walls in the living room, their banging loud. A paint-splattered radio in a corner of the bedroom began to broadcast Kline's description. The painter was explaining over the din that the two apartments were going to be re-joined into one huge penthouse, the way the top floor had been originally.

"The pocket door. Was it operable when you found it?" Kline asked, speaking up over the radio.

"Yeah. Using it makes it easier on us," the man said. He talked in a loud booming voice over the announcer's description of Kline on the radio. "Do you want the clothes or not?"

"Yes, leave them," Kline said.

Kline thanked the man and they walked back down the hallway and into the room that had been connected to Martin's bedroom by the closet pocket door. Kline went to the window and looked out. He realized it was here at this window that he'd seen the blonde girl the day he'd been attacked. He turned around.

"I was right. They were driving him crazy," Kline said. "The dog, the files on his computer, the bloody clothes, all of it done right from here. I missed the pocket door because of the mirror. You see yourself and it distracts you. It's brilliant and so simple. That's why the girl tried to kill me, so I wouldn't try and follow her back into the closet because the mirror was probably pulled away from the wall. I would have seen it. When I came back afterwards, I missed it. I looked right at it and didn't know what I was seeing. Stupid."

"But Michael bought the apartment next door *for* Martin," Cindy said. "Martin called me and told me all about it, just before he died. It was *his* idea. Martin knew all about it. I don't get it?"

"He *did* know about it, but he *didn't* know that Michael had *already* bought it for him when he'd first bought Martin's place," Kline said. "That's my guess. It would have given Michael access to Martin's place from the day Martin moved in."

"And if we told the police someone was using the other apartment to drive Martin crazy, they'd never have believed it," Cindy said.

"Probably not. And even if they did, it wouldn't prove I didn't kill Rosenthal. Or that Martin was murdered, would it?"

Kline looked around the bedroom. They walked back through the pocket door into Martin's apartment. As they came down the hallway, they saw Michael come through the front door.

"Good, let's finish it," Cindy said. She took the gun out from her purse, the one Kline had given her the day he'd been attacked. "I'm going to kill him. It's the only way. He'll get away with it all otherwise," she said.

"No. Wait," Kline said. He stepped in front of her. He could feel Cindy following behind him. Michael was wearing an overcoat, his hands in his pockets.

"Michael," Kline said.

"Paul. I thought you might come here. It seemed logical. I'm going to appeal, Paul. I promise. But you aren't helping things if you run away. Turn yourself in," Michael said.

"I want to see Virginia before I do," Kline said. As he got closer, Kline could see the look in Michael's eyes now. It was what he'd hoped for; his look was suddenly keen.

266

"Do you think that's wise? I mean it could be dangerous. You're a wanted man now, Paul. I have to tell the police I've seen you. She can visit you in jail if you want to see her."

"No. I want to see her tonight. Please. I want to say good-bye. You and I know I don't have a chance. I'm going to the gas chamber."

"Not necessarily. It's not over yet," Michael said. "What's wrong, Cindy, are you afraid of me? You haven't been listening to Cindy, have you, Paul? She's a hopeless romantic, our Cindy."

"No. She's all wrong about you, Michael. I want to see Virginia. Then I'll turn myself in. I promise you."

"All right, Paul. But you have to promise to turn yourself in after you see Virginia."

"You have my word."

"You asshole, Michael." Cindy came out from behind him then. She had the gun out pointed at Boon. Kline knocked her against the wall with his left arm. She dropped the gun. Kline kicked it away. It slid out across the hard wood floor stopping against Boon's tasseled loafer. Kline turned to look at him unsure of what he would do.

"She has always been a crazy, stupid bitch," Boon said. Then he turned around and moved toward the front door.

"Coit Tower at ten o'clock tonight," Kline said. Boon stopped for a movement without bothering to turn around. "Tell Virginia to meet me on the observation deck alone, Michael. She has to come alone." Kline spoke to Michael's back. He kept Cindy pinned against the wall with his left hand as she cursed Boon.

"Are you sure, Paul? Coit Tower?"

"Yes. It has to be there," Kline said. "Coit Tower."

"All right, I'll tell her."

267

"Why didn't you let me kill him?" Cindy said after the door closed. Kline looked at her and at the gun on the floor. He'd intended to kill him for weeks now. The idea of it had kept him from going insane. But he couldn't, not yet. Not if there was still a chance he could win it all.

"If you want to get him, you have to trust me and do it my way. Can you?" He looked at her. "Cindy, I have a real chance to save myself now. Will you let me try?"

• • •

Cindy had been waiting for him on the corner. They'd taken her car, leaving the Cadillac at Martin's in the garage.

"It's me, Kline. I have to speak to you." He wasn't sure the old man would open. For a moment that seemed to last an eternity, he waited for an answer. The buzzer went off suddenly, and Kline pushed open the heavy glass door to Count Moro's apartment building. The afternoon paper had been shoved halfway through the mail slot. He could see his name in banner type. The paper tumbled onto the lobby floor as he opened the door. He bent down, pulled off the rubber band and unfolded it. His picture, in color, was below the fold. He took the paper with him and went up the stairs, trying not to run. Frightened, he knocked on the door to the Count's apartment. Kline heard the security chains fall away one at a time. He announced himself, a little out of breath from the fear of how the old man would react to him, now.

"It's Kline. I have to talk to you," he said.

The door was pulled open. "It's *you*, dear boy." Kline looked at the old queen. "You really are *everywhere* these days. I just saw you on TV." The Count was without wig or much make-up, obviously not well. His pancake makeup was only partially removed, and left him looking like some kind of stage actor caught between acts. He was just an old man in a rather moth-eaten women's pink bathrobe, moribund, holding onto what was left of his tattered life. His skinny shins were flaking and very white. He was wearing worn old-fashioned leather slippers, some kind of nod to his masculine needs, perhaps, as he was getting close to the end, something to belie the years of cross-dressing. Perhaps death was bringing out the masculine in him, Kline thought, some last awkward spasm of guilt or pride that he'd been both male and female. "It's too early for sex, dear. I'm sorry. But we could watch a film or something. I have some old sailor films from the fifties, if your tastes run that way. If you're worried about me telling the police you're here, don't be. I hate the bastards. They used to spy on us in the old days. They would ruin people—cart them away for holding hands in a bar. We used to have to go to the toilets. Can you imagine being forced to make love in a toilet at the Black Cat? I mean the old Black Cat, dear. The new one is all young heterosexuals with cell phones now. The old Black Cat used to be filled with artists and homos and reds in my day. Some were all three if you can imagine it. It made for busy people," the Count said. His voice trailed off. "Well, are you coming in?" A parakeet chirped in the kitchen. Kline walked through the door. The Count ushered Kline in with one hand on his hip, trying to be forever youthful, the gay curse.

"I have to ask you something," Kline said, watching the old man close the door behind him.

"You could have called, honey. I've been reading all about you. You're becoming quite the celebrity, I think. Are you a brute? That's what they're calling you. But I suppose it's not the kind of fame one wants. Not like Liza. I felt awful for your dear mother. People are so quick to judge, aren't they?" The Count leaned against the door. He looked exhausted.

"You see, queer love is kind of like hers, isn't it? Or is that going too far? It was awful, though, in those days, lots of fear. *Here,* I mean, if you were homosexual. But everyone has forgotten that now. We had our Gestapo too–the vice squad. Little men. Half of them were faggots themselves. They liked to watch."

He started to hack, a deep wrenching damaging smoker's cough. "I'm out of air. They're supposed to send me a bottle today, or was it yesterday? They're always late anyway," he said. Kline followed the old man through the living room into the tiny kitchen. It was the only room in the apartment that got any natural light. The coffee pot was on and the white enameled kitchen table was scattered with breadcrumbs. "It seems it's the maid's day off," he said. Kline pulled back a chair and noticed the red Naugahyde was torn. The Count poured him a cup of coffee, his hand shaking, and sat down across from him, pulling the worn robe tightly around him. He seemed to be glad for the company, even if it were that of a wanted man. Kline supposed the Count was going to die alone here, perhaps at this very table, looking at his photographs from the past.

"There was another child in the car that day besides Martin Kolsrud, wasn't there? Why didn't you tell me?" Kline said. The Count reached for his cigarettes. He coughed while he lit one with trembling fingers. He managed to cough and get a drag off before he really started to hack. He turned to look at the empty green-metal oxygen bottle in the living room, then back at Kline. "It's such a bore when I can't breath," he said.

"Why didn't you tell me?" Kline said again. "Will you tell me *now?* It might make all the difference, I mean to me, to my case."

"Are the two connected?" Kline nodded. "Well, because it was so sad. And I didn't think it would do anyone any good. And I made a promise a long time ago. Kitty doesn't even know, poor girl, so I couldn't very well have told *you,* could I?" he said.

"She didn't know Marguerite had another child?"

"No. Marguerite and her mother had been estranged for over three years before the poor girl killed herself."

"Who was the father?"

"The boyfriend. He'd come back. He'd been in Vietnam and cleaned himself up. They had moved in together again. It was a happy family except that Marguerite was taking too many drugs and drinking, and he couldn't stop her."

"What made her do it? Something happened, didn't it? Something happened that made her go to the tower that day." The old man looked at him. The cigarette was in his mouth and his fingertips were touching his face pensively.

"They got into a fight that day. Kitty had come to the house and threatened to have the little boy taken if Marguerite didn't straighten up. They had a terrible fight."

"You said they were estranged," Kline said. He felt instinctively that he was being lied to. Maybe he was too aware now of lies. The Count looked at him, his old blue eyes focusing. He coughed a little and reached for another cigarette, pulling one from the pack, forgetting he already had one going. "Marguerite found something out," the Count said, finally.

"What?"

"Let's call it one of life's little mysteries," the Count said, looking at him with men's eyes, a flash of intelligence lighting them.

"What the hell does that mean? Was it his? The old man's? The little girl?"

271

"God, *no.* Don't be ridiculous."

"Then what?" Kline said. He watched the Count light the end of the cigarette.

"Marguerite found out her husband had a *special* friend. I'm afraid it was a little too much for her."

"Who was it? Why would it matter so much she had to kill herself?"

"Because it was Jay, her father. She caught them in bed together in their apartment, I'm afraid."

"That *day?*" Kline said. The Count nodded. "What happened to the little girl that day at the tower? The police would have known she was the sister. They must have told *some*one."

"Kitty had already taken the boy with her from the police station. She didn't know anything about the little girl. I told you they were estranged. She told the police the little girl must belong to someone else. Marguerite had kept her daughter's birth a secret from her parents, you see, so Kitty just assumed the little girl wasn't her daughter's. Marguerite's boyfriend found out where the little girl was and got her back. He *was* the father, after all. Even Jay Kolsrud couldn't get between that. The young man left town. He went back to New York with the child. But he felt guilty. He blamed himself for what happened to Marguerite. He took up his bad habits again and overdosed finally. Jay Kolsrud got the little girl in the end. He never told Kitty she had a granddaughter. He'd known about her all along, you see. That's what kind of man he was. He won it all in the end. The rich usually do, you know."

"Why didn't Martin say anything about his sister?"

"He was just six. They'd been living in a commune most of his life. There were lots of children around. All the kids called each other sister and brother."

"How do you know all this?" Kline asked.

272

"Pillow talk, my dear boy. Jay and I were the best of friends, you might say. I helped keep it from Kitty. I helped find a family that would take the girl. Jay wanted her to go far away, so Kitty wouldn't ever find out, but the girl ended up here in the city, ironically."

"What was the family name?"

"Elders. That was the adoptive family's name. Jay would visit her sometimes and pretend he was just a friend of the family. The girl looks just like Marguerite, the spitting image. I think it drove Jay a little mad," the Count said.

"You never told Kitty?"

"No, of course not. Why should I? Jay never wanted her to know. He never told anyone he was gay. I promised Jay I wouldn't tell her. . . . You see, I loved Jay. Go figure, dear. I always thought it was the opposites attract thing. What do you think? Not too different than your mother and father, I suppose."

"But Kolsrud must have told *some*one else?"

"He told his lawyers. His lawyers knew. But they're paid to keep secrets, aren't they? He set up a trust for both kids." The Count smashed out his cigarette. "They say the worst toxins are in the last half. . . . Jay told me the boy went back to wait for his mother in the car despite what he'd seen. He was holding his little sister when someone from the tower found the two of them and put it together. It's not fair what happens to children, is it?" the Count said.

Kline drove his Cadillac to the tower on purpose. When the police came, he wanted them to be certain they'd found him. Headlights blazing, a double-decker tour bus, its interior lights on, was being loaded with the last of the day's tourists hunching in the darkness; the rest of the Coit Tower's circular parking lot was empty. Kline pulled the Cadillac past the bus to the place Martin had gone to stand each time Kline had followed him to the tower.

Turning off the engine, Kline wondered if it was here, in this very parking place, where Marguerite had left the children that day. Was this where she'd taken Martin by the shoulders and kissed him goodbye? It seemed as if he'd gotten to know the young woman now that he knew her history. He wished he could travel back in time to that dimension and pull her back, hold her, walk her back to the car, and talk to her about a future. He looked out on the moonlit bay in front of him. Glancing in the rearview mirror, he saw the statue of Christopher Columbus at the center of the parking lot on its white plinth, the statue's bronze turned blue by the moonlight.

And what about me? I'm the son of a Nazi and the son of a Jew. The two seemed impossible to reconcile. *Which am I? Both?* He tried to imagine that moment when his father first set eyes on his mother. What had they said to each other? They were about the same age and both culturally German. He supposed they must have had that in common. Were they just two young people—even there, in the midst of that horrible nightmare—meeting for the first time? Was it *possible* that something innocent could have existed in that awful room, an innocent attraction? He *wanted* to believe it, but couldn't. His Aunt Carmen was right, he would never understand, and yet he felt he had to or he would go mad.

He glanced up at the tower that was lit up brightly from below by several floodlights; its bottom section was reminiscent of grandiose Weimar architecture. Could he blame his mother? The thought of suicide had been with him now constantly; it had crept into his soul the moment he'd heard the horrible news about his father. There are some things that are too awful to bear. Why not? Is that what Marguerite would have said?

Cindy knocked on the car window. She came around to the passenger side and slid into the seat next to him. She'd changed into black overalls and a black velour cap.

"Are you all right?" she asked. "You don't look too good, Kline."

"Yeah, I'm alright," he lied.

"My uncle's inside. He'll keep the tower open, and he'll run the elevator for Virginia when she comes, the way you asked," she said.

"You told him that I have to take the stairs to the top. That the stairwell has to be kept open?" he said.

"Yes. Are you going to explain all this to me, Kline?" she asked. Kline looked at her trying to get a hold of himself.

"I can't. Not yet. You have to trust me, just for one more hour. That's all I ask. You have to stay down here in my car. Call me on my phone if you see the police or anyone else, but don't try to stop them, whoever they are. Promise me that no matter who you see go inside, you won't try to stop them. Just ring my cell phone to warn me," he told her.

"All right," she said. She reached over and gave him a kiss on the cheek; it surprised him. He'd assumed he was repellent to people now, an untouchable.

"You're wrong about Hemingway," he said, trying to joke. "He's not so bad. When Virginia comes, don't let her know you're here."

"All right. Whatever it is you're trying to do tonight, I hope to fuck it works, Paul. But if it doesn't, I'll kill Michael myself," she said.

THIRTY-THREE

Cindy's uncle, slightly stooped, his hair completely white, stood by the open elevator doors. Neither man said a word as Kline pushed through the building's front doors. The lobby was deserted. Most of the lights had been turned off so the building would seem closed from the outside. The souvenir shop window, usually lit up, was dark. Kline nodded to the old man, who snapped off a salute.

"Korea, '52," the old man said. His voice echoed in the empty lobby. *"Semper Fi,* Captain." Kline, surprised, saluted him back, then turned and went to the stairway and pulled the door open, checking the lobby behind him one last time. He hesitated a moment, looking up at the mural by the door, the one with the blonde, and then he stepped inside the stairwell and let the heavy metal door close behind him. He started climbing the winding narrow staircase. His phone rang suddenly and he answered as he climbed.

"Virginia." He heard Cindy's voice.

"Is she alone?"

"Yes."

He closed the phone. He listened for a moment, waiting to hear the elevator door close. He heard it through the wall; then the sound of the elevator's motor engaged as the elevator began its climb up to the top. He heard the elevator pass him, unseen, behind the unpainted concrete wall. He started up the winding stairs again as it passed. Near the top, he heard the elevator motor stop for a moment, and then, with a rumble, the motor turned on again as the elevator descended. He got to the top and pushed open the door that led to the observation deck.

Dragging wisps of fog blew across the well-lit observation deck. The deck's red concrete floor was bathed in a bright light. Kline stood for a moment on the last stair. He saw that Virginia was alone. She was standing with her back to him where she'd stood the day he'd stopped her from jumping. San Francisco stretched out in front of her, its multicolored lights punctuating the darkness. Everything that had happened since the first day he'd seen her seemed like a dream. He heard his own footsteps on the concrete deck as he walked towards her. She turned around before he got to her.

"I'm glad you came," he said. "I wasn't sure you would." His words seemed to be pulled apart by the wind.

"Paul, I'm so sorry." She ran to him. He felt her hold him and he was unable to speak for a moment.

"It's all right," he said. "It doesn't matter now."

"Michael has done everything he could for you," she said. He let go of her. "He said he'd keep fighting for you."

"I know," he said.

"I want to marry him, Paul. Do you hate me? Please don't. Can you understand?"

"Yes," Kline said. He held her again. "I don't hate you."

"I'm glad he wants to marry me. I don't want to be alone anymore." She looked at him. He could see her pretty face in the strong electric light.

"I still love you," he said. "More than ever." She looked at him a moment.

"I'm glad you don't hate me," she said.

"If I were younger, would that have made a difference?"

"You aren't old, Paul. And I *do* love you. If things had been different, maybe, but Michael understands me."

"You and Cindy were right about Martin's being murdered."

"I don't want to talk about Martin anymore."

"We have to, Virginia. You see, that's what it's been about, all of it, since the beginning. Rosenthal, Martin—they were connected."

"I don't understand." She moved away towards the rampart, holding his hand, then letting it go. "Paul, Michael told the police about you being here. He said it was for your own good. He's afraid you'll ruin any chance you have of an appeal if you don't turn yourself in."

"Virginia, don't believe anything Michael says. Michael doesn't love you. He's been lying to you all along!"

"Paul, stop it. Not now. We don't have time for this."

"He's going to kill you! The way he did Martin and Rosenthal! That's what he's going to do. I'm sure of it." He walked toward her, her white suit brilliant in the light. She was leaning against the rampart and looking out on the city, the wind blowing her hair. He heard his phone ring but didn't answer. "That's him. Michael. He's here," Kline said. "I'm sure of it."

"He promised me he wouldn't come. I didn't want him to spoil it." He turned away and looked toward the closed elevator door, waiting for it to open. He was sorry suddenly that he'd put her in danger.

"It's Michael," Kline said. "Michael murdered Martin."

"Why do you hate him, Paul? After everything he's done for you?" He thought he heard the distant sound of the elevator start up, the rumble coming from below.

278

"I'm sorry I had to do this. I had to prove it to you once and for all. You see, I knew you'd never believe me, so there was no other way. I'm sorry," Kline said.

"What are you talking about?" The elevator sound got louder. She turned and looked out on the city not wanting to hear what he had to say. He walked up behind her and spoke into her ear.

"I knew during the trial that I'd been right about him, because he never asked me how the gun he gave me could have gotten into Rosenthal's car. I wanted them to find me guilty from the start, because then I knew I had him. But now that we're here, I'm afraid of what will happen next," he said.

"I don't understand." She turned around and faced him. He put his arms around her tightly. She looked frightened as if she thought he might have gone mad.

"Michael is going to kill you because you've inherited Martin's money. I want you to leave before he comes. You can take the stairs." He pulled her back from the rampart and tried to get her to leave, but she wouldn't, she held onto him.

The elevator door opened. Michael stood below them for a moment in the warm yellow light of the elevator. Then he stepped clear of it. He was alone. He was holding a pistol and smiling a half-smile as he climbed the steps.

"Michael?" Virginia said. She started to walk towards him. "You promised me you wouldn't come. What are you doing? You don't need that, Michael, for godsake."

"Shut up, dear. I don't have much time." Boon crossed the deck pointing the gun at Kline. "I lied about guns, Paul. I'm not frightened of them as it turns out." He pushed Virginia back towards Kline.

"You see, I knew he'd come, Virginia. It's the last chance he has before I'm arrested to have me do one more little job for him. I'm a wanted man now. I'm guilty of one murder, why not two?

"Michael? What is he talking about?"

"Shut up, Virginia. Take off your coat, Kline." Kline dropped his coat. "Now turn around so I can see. Good boy. Now pull up your pant legs. One at a time. That's it." Kline did as he was told.

"What are you doing, Michael?" Virginia watched Kline pull up his pant legs showing Michael he was unarmed. She went towards Michael and tried to grab the gun. Boon turned and struck her with the back of his hand. Kline jumped forward, but Michael took her around the neck and put the gun to the side of her face, pressing her against him. Kline stopped a few feet away.

"Now, Paul. You're going to jump. If you don't, I'm going to shoot Virginia in the face. Do you want to see that?"

"You're going to shoot her anyway," Kline said. "So why should I jump?" Kline watched Boon press the barrel of the pistol against her cheek harder, his face grim.

"Oh, my God. You killed him. You killed Martin." Virginia's face moved against the barrel.

"That's right," Kline said, moving closer. "Michael got Martin's case out of the blue and saw a chance for the really big money, the kind of money he'd always thought he should have but never would, not from being a lawyer. And he decided to take it. He interviewed the sister first, you see, and decided that he'd just marry her. Why not? She was beautiful and she fell for him. But there was one problem. He needed it all and she had a brother who was supposed to get half. So Michael decided to kill him." Kline stepped closer.

"In fact, the idea came to me after I met her. I realized after that first meeting that Susan didn't know about Martin. Not a thing. No idea she had a brother. You see, I assumed they knew about one another. That's when the idea hit me of course. I just saw it all in front of me. I must say I was shocked when I found out that Martin Kolsrud was *our* Martin, but that only made it easier. Now get up on the damn wall, or I'll shoot her in front of you, so help me God."

"You see, Virginia, he never loved you," Kline said. "I knew if I went to jail he'd kill you and get away with it."

"Get up on the wall," Boon said again. Kline watched Michael pull the hammer back on the pistol.

"All right. All right. But it must have been a shock when they found the will and you realized Martin had left his share to Virginia." Kline moved toward the rampart, slowly walking backwards.

"It was a problem," Boon said. "That's all. Every problem has a solution, Paul, and you were mine with your ridiculous love for Virginia. I really had to laugh when I saw you watching her that first night. It came to me then that this stupid middle-aged fart was in love. It was really too good. You see, dear? He doesn't love you either or he wouldn't have ever asked you to come up here. He knew he'd be tempting me. He just wants to clear his name."

"You're going to kill Susan too, aren't you?" Kline said.

"I'm afraid Mr. Kline has ready done that."

"Oh, my God." Virginia began to shake.

"You see, we were secretly married months ago in Mexico. I told her we had to keep it a secret until after the trial. She agreed of course. She wasn't very bright, Susan. Good hearted, but not very bright. I called the police just a little while ago and told them my wife was dead and that I thought you'd broken into our house and shot her, with this gun, in fact. I said you'd called and asked to meet me here. Now get up on the damn wall. You're going to kill yourself because of who you are and what you've done." Kline stopped, his back to the rampart. Virginia was shaking uncontrollably, the gun smashed against her face.

"My guess is that the trust is still in limbo, that somehow you'll collect it all once Virginia and Elders are dead." Kline said. He stole a glance over his shoulder down at the parking lot but it was empty, just his Cadillac alone in the lights.

"That's right. You can't trust lawyers, I'm afraid, Paul. It would all revert to Susan, you see, if something happened to Virginia, and it's a community property state. Now climb up."

"And *I* killed Elders. Why?" Kline said. "What are you going to tell the police?" Kline turned around and faced the city.

"Well, because I failed you, didn't I? You were found guilty and couldn't stand it. You're a vicious killer and son of a war criminal. You came to our house looking for me and killed my wife instead."

"It's almost over, isn't it, Michael. And you've won. I commit suicide after killing Virginia and your wife. You had to kill Rosenthal because you needed to stop me before I found out about the sister. I'd gotten close in Bolinas, hadn't I, with the reading."

"That's right. And then I saw on the news what had happened, and lo and behold, a few minutes later Rosenthal was at my door looking for you. He told me you two had argued at your mother's house and that you'd threatened to kill him. *Well, Jesus. Another* plum fell into my lap, and I *did* have to stop you after all. Now get up on the wall." Kline's cell phone rang.

"Throw it over the side. *Now,*" Boon said. Kline lifted the phone off his belt and dropped it over the side of the tower.

He pulled himself up onto the rampart and stood up turning to face Boon, his back to the city. The wind was blowing harder. He looked down at the two of them. "Now turn around and jump, you ridiculous man," Boon said.

"O.K., Michael, I'll jump. But the police are coming. I called them too. They'll be here any minute. I can hear them now." Kline glanced over his shoulder. He heard sirens on Lombard coming toward them. Directly below him he saw the Cadillac. The wind buffeting him, he fought to keep his balance; he heard Virginia scream.

"You bitch." Virginia was struggling, trying to stop Michael from coming forward and pushing Kline off the wall. Boon slapped her with the gun. Stunned, she stopped fighting and sagged against him.

"You see, he can't afford to shoot me because that wouldn't quite fit. Would it, Michael? Can't afford a mistake now, can you?"

"Please! God, Michael, please! *Michael, don't!* Virginia begged him as he dragged her towards the wall.

"The gun. The one you used to kill Rosenthal wasn't Martin's gun, because I took that one home from your office and it's still at my place. I told you during the trial but you ignored me. That's when I knew for sure you'd killed Rosenthal. How did you do it?"

"That day you came to my office I had a second gun in the drawer that was identical. I simply switched them. The one I kept was the one Martin had bought, the one you so obligingly got your prints all over. I made you the gift of a gun I had purchased anonymously at a gun show. You see, I'm smarter than you are, Kline. You can take that fact to hell with you."

Kline looked behind him. He saw a squad car crest the hill and pull into the parking lot, its lights going blue-red. He heard

283

heard their doors open and close. The Cadillac's passenger door was open; the interior lights were on.

"And you were going to use Martin's gun on Virginia at some point and blame me but ended up using it to kill Rosenthal instead. A change of plans. You'll have to push me," Kline said. He turned and faced Boon.

Kline saw the door open to the stairs. He saw the blonde in the polka dot dress appear and stop for a moment in the shadows, then come slowly up the steps to the deck, holding something tightly in her hand.

"You don't have much time now, do you, Michael? You'll have to use the stairs. Or are you going to let them find you here?" Kline suddenly flung himself off the wall at Michael. He heard a shot. Michael, firing at him, moved back.

Lying on the ground, pain racing through his body, Kline looked at his shoulder where he'd been shot. He saw a bullet hole in his white shirt. When he looked towards Michael he saw the blonde walking toward them, just a few feet away now.

"All right, Michael. You win." Kline staggered to his feet, the blood oozing from his shoulder wound. "You wouldn't really kill Virginia in cold blood, would you?" Kline said into the wind. He watched as the blonde stopped behind Michael.

"I'm afraid I have to, old boy," Michael said. Kline saw the hammer move back on Michael's pistol.

The blonde suddenly jerked Michael's head back from behind and stabbed him in the neck. Kline heard a gunshot and saw the muzzle flash. Kline lunged for Boon's gun hand at the same time, knocking the pistol out of his hand.

Michael backed away, holding his neck, an ice pick stuck completely through it. Blood began pouring out of the wound. He brought his hand up to the sharp end protruding out the other side, his face in shock. Kline looked at the blonde. She had gone to the rampart and was climbing over. He ran for her, managing to get hold of her arm as she dropped over the side.

Kline looked down into the night and saw Kevin's face, his blond wig falling away toward the parking lot. The police, right below them, were running up the stairs into the building.

"Let me die, Kline. Let go." Kevin was looking up at him. "Let go of me, please." Kline had grabbed him with the wrong hand. His shoulder wound was pumping blood. The blood rolled down his arm to the fingers that were clutching Kevin's arm. He tried to pull him up. Kline's good arm held onto the rampart. As he pulled, his grip slipped on the blood running down in waves from his shoulder; the fingers of his hand slid up Kevin's arm, unable to hold on.

"Let go! Let me die!"

Kline looked down into his eyes. "No. Take my other hand. Come on, reach for it," he said. Using his knees to keep himself from going over the wall, Kline reached down with his good hand. "Take it. Come on, damn it. Take it." He could feel his grip giving way. Kline saw the expression on Kevin's face change.

"Cindy, shoot him! Do it! Do it," Kevin yelled. *"Do it!"*

Michael's bloody fist came from nowhere and punched Kevin in the face, then again. The force of the second punch broke Kline's grip. Horrified, Kline watched Kevin fall away and heard him scream as he fell. Kline was picked up from behind by his belt, his feet losing contact with the ground. Michael was trying to send him over the side.

Kline heard a shot, then another. Michael's grip around him relaxed suddenly. When he turned around, he saw Cindy looking at him, Michael's gun in her hand, and the police rushing out of the elevator door. He turned to look at Michael, who was slumped dead on the rampart. His face was turned toward them, his eyes open in surprise.

• • •

They were married six months later, on the seventh of April. It was a glorious day in San Francisco, one of those few really warm days. The newspapers had reversed now. Kline had been rehabilitated in the press and was officially Paul Kline, the victim now *and* the hero, who had risked his life to save the woman he loved. Susan Elders had survived her wounds, and she and Virginia had been able to tell the D.A. what Michael had done. Kevin had left a suicide note confessing to Martin's murder and implicating Michael. Kline's guilty sentence was overturned by the judge, and the D.A. was forced to drop the case against him.

Kline's powerful friends had come back, one by one, and apologized for abandoning him during the trial. He'd been polite, but he hadn't invited any of them to the wedding. He was through with the past. His Aunt Carmen had come, and his mother, but the rest were young people, friends of Virginia and Cindy, people who had no idea of history's long reach. The wedding was gay and happy, full of only the future. After they got home from their honeymoon, after he'd put the suitcases in the closet, he found Virginia standing out by the window looking out on Coit Tower. They could see the deck with its crowd of tourists.

"That night. Were you sure Kevin would come?" She turned around and looked at him. She'd told him in Mexico that she loved him. He wasn't sure yet if it was true or not, or if she was just tired of being alone. He hoped it was true. But it didn't matter really. She was all he'd ever wanted. He loved her like he'd never loved anyone and he supposed that was good enough.

"No. I just thought he was probably following the trial. I knew that he'd failed as a screenwriter and had come back to San Francisco. Betsy had kept in touch with him. I figured he was probably in love with Boon, but I knew that he loved you too much to let anything happen to you. I called him and told him that I was meeting you at the tower. He knew Michael would have to try and kill you, too. Kevin knew Michael better than anyone. He knew what he was capable of, and he knew it was going to be Michael's last chance to blame it on me. I never realized Kevin was the blonde that I'd seen following Martin and who attacked me in the apartment," he said.

"Michael used him the way he did me and everyone else," she said. "Poor Kevin. I never guessed he was a switch-hitter."

"Michael knew Kevin couldn't possibly tell anyone what he'd done because it was Kevin who had pushed Martin off the tower. I think Kevin was jealous of Martin, jealous of Martin and Michael's friendship. Maybe he was afraid it was more than that even," Kline said.

"And Susan Elders never realized she was Martin's sister until that night in Bolinas?" she asked. Kline nodded.

"Not until I read Martin's piece. That's when she started to finally remember what had happened to her mother," he said. "Michael had to have been afraid she would figure the rest out eventually. That's why he had to kill her, too."

Kline had been afraid to bring up Martin and everything that had happened, even in Mexico, in bed, when he felt safe holding her, feeling that he'd won and that she was his now forever. It was the first time they'd spoken about that night since it all had happened.

"Should we move? From here?" she said, turning to him. "I don't think I want to become a mother here."

"Maybe," he said. "But I like the view." He walked up to her and put his arms around her. "Just kidding."

"I don't want the baby to grow up and be an artist," she said.

"I don't want her to be a soldier," he said.

"There's too much history here at Martin's place."

"Probably," he said. "Probably too much history."

A week later, Kline had his mother's camp number tattooed on the inside of his wrist so he'd never forget, and he had his name changed legally to Kline for the record. Then he forgot about it all, except whenever he went to pay for something and saw: *0125411*.